THE DOMINO ENIGMA

'Beg for forgiveness,' he told her.

'Forgive me, master!'

He laughed. He had tricked her.

'Beg for punishment,' he said.

'Please punish me, master! Punish me as I deserve!' Her voice echoed from the high ceiling and bare walls. It astonished her with its sincerity.

The crop fell. She screamed. It fell high on the crown of her left buttock, biting her with teeth of fire. She heard it swish back, up into the air, then heard him exhale with a grunt as it fell again. The crop rose and fell, dancing on her flesh. It laced her hips, her thighs. She pulsated and moaned, white-hot with pain. She thrust her bottom at him, crying inarticulately.

The beating stopped. She heard the sound of a zip fastener opening.

'What do you want, Josephine?' he asked. His voice was lazy, ironical. She did not speak.

Everything, she thought.

But she would not tell him.

By the same author:

THE DOMINO TATTOO
THE DOMINO QUEEN

A NEXUS CLASSIC

THE DOMINO
ENIGMA

Cyrian Amberlake

This book is a work of fiction.
In real life, make sure you practice safe, sane and consensual sex.

This Nexus Classic edition published in 2006

First published in 1991 by
Nexus Books
Thames Wharf Studios
Rainville Road
London
W6 9HA

www.nexus-books.co.uk

Typeset by TW Typesetting, Plymouth, Devon
Printed and bound in Great Britain by Clays Ltd, St Ives PLC

ISBN 0 352 34064 9
ISBN 9 780352 340641

A catalogue record for this book is available from the British Library.

1

He was not Josephine's type at all, really. He was in the seat next to her on the flight back from Edinburgh and he made a pass at her. He was young, not out of his twenties, she'd have bet on it. She didn't see any reason not to take him home and play with him.

Francis was waiting in arrivals. 'Evening, madam,' he said, taking her luggage. 'Did you have a pleasant flight?'

'No, I didn't, it was bloody as usual. Francis, this is Russell.'

'Evening, sir. Would you like me to take that for you?'

'No,' said Russell, holding tight to his briefcase. 'Thanks all the same.' He hesitated. 'All right, then, there you go,' he said and loaded it offhandedly onto the barrow. Francis and Josephine exchanged a glance of amusement.

Russell was impressed by the Mercedes. The very word 'penthouse' had him wriggling in his seat with eagerness. It probably reminded him of his favourite magazine. When he saw where it was, which building it was on top of, she saw him grin with admiration. She could see he was dying to ask how much it cost.

Francis loaded the luggage in the lift and stood aside. 'Will you be wanting the car again tonight, madam?'

'Not tonight, Francis, thank you.'

'Then I'll wish you a pleasant weekend,' he said expressionlessly.

Josephine cocked her head. 'And you,' she said lightly.

The doors slid shut. Josephine inserted a plastic card in a slot and they began to move upwards, smoothly, at speed. Freed of the intimidating presence of a uniformed chauffeur, Russell slid an arm around her waist and tried to kiss her. She didn't respond. As he drew back, questioningly, she gave him a look of cool admonition that made him take away his hand. He straightened his tie, murmured something

1

charming, and looked uncomfortably at the floor indicator.

As soon as she entered the combination and the doors slid open, Russell was looking round alertly, taking in all the details — the concealed lighting, the gold-flecked black paintwork, the lacquered furniture. She could see him memorising them for use in future anecdotes at drunken office shindigs. There was a smell of fresh coffee brewing. Russell stood on the balcony with the wind in his hair, identifying all the buildings he had worked in.

Josephine laid her hand on his shoulder, put a drink in his hand, excused herself. She went into the bedroom, unlocked a drawer, and laid a few items out in readiness. She slid up her pencil skirt and adjusted a suspender. Then she went back into the lounge. For a moment she stood watching him through the glass doors. He was marvelling at the riches of the city spread far beneath his feet.

She had decided he looked like the young Peter Fonda, rangy, with deep lines either side of his mouth and that long upper lip. His eyes were confident behind a pair of tinted glasses in Swiss frames with elaborate cornerpieces. He was some sort of management consultant, she had not listened. She had been watching his mouth.

She went out and joined him. 'You can see fourteen banks from here,' he said, congratulatingly. His tie fluttered in the breeze.

She put her hand behind his head and kissed his mouth rather hard and deliberately. She could feel his excitement, his fear; she liked that.

He was three inches taller than she. She reached up and took his glasses off, folded them and slipped them into the breast pocket of his Brooks Brothers suit. She kissed him again, more slowly. His eyes were blue-grey, like storm clouds in spring. They watched her steadily.

'Gloves,' he remarked, taking her hand and toying gently with her fingers. She wore black satin elbow-length gloves with a tailored fit.

Josephine crooked a finger and ran the knuckle down his smooth tanned cheek. Suddenly she dropped her hand to his neck, spreading her thumb and forefinger and pressing them lightly against his throat.

He caught his breath. His eyes widened. She could see he was unnerved, trying to stay cool. He was searching in vain for somewhere to put his drink down. He put his free arm around her waist again and lightly kissed her earlobe, then lifted his glass behind her back and took a sip over her shoulder. She could smell his aftershave, and beneath it, other scents; human, animal.

Lightly she pulled out of his arms, away from him. He responded,

2

taking a step towards her, then restraining himself. She gave him a conspiratorial, seductive look, then turned away and went back inside.

He followed. He was already helpless, whatever he thought.

She was at the counter, mixing herself a drink. She poured coffee over ice cubes, watching them crack and steam furiously as they melted in the thick brown stream. She took more ice, crushed, out of a bag, put it in a tall glass, and put a generous shot of golden demerara rum over it. In the fridge she found a fresh carton of apple juice, inverted it in her hand, looking at Russell who was standing beside an armchair, fingering the leather and watching her with wary interest. He had put his glasses back on.

She gave him a slow smile, turned the juice carton the right way up and tore the corner off with a forceful tug. She poured the chilled coffee into the rum and topped it up with apple juice the colour of liquid honey. She tasted it, tightened her lips.

She put the glass down on the counter and began to take off her right-hand glove.

With the forefinger and thumb of her left hand she pulled the thumb loose first, then the little finger. She slid the glove off and laid it carefully aside. Straightening her right forefinger, she stuck it in the drink and stirred it, clockwise.

Russell stood frozen, alert, leaning towards her from the waist. He couldn't keep his eyes off her.

'Do sit down,' said Josephine.

He came around the chair and put his glass down on a side table, plucking the creases of his deep grey trousers as he sat down.

Josephine slid her finger out of the drink, gave it the tiniest possible shake, then lifted it to her mouth.

She put out her tongue and licked it, deliberately, starting at the root and sliding up to the tip.

Then, delicately, she slipped the whole finger into her mouth and sucked it languidly, savouring the cold sweet taste. She was staring into his eyes, expressionlessly. She saw him shift unconsciously in the chair, rearranging himself.

He said something. She ignored him, pulling her glove back on and turning to the counter, picking up the carton again. More apple.

Then, before he could get restless, she came swiftly out of the alcove and crossed to the couch facing him. She sat down neatly, lifting her glass and pausing an instant, as if toasting him.

3

He looked for his own drink, found it on the table, picked it up, turning to her to return the gesture; but she was already drinking deeply, feeling her throat constrict at the touch of the cold liquid, willing herself to contain the sensation, not to show anything on her face that was not considered and intended.

'What do you call that?' He nodded to her glass.

'A drink,' said Josephine. She tilted the glass again, swallowing half of the cocktail in one.

He smiled uneasily, and glanced at his own gin and tonic as if it had suddenly turned to lemon squash,

Josephine said nothing. As far as the skirt permitted, she stretched one foot towards him, flexing her ankle and pointing the toe of her little back calf boot at him, turning it this way and that.

'What were you doing in Edinburgh?' he asked. There was a faint note of anxiety in his voice now. He'd already asked her on the plane, but she'd deflected it.

'Being nice to boring people,' she said.

'Not too nice, I hope,' he said automatically, recovering his self-assurance.

She considered. 'If you're too nice, people don't give you money,' she said.

She was close enough to see his brows contract a fraction. She realised she had produced an unintended effect. Now he was wondering if she was a hooker, a high-class tart! How very amusing.

She wondered what he would do now. She was sure he was neither coarse enough nor sophisticated enough to pay for sex and think nothing of it. It wasn't just a matter of pride. He was a properly brought-up young son of the home counties and he had the vestige of a conscience.

That was one of the holds she had over him.

Forgetting her display, Josephine sat back more comfortably on the couch, watching him in the pale light from the dull grey sky outside. She had spent a lot of time reading the hungers and fears on the faces of men and women by dim light. Young Russell was an interesting study – controlled enough to have some poise, an acquired, conventional style – but inside so bewildered and unaware that she might have been playing with a puppy. Which way would he lurch?

She summed him up. Russell was the sort of man who equated money and sex. To him, money *was* sexy. But that didn't extend to

4

exchanging money *for* sex. About money, a man like Russell understood everything and nothing. He did not understand the principal truth, that money was extremely boring. It was extremely useful, but extremely boring. Russell's type thought that money was the most interesting thing in the world, because money was power, and power was sexy.

He didn't understand that when it came to sex and power, money didn't enter into it.

Josephine had hopes for Russell. She thought he might understand a little more soon.

Meanwhile, he was still on the hook. He was trying to find an acceptable, inoffensive way to ask if she was expecting him to pay for what they were going to do. If the answer was yes, he would be out of here like a shot.

'Can I get you some more gin?' she asked him, emphasizing the last word with a very slight hint of scorn, as if gin was something she would never dream of drinking herself.

He looked in his glass, swallowed the remainder, held the glass out to her. 'All right,' he said.

She stood up gracefully, bending over him to take his empty glass, taking another long kiss from his narrow, supple lips. Then she went back into the alcove to mix gin and tonic, turning her back on him to give him a chance to get the nerve to ask his question.

Josephine was not a cruel woman. She was only accustomed to cruelty, as she was accustomed to pleasure.

'It must cost you a bit, this place,' he said.

She felt a flash of anger. He was banal, he had no spirit. There was not a spark of imagination in him. She was tempted to take him, and his money too, and laugh about it afterwards with Jackie.

She came back to him with his drink, stood before him holding it suspended in the air, out of his reach. 'Why don't you make yourself comfortable?' she suggested.

He looked at her. 'Okay,' he said jauntily. He looked at his glass. She gave it to him. He tilted her face to kiss her again, but she evaded him.

'Don't you feel like a shower after flying?' she said.

'Yes,' he said, positively, a touch too quickly. He sat forward in his chair, taking a mouthful of gin and running his hand down the sleeve of her blouse. His movements were becoming unco-ordinated, impulses contradicting each other in his brain and body. She kissed

5

him again. His mouth tasted of juniper and quinine.

'Good,' she said. 'So do I.'

His nostrils flared.

'Drink up,' she said.

'I'll bring it with me,' he said.

She shook her head.

Obediently, he swallowed another gulp of gin.

As he did so, Josephine went back to her seat, smoothing her skirt under her bottom as she sat down.

Russell sat there, finishing his drink in a hurry, trying to look nonchalant.

'Take your clothes off,' she said.

He smirked. He finished the drink with a flourish and set the glass down with exaggerated care.

He took his glasses off and folded them, slipping them in his breast pocket exactly as she had done. He took off his watch, took out his corporate emblem tiepin and slipped them together into his hip pocket. Then he loosened his tie, unfastening the top button of his shirt before he took the tie off. He put the tie in the pocket with the tiepin and got to his feet, shrugging out of his jacket.

Josephine got up again and took the jacket from him, laying it carefully across the back of the couch.

Encouraged by her attentive action, he took off his shirt. She did not offer to take it, and saw him hesitate, wondering whether to hold it out to her, before discarding it on the back of the chair behind him. He was wearing a grey singlet, which he quickly and easily slipped out of. His chest was narrow, sparsely haired. His nipples were flat and broad and almost colourless.

He sat down again, smiling slightly, and without looking untied his laces and tugged off his shoes. He slipped his thumbs into the top of each sock, working it down off his foot and depositing it inside its shoe. He opened the buckle of his narrow belt of maroon leather and unbuttoned the waistband of his trousers.

He stopped.

'Are you going to join me?'

Josephone considered. She stood up, unfastening her skirt as she rose. She slid it down to her knees, stepping out of it carefully, without taking her boots off.

Beneath she wore a black half-slip. She took that off too, and stood

6

holding it in her hand for him to look at her. She was wearing her black Armani blouse, the gloves, plain black panties and suspender belt, and plain black stockings, very sheer. The boots had no heels to speak of; still, even boots so soft and feminine preserved her authority. She saw Russell feast his eyes on her stockings, the strips of golden thigh visible above, the curls of dark hair escaping from the crotch of her panties. He gazed frankly at the full swell of her breasts beneath the blouse.

He unzipped his trousers and lowered them. Beneath he was wearing boxer shorts in a bold red and gold stripe, quite out of keeping with his smooth but formal outer appearance. Obviously he thought of himself as something of a buck, sexually; or whoever bought his underwear did.

He looked at her intently and slid down the shorts.

His pubic hair was thicker and more profuse than the rest of the hair on his body. His penis was dark, reddish and soft, circumcised. Josephine came swiftly and took it in her hand, feeling it stir silkily in her palm. It was very warm.

She stooped on one knee and kissed it. It smelt salty and sour. She touched the shaft, just behind the head, with the tip of her tongue, feeling him shiver, hearing him catch his breath.

She rose, looking into his eyes with a slightly mocking smile, still holding him in her hand.

He looked calmer now. The slightest attention to his genitals and he had forgotten all about fear and money. He had accepted that he was in her power, just like the puppy he reminded her of; he didn't know it.

He kissed her. It was a nice kiss. 'I need to use your bathroom,' he said, his voice intimate and low.

'The shower?'

'The loo.'

Josephine gave him a stern look, forbidding him silently to do anything, require anything. She led him along the hallway by his penis. He tried to laugh; she ignored it.

She led him into the bathroom, lingeringly let go of him. He was still flaccid, overcome by her, by things happening that had never happened to him before. She sat on the bidet, folded her hands in her lap.

He lifted the seat, pointed his penis into the loo, waited. He looked

7

at her, sidelong, embarrassed.

'I can't go with anyone watching.'

She had reduced him to childhood, back to his potty-training. She looked impassively at his face, then at his penis. She didn't move from where she sat.

He laughed shakily, swore under his breath. He jiggled his penis.

Josephine rose and stood close behind him. She reached around him with her gloved left hand and removed his hand from his penis. Then she cupped it in her hand, stroking his testicles with her little finger, pressing lightly on his penis with her thumb to point it down into the blue-tinted water below.

His body was tense now.

She stroked his neck with her right hand, pressing her breasts and pelvis against him, moving gently, caressing him with her body.

'Relax.'

He did his best.

Thoughtfully, she put her right hand palm up beneath his buttocks and slipped her middle finger between the cheeks. She squeezed between the muscles, working through the hair, and found his anus with the tip.

Firmly, forcefully, she put her fingertip against the sphincter and pushed.

He was gasping, panting — he even sounded like a puppy now. He said something incoherent and tried to take hold of his penis. She smacked his hand. At once, convulsively, he began to piss, at first in spurts and dribbles, then in a clear, grateful stream.

Josephine removed her hands from him at once and left the bathroom.

She went back to the lounge and picked up her drink, finishing it in one long swallow. She checked her hair in the black mirror of the TV screen; touched her throat, slipped her hand between her legs.

She heard the toilet flush and went quickly into the bedroom.

Through the wall she heard the basin taps run briefly, then stop.

He came in the bedroom, looking embarrassed and relieved. He tried to apologise. She shook her head. He fell silent, looking at the things she had laid out on the vanity unit. The leather straps with buckles on; the handcuffs; the other strap, of black leather with silver chasing. He flashed her a look of fear that was just on the point of turning into a self-protective sneer. She lashed out with her hand and slapped him hard across the cheek, knocking his head sideways. He clapped his hand to the place, staring at her in pain and outrage, his eyes watering. She lifted her hand again and he flinched. She took him in her arms and hugged him tightly, kissing him hard, thrusting her tongue into his mouth, finding his own tongue, flicking over it, drawing it down between her lips.

This he understood. He quieted, responded.

She kissed him for a while, then broke off. She was still hugging him, running her hands down his smooth, narrow back.

'We have plenty of time,' she said.

She kissed the red mark of her hand on his cheek. His skin was pale beneath his tan. He was struggling to keep up with her.

She let go of him, turning to the bed and stripping off the covers.

'On the bed,' she told him.

He got up and lay down on the sheet, warily docile.

At that moment the phone rang on the bedside table.

Josephone ignored it. It rang again, then stilled as the answering machine cut in.

'Nobody can disturb us now,' she told him.

And she took one of the buckled straps from the unit and fastened Russell's right wrist to the corner of the bed.

'I don't −' he said. 'I've never −'

'Quiet,' she told him.

Patiently she fastened his other limbs. He lay beneath her, face upwards, spreadeagled. A light sweat filmed his forehead.

'Josephine, listen, I −'

She smacked his leg, hard. He bared his teeth in pain and frenzy.

She climbed up on the bed, straddling his legs, and buried her face delicately in his crotch.

Gently she nuzzled his penis, holding the skin very lightly between her lips and running her mouth lengthways down the back from root to glans. She ran the tip of her tongue quickly over the glans, hearing him cry out, feeling him stir.

Josephine sat up and looked at him, admired him. She liked her slaves attentive, reactive. This one was straining his neck, lifting his head to watch her; his expression was rapt and wild. The marks of her fingers were still clear on his cheek.

She knelt astride him, fondling his penis, pulling it gently back and forth, encouraging it to swell for her. She cupped her gloved hand

9

beneath his scrotum and ducked her head to take the head of his penis in her mouth. Lightly and quickly, she licked it. His balls crawled excitedly against her hand. She bobbed down, plunging the stiffening shaft into her mouth until the head touched the back of her tongue, then drawing it out again at once.

She explored the shaft with her tongue and fingers. It was smooth, still not quite full, developing a distinct upward curve as it rose. She tugged gently on it. A bead of moisture formed at the tip. She put her mouth to it again and spread the juice with her tongue, mixing his lubricant with her own saliva. She reached behind his testicles and stroked the skin between his genitals and his anus. He was wonderfully sensitive there. He was breathing hard, shifting restlessly on the bed, pulling on his bonds.

'Josephine, can't we —'

She squeezed his balls and he squealed.

She pulled off her boots and sat back on her haunches, reaching for her equipment.

'If you can't be quiet you will have to be taught,' she said, and leaning forward, gripping him with her thighs, she put a black slave collar around his neck.

The collar fastened at the back, with a silver ring in front. When it was buckled up, Josephine slipped her index finger through the ring and pulled his head up off the bed. He grimaced. She lowered her face and kissed him, then pressed her breasts against his face.

She sat back again, fastening another collar around her own neck. This one was narrower, and set with a row of diamonds alternating with little silver studs.

His erection was waning from fear, tension, lack of stimulus. She coaxed it upright again, licking and mouthing it until he began to moan.

She moved until his penis stood upright in her own groin, pressing against the straining fabric of her panties and the narrow band of her suspender belt. She moved her hips, oscillating in little circles, rubbing ceaselessly against the underside of his penis.

She peeled back her gloves and unbuttoned the cuffs of her blouse. Then, straightening her gloves again, she unbuttoned it slowly all down the front, pausing when her hand reached his cock to tease it with her fingers. Then she flapped the blouse up behind her, uncurtaining her breasts. Her bra was cut deep between the cups. She pulled back her shoulders, reaching behind her to draw the blouse off, letting Russell study the small black tattoo she revealed, nestled in her cleavage: a shape like an infinity sign, like a lop-sided figure of-eight. It was a carnival mask. It had been hard to earn. She knew it would mean nothing to him, he would be unable to understand it was her proudest possession.

But he did understand now that he was not to ask; that he was not to say anything without her permission.

She regarded him, lying stretched out between her thighs. She caressed his penis with her stomach.

Leaning over him, she took off her bra. She let her breasts spill forward into his face.

Gamely he turned his head from side to side, caressing her flesh with his lips, straining to reach her nipples with his mouth. She taunted him with them, holding them out of his reach, rubbing his own nipples hard between her thumb and forefinger.

She pinched his right nipple hard. He was not distressed. He was there. He was hers, she had him.

She engulfed his face in her breasts, pressed her cleavage to his mouth. 'Kiss it,' she commanded.

He kissed her tattoo. He licked the light sweat that had begun to form between her breasts. She was pleased with him.

She kissed his chest, his stomach, his outstretched arms. She kissed his throat, planting a line of little kisses up the line of his jaw. She tongued his ear. She worked her way back down his breastbone and into the forest of his pubic hair, nibbling and nuzzling around the edges of it, kissing his open groin, but not touching his penis or his testicles, withholding that pleasure. She ran her tongue down through the hairs of his thighs, pressing her cheek into the mattress to kiss the backs of his knees. She bit his thighs, sat up astride him again and slapped his thighs sharply with her hand.

She reached for her black and silver strap, to acquaint him with that. She lifted it and smacked it down across his thigh. He cried out, more in alarm than pain.

'Silence!' she cried, and struck him again.

Tightening his lips, he jerked under the blow.

She worked her way up his body and raised her hips over his face, tantalizing him with her crotch. He must smell her now, see the sticky moisture seeping through the black cotton; but struggle as he might he could not reach her.

Josephine balanced carefully, poised above him, gyrating her hips slowly. He snuffled and groaned. His eyes were starting from his head. Quickly she glanced at his bonds to make sure he wasn't damaging himself. If she had known he was the type to writhe, she would have padded them for him. Perhaps later.

She sat back on her heels. 'I might,' she said, 'take off my panties. I don't know if you deserve it.'

He pleaded with his eyes.

'The consequences might be painful.'

He bit his lip, closed his eyes. His face was flushed with anguish and desire.

'Six strokes of the strap without a sound,' she instructed him. She brought her face down to kiss his face, to murmur in his ear: 'And I might take off my panties.'

She sat back and studied his face.

He had turned white with apprehension.

She breathed in, feeling her power rise through her, feeling his body pinned and supine between her thighs. She smacked the strap down on his stomach, not very hard. He bucked.

'One!'

She knelt over him and hit the right side of his chest — 'two!' — the left side — 'three!' She hit his left thigh, hard.

'Aah!'

Josephone paused in her discipline. She looked sternly into his face. His eyes were beginning to water.

'We begin again,' she said, and lifted the strap.

She smacked his left thigh, then his right. Left again, right again. She paused, looking into his eyes. He was silent and sweating, the muscles of his face tight and trembling. She kissed his mouth. He came urgently up to her, feeding on her tongue, crashing their teeth together in passion.

Josephine gave him just so much, then no more. She pulled away, and strapped him again.

And again he cried out.

His thighs were striped with burning marks, his cock was straining. She clamped her mouth over it, almost gagging from the heavy stink of it. It was hot on her tongue. She sucked it slowly and soothingly, calming him. Already it began to quiver in her mouth and she with-

12

drew in a hurry.

She stroked the rim of his collar with her finger.

'We begin again,' she said.

She raised the strap.

He took the six strokes in silence.

His torso was slashed and patched with red, his thighs were quietly blazing. On either side of his face, a tear trailed down into his ear. His lips were feverish under hers.

She raised her hips and slid off her panties. Her quim was pouched, her labia swollen and oozing. Strings of clear mucus left her as she pulled one leg out of the sodden panties, then the other. She squatted over Russell once more and pressed her wet crotch gratefully against his chest. Then she turned around, letting him mouth her crotch while she licked again at his hot penis. She pressed her breasts against his flat stomach, raising her hips to give him air.

'Josephine,' he complained, 'my arms hurt! Untie me.'

Josephine got off him, off the bed. She stood looking down at him dispassionately in her black gloves, her black stockings and suspenders.

'You were not given permission to speak,' she said quietly.

'Josephine, enough's enough! I can't take any more!'

He really did have a great deal to learn.

'Disobedient slaves end up across my knee,' she said.

He look irritated. 'Come off it, Jo –'

'One more word,' she said sharply, 'and I shall give you such a spanking you'll beg me to put you in restraint again.'

Their eyes locked, each glaring fiercely at the other.

'Now then,' said Josephine.

Russell didn't reply.

She reached for his penis and worked it gently and expertly to a tight, full erection. Then she got up on top of him again, squatted above him, held him upright in position and lowered herself down onto his quivering flesh.

He gasped and wailed with gratitude.

Josephine lowered herself onto all fours, slowly and carefully so as not to lose him. She rocked from side to side, backwards and forwards. Helplessly he thrust up at her, harder and more insistently than she liked. She thought dreamily of more elaborate restraints, full-body harnesses, bondage suits of rubber and metal. In her mind's eye she

13

could see him, immobilized, blindfolded, gagged and hooded. Nothing of him would remain untrammelled but his penis, naked and erect, presented for her pleasure; he would be able to feel nothing but her mouth, her hands, her vagina.

She swayed above him, leading him onwards with her hips, feeling him snug and wet inside her, fitting as close as if they had been tailored for one another's tolerances. Lights began to drift down into her skull, one, two, three, red and silver. Russell panted and snarled.

She opened her eyes and stroked his chest. 'Hold still,' she told him. He couldn't.

In the flat an alarm went off, an urgent, shrilling squeal.

In shock the couple on the bed froze, staring at each other. For a moment Josephine didn't know what it was. Then, riven with anger and frustration, she grabbed a tissue from the bedside table, tugged herself free, and clamped the tissue to her crotch as she clambered to the floor.

'What is it?' Russell was asking. 'What's happening?'

She didn't answer, she was in too much of a hurry, too much of a rage.

It was the intruder alarm, something had set it off. Unless one of the idiots down in reception had turned it on by mistake. There was no other way the intruder alarm could go off, no way someone could have got a card for the lift, could have opened the doors at the top, could have actually set foot in her flat. It had to be some malfunction, some stupid human error. She made a grab for the phone.

The bedroom door opened.

Josephine's head snapped round. She dropped the phone and crouched down on the floor beside the bed, her arm thrown across her body. The noise went on and on.

The intruder was a young man, a boy — he couldn't be more than twenty, or more than five foot six. He was white, with a peaked cap on his fine blonde hair, and wearing a very smart uniform, a crimson jacket with a mandarin collar, black frogging and polished buttons. Ignoring the man tied to her bed, he walked straight up to Josephine and held out a tiny gift-wrapped package.

Russell was spluttering. 'What the hell —'

'Who are you?' shouted Josephine, standing up and glaring at the boy. 'How did you get in here?'

He made no reply, just stood there stony-faced, offering her his minute delivery. It was wrapped in black foil and tied with a beautiful lacy ribbon the exact red of the delivery boy's uniform.

At a loss what else to do, she took it. 'What is it?' she demanded, though she already knew.

Russell was craning his neck on the bed, hauling at the straps, cursing in frustration. 'Who the hell is this, Josephine? What the fuck's going on here?'

Josephine didn't answer. She jerked the ribbon from the package, tore the foil away.

Inside was a domino. There was nothing on one side but a low-relief design like fishscales. She flipped it over, but there was nothing on the other side either. A double blank.

She looked up.

The boy had gone.

2

Josephine dashed out of the room and into the hall just in time to see the lift doors sliding closed, the flash of a red uniform between them.

'Damn!' she swore. She seized the nearest phone, punched the code for the lobby of the office block that towered beneath her feet. The phone rang, and rang, and rang. The siren of the intruder alarm wailed like an insane beast.

'Josephine!' called Russell angrily from the bedroom.

With her free hand Josephine pushed back the sweaty fringe from her forehead. She cursed into the softly chirping phone as the lift indicator flipped silently and steadily through the numbers of all the other floors.

She was just about to throw the receiver back on the hook when the phone was finally answered.

'Reception.'

Josephine stuck a finger in her other ear. 'Stop the lift!'

'I'm sorry?'

'Stop the fucking lift! There's an intruder in the lift!'

'Who is this, please?'

Josephine seized a fistful of her clammy hair and tugged it in anguish. 'This is Josephine Morrow in the penthouse. There's a man in the lift, he broke in up here —'

'One moment.' The woman spoke to someone else, then came back on the line, cool and uninterested as ever. Josephine had to screw her finger in her ear again to hear what she was saying.

'I'm afraid we can't stop the lift, Ms Morrow. It's going down to the garage. I've alerted security, there'll be someone there in a second.'

Security, hell. That probably meant the stupid lout who hung around the lobby reading the *Star* and trying to chat up the secretaries

16

as they flocked in and out.

'Did he take anything, Ms Morrow? Can you tell me? Is he armed?'

'Yes. No. I don't fucking know!'

'We're calling the police in any case.'

'No,' said Josephine at once. 'No. Don't do that. The police mustn't be involved.' What could she tell this company moron? 'It's personal. Just don't let that man leave the building!'

She went to hang up again, then yelled: 'And you can turn that bloody noise off!'

She hurled the phone back on its hook. It began to ring immediately. She swore at it, ran from it back to the bedroom. The alarm was still squealing fit to break every window in the building.

Arching his back, standing up off the bed on his heels and shoulders, Russell shouted at her over the hideous noise.

'Josephine! Let me out of this, God damn it!'

'There isn't time,' she said, sweeping open the wardrobe and grabbing the first thing she saw. It was a flimsy kimono, a present from a grateful Tokyo trade commission. She pulled it off its hanger and had it on in a second, tying the obi firmly round her waist.

Russell was swearing and gnashing his teeth. 'Josephine, what the hell is going on?'

'I don't know,' she said, sitting on the bed and pulling on her pixie boots. 'Just wait here for me,' she said redundantly, snatching the domino from the table and dropping it in her handbag. 'I'm going to lock you in.'

As she rose, whirling from the room on a torrent of complaints and abuse, the siren finally stopped. The air rang with silence. The phone had stopped too, cut off by the answering machine. The lift indicator showed the car was passing the third floor and heading for the second.

Josephine caught sight of herself as she rushed past a full-length mirror. The kimono was better than nothing, but not much. It wasn't designed for large-breasted western women in energetic motion. Or perhaps it was: you could never tell with Tokyo businessmen.

She hurtled to the door to the stairs, shoved it open and slammed it locked behind her. She swung down one flight of stairs, then raced along a corridor of senior offices to the staff lifts. Two elderly directors standing chatting over the *Financial Times* stopped and stared at her open-mouthed, this odorous apparition in her long gloves and flowing, filmy robe, breasts bouncing juicily and black stockings flashing as

17

she ran for the lift that was just arriving at their floor. 'Excuse me!' Josephine shouted determinedly, and they did. The two men hesitated just long enough about getting in with her to find the doors closing in their faces. They lifted their hands and patted ineffectually at the doors with expressions of pained distaste. Then she was gone.

The lift was fast down to the twentieth floor, then Josephine rode down all the way to the basement with her finger jamming the Close Doors button, hopping it would be enough to prevent anyone else stopping the lift. It was, or she was lucky. The car reached the bottom of its shaft and settled with a whisper of brakes and a soft clunk. Forcing the opening doors with a shove of her arm, Josephine was out in a second, running across the stained tarmac from pool to pool of feeble amber light.

The basement garage was a system of drab concrete caves stretching beneath Josephine's building and most of the neighbouring buildings too. Raw slab walls and square columns divided it into a series of identical rectangular bays, each filled to capacity with cars of all descriptions, secretarial Metros and 2CV's, executive saloons, salesmen's hatchbacks, trade vans and nondescript Volvos, Renaults and Escorts. The place was uncomfortably warm in summer and an absolute fridge in winter, and the air stank of exhaust fumes, oil and metal. Five minutes down here and Josephine's head would begin to throb.

She had no intention of hanging around for that long.

Cutting from bay to bay, she made her way back in the direction of her lift, the lift the boy had used. Francis and the company Mercedes were long gone, but there was her own car, the little red MR2. Where the hell was the lift?

Squeezing between a sleek Peugeot and a Sierra that looked as if it had seen better days, she caught sight of it. It stood there immobile, its doors standing open, its interior light shining bleakly on the wood-grain formica and black trim of the empty car.

At once Josephine changed direction, running for the nearest exit. Loosened by her exertions, the obi came untied at her waist and her kimono flew open, flapping out loose behind her like great gauzy flower-patterned wings. Her breasts hurt from bouncing, her feet from slapping hard on greasy tarmac through thin bootsoles. She grabbed uselessly at the kimono as she ran, trying to pull it closed around her without slowing down.

18

Ahead she heard the booming sound of a powerful engine. Cursing, she made a sprint between two pillars and saw a long low strip of daylight ahead. There was a pain in her chest. Her bosom heaved as she stood there, breathing hard. The gate was raised. A big black car was pulling out and turning up the ramp. The security guard was standing there looking dazed, pushing buttons on a telephone.

'Stop him!' she yelled, pointing. Her voice echoed flatly from the bare walls of the grimy garage.

The guard lifted his head, startled, frowning, unable to tell what direction her voice was coming from. He stood there looking all around with the phone in his hand, trying to find her, staring everywhere among the ranks of parked cars.

The black car turned the bend and was out of sight, going up into the street.

Josephine turned her back and ran to her own car, pulling the keys from her handbag. 'Come on, come on,' she berated herself, clenching her teeth. She unlocked the car, hauled open the door and dived inside, throwing her handbag on the passenger seat and stabbing the key into the ignition, shoving the car into gear and into motion by sheer force of will.

The automatic gate had come grinding back down. The guard was still standing there fumbling with the phone buttons as Josephine swerved to a halt beside him, powering down the windows. 'What the hell are you *doing*? Why didn't you stop him?'

All the guard could say was, 'He had a card! He had a card!' As far as he was concerned, that was the beginning and the end of legality. He shook his head in bewildered dismay. 'I'm calling the police,' he promised, listening to the phone and frowning.

Josephine swore. 'Leave it!' He looked even more startled, then suspicious, belligerent. She tried to calm down, to fix him with a straight command. 'Look, it's all right. We don't need the police, this is just personal. Go back up to the lobby and tell them everything's all right now.'

The guard looked blank, looked at the phone, hestitated. He focused on what she was wearing, or not wearing, and goggled at her instead.

She gunned the engine. 'Did you get the number?' she asked him.

'What?' He glanced at the phone, confused.

'Of the car! The number-plate!'

19

He shook his head.

'Fucking security!' she snarled, and with a screech of abused rubber jolted out of the garage, up the ramp and into the grey street.

It was noon. The lunchtime traffic was beginning to thicken. She had to wait, drumming her gloved fingers on the wheel, while a herd of taxis and bikes puttered past, before inching her way into the flow to a chorus of angry horns. She could see the black car, or what looked like it, some way ahead along the street, between a couple of lorries.

Stuck for a moment, she tried to adjust her dress, and thought to put on her seat belt. She opened her handbag and took out the domino to look at it again, then put it in her lap as the car in front of her moved forward a yard.

She released the brake and crept along the streets in fits and starts. Pedestrians sped past heedlessly, pushing prams, talking business, chewing hamburgers. At this rate, Josephine realised, she would have been quicker chasing after her quarry on foot. She lost sight of the black car for a while, but there was nowhere it could have gone. The traffic closed in around her like pack ice shouldering in around a struggling ship.

She took advantage of a lorry pulling out of an entrance ahead to overtake a couple of cyclists and an old man in a moribund Morris. She spotted the car again. She hoped it was the same car. As they crawled along she kept craning out of the window to see if she could get a look at its driver, but she never managed to see anything before she had to duck back inside, rather than lose her head to a bus or a van shaving insolently past. She thought it was a Rolls or a Daimler, probably with smoked glass windows. She wished her Toyota had. Stuck in a jam at the lights she was aware of a van driver leering in the window at her ill-covered breasts, her bare left thigh and the top of her stocking clearly visible in the gap of her kimono. She had the urge to reach up through the window and stick her fingers in his eyes. Instead she wound it up and sat in heedless contemplation, fingering the domino.

The double blank. What did it mean?

Josephine was more than familiar with the dominoes the members of the association exchanged as tokens among themselves, announcing the secret terrors and forbidden delights to which they gave — no, compelled — entry. No one had ever given her a double blank before. No one had ever violated her privacy before either, walking into her home in broad daylight, to deliver their message. Whose message was it? Who was the boy working for? Was it a man or a woman? Someone she knew already, who liked to hide behind elaborate façades of organisation and schemes of power? Or someone new, someone she had never met, never even heard of? The members were many, in many countries; and there were many more people who worked for them, for money, or under some false apprehension of who their masters were, and what their purpose was.

Which was nothing other than the steeper, more arcane heights of pleasure.

There were many places where they met, she and her companions, for their games and parties and intimate masquerades. Some were secluded and obscure, in the depths of the country or the vaults of the city. Then there was at least one yacht and several private planes; peramently booked hotel suites whose occupants changed, though the activities they housed didn't; discreet clubs in foreign capitals. Josephine knew of a soundproofed house in a suburban close; the crypt of a deconsecrated church; an anonymous clinic in an ordinary industrial estate. To all of these, entry was by consent or sponsorship only. No one went in who did not wear the tattoo of the domino mask on their chest; unless on purpose to come out wearing it.

Josephine had been to ten or twelve of these places, in Britain and Italy and once in America. Time seemed to stop there, to be replaced by laws of obedience and desire that became no less physical, no less implacable. In these cunningly appointed antechambers to hell, she had glimpsed a private heaven. She had tasted iron and leather; she had swallowed blood and sweat and other secretions. She had been abased and degraded, and exalted to eternity.

She knew that the more elevated, powerful members walked at will in and out of the lives of others, pursuing their games. Yet secrecy was close, and all-important. No one had ever burst in on her before, and in the presence of an outsider, compromised and compromising. The danger made the hair prickle on the back of her neck.

She had received many dominoes, and obeyed their summons; and she had given many in her turn, whimsically or earnestly, in play or in the frenzy of compulsion.

Many of them had been the key to secrets.

None of them had been blank.

When someone gave you a domino, it meant they were your master

21

– for the hour, or the day, usually, or for a specified sequence of games or ordeals. In a garden in Rome, an old priest had sent her a double one nestling in the centre of a gold-foiled box of handmade chocolates, each a miniature wafer in the shape of a domino, its pips picked out in coloured icing. He had used a go-between, a mute manservant with a strange disfigurement that left his skin hard and shiny as the back of a crab. Accepting the gift, Josephine had undertaken to visit the garden at the same hour every day for four days, dressed in a plain penitent's shift of coarse, unbleached cotton. There she had suffered herself to be hung by her hands from the branch of a tree and whipped with a bunch of well-pickled birch rods for ninety seconds. The servant wielded the birch while his master sat a little way off, watching from a seat among the bushes. Her cries had startled the birds. Back at the convent a nursing sister had bathed and salved her lacerated back, her bottom and thighs, and ensured with her well-schooled hands that Josephine did not go to sleep unsatisfied.

In an airless hotel room in Swansea, a young Israeli had made her dress in the uniform of an El Al air hostess, then spanked her across his knee with the back of a hairbrush. She remembered his penis, its glans so purple it was almost blue. Though she had desired it, he had refused to spill his seed inside her, and had pulled out at the last moment to ejaculate on her reddened bottom. After that he had lain beside her all night, stroking her hair and murmuring confessions while she drifted in and out of a confused and shallow sleep. The domino lay on the night table: a double two, she remembered.

With a double three, she and another woman, a chubby blonde called Maureen, had been stripped naked on a cabin cruiser somewhere off the Dorset coast. They had been led up on deck and tied up side by side, bottom up over the stern rail, where they had endured the tongues, vibrators and lashes of a party of excitable young Americans. Josephine remembered staring into the blue sea, the shadow of the boat, hearing the whimpers of the woman at her side and the brash, slurred remarks and insults of the tormentors at their backs. Neither of them knew at any moment what was coming next, pain or pleasure. The party that had followed below deck had turned into something of an orgy. Josephine remembered Maureen, drunk, stuffing maraschino cherries into her vagina and demanding that an Olympian youth dressed only in ankle socks and sneakers eat them out of her.

On a week at a chalet in Cumbria Josephine had given a double four to a young girl whose cheerful, effervescent personality and sleek black body made her dizzy with lust, and whose shriek of wild apprehension made her sure she had chosen aright. Judy, her name had been. She had been difficult to master. A whole day's training ensued, with complex rituals and many severe chastisements for failure and indiscipline. They had spent that night in one another's arms; and in the morning Josephine's heart had been broken because Judy decided to give her double four to someone else.

The double five her original mentor, Dr Hazel Shepard, had given her as a surprise one Friday evening after a dinner party, when the other guests had gone. Instead of breakfast the next day she had dosed her with a drug that had made her feel detached and highly sensitized; and she had made her masturbate slowly, on and off for hours, while they talked and talked in infinitely indulgent detail of all the exciting and arousing things they could imagine, sharing experiences and fantasies. When Josephine's arousal waned or her clitoris grew sore, Dr Hazel had worked on her flesh with such expert instruments of pain and pleasure that Josephine could hardly tell which was which. Later Dr Hazel had sat in a chair, twining her strong fingers in Josephine's hair as Josephine crouched between her thighs, tonguing at her thick and fleshy vulva. She had slept all day Sunday, not waking until late in the evening.

A double six she had given once to a man, a poet who was short and fat and rather ugly, but who had the most sensuous voice she had ever heard. She closed her eyes and had him read erotic poetry to her on the veranda of a Neopolitan summerhouse; when she wearied of the touch of her own fingers she beat him with a cane. His cries chimed with those of the seabirds calling plaintively around the bay. He claimed he had never once performed the act of cunnilingus, so she had pressed his face to her crotch and encouraged him to greater and greater efforts with random cuts of the cane across his broad back and buttocks. Afterwards she condescended to let him masturbate with a pair of her panties while she sat on the far side of the room. Then she beat him again.

A double blank she had never seen. The fact had never occurred to her until today.

An air horn blared. Two young men on a motorbike were cruising alongside, making eyes at her and laughing. She sat forward and pressed her legs together, trying to make her bare crotch less visible, steering with one hand and with the other once again attempting vainly to close the front of the kimono over her breasts. Shiny and loose, it kept working its way out from under the seatbelt and allowing her right breast to slip out.

The mystery car was gaining on her. She was losing ground, unable to throw her weight around in traffic the way the unseen driver was evidently doing. She saw the car leave the roundabout heading north past Old Street station. She tried to cut across a lane to catch it and almost went into the side of a bus. By the time she'd sorted that out, she'd lost it completely.

She drove at random for a while, fingering her domino and thinking. The anger and impetus that had driven her out in pursuit of her intruder had evaporated, burned off in the thrill of the chase. Confused in the moment of interruption, her appetite began to turn away from Russell the yuppie towards the unknown master who had so brusquely commanded her obedience. Perhaps she had done the wrong thing by leaping onto the offensive. Perhaps she should have submitted meekly to the fate he had in store for her. Still, it was him — she kept thinking of him as a man, for some reason — that had broken the rules first.

Or perhaps this was an entirely new game.

She felt her vagina moisten at the thought.

Russell, she decided, could wait. On a sudden impulse, she took a turn and turned back to the City Road, heading west through Camden Town to Hampstead. There, in a large, secluded house set behind walls among an orchard of cherry trees, lived a woman who might be able to answer her questions. If she chose.

Pink marble chippings crunched under her wheels as she turned the Toyota in through the gateposts and parked outside the house. There were no other cars in sight; it could be that the doctor and her housekeeper were away from home, as they so often were.

Josephine stepped out of the car, leaving her handbag but bringing the domino with her. She was careless now that her obi had come untied and her kimono was hanging completely open. Here, it wouldn't matter. Dr Shepard would forgive her — or admire her — or, if she was feeling sprightly, punish her: in her present nervous mood of light arousal, whatever happened would be welcome.

She rang the bell.

At first she thought there was no one at home. Then, looking through the bulging lights of the leaded window, she saw a movement, a shape arriving at the door.

It was Annabel Taylor, the housekeeper. 'Miss Morrow,' she said with a cheerful smile of surprise. 'How nice to see you.'

Her bright eyes took in Josephine's less than modest attire. She had seen her naked before, several times, and in much more disadvantaged situations than this. Josephine leaned forward and kissed her gently on her soft, powdered cheek.

'Have you come to see Dr Shepard?' asked Annabel. 'I'm afraid she's not here at present. But come in for a bit, do.' She opened the door wider, and Josephine stepped past her into the cool hall.

There were artfully crooked black beams overhead, hessian flooring underfoot. The walls were whitewashed plaster. There was a gentle fragrance in the air from a china bowl of pot pourri standing on a dark, lustrous redwood chest, an ancient black bakelite telephone beside it. On the wall above it was a noticeboard completely obscured with postcards, leaflets, coupons, yellowed scraps of paper and ancient envelopes with scribbled phone numbers fading into illegibility. On the wall opposite hung a big oval mirrow in a twenties pewter frame that would have fetched a handsome price at any antique auction. A hallstand almost invisible beneath its immense accumulation of coats, jackets, scarves and hats stood nearby, just inside the door.

'Shall I take your things, miss?' asked Annabel, innocently.

Josephine smiled, hesitated; then succumbed. With quick, economical movements she pulled off her gloves and laid them neatly on the chest beside the bowl; then, thinking what a strange striptease this was, slipped the kimono from her shoulders. 'I came out in a bit of a rush, I'm afraid, Annabel,' she said.

'So I see, miss,' said Annabel, taking the flimsy garment from her and adding it nonchalantly to the precarious heap on the hallstand. 'You could take off your other things too, miss, if you like.'

Josephine looked down at her suspender belt and stockings. For the first time she noticed she had laddered the right one somewhere; pushing between cars in the basement garage, probably. A long streak of golden thigh peeked through the sheer black nylon.

'I really mustn't stop, Annabel, thanks. I left some, um, unfinished business.'

Annabel's expression didn't change, but it was perfectly clear she had a very good idea what sort of business Josephine meant. She appraised Josephine's nakedness with a frank glance. If she was disappointed that her surprise visitor was declining to strip off completely in the front hall, she didn't admit it. She said, 'You're looking well, miss, if I might say so.'

'Thank you, Annabel. It's nice to see you.' Josephine turned deliberately, letting the older woman view her body from the side and back. She glanced at herself in the mirror, exclaiming at her appearance in rueful displeasure. Was it her imagination, or was there still a tell-tale flush of passion glowing on her cheeks? Her blonde hair, cut in her usual shaggy, face-hugging style, was terribly untidy. She tried to comb it out with her fingers. The domino was still in her other hand.

'Can't I persuade you to stay for a bite of lunch, at least, Miss Morrow?'

'Thank you, Annabel,' she said, 'no, I mustn't. I only called to ask Dr Shepard if she knew anything about this.' And she held out the double blank.

'What's that you've got there?' asked Annabel, coming across to take it from her.

'A domino,' said Josephine, needlessly.

'And who gave you this, then, or shouldn't I ask? Is that your unfinished business?' She turned the stone over in her strong fingers, examining both sides.

'It's blank,' Josephine pointed out. 'A double blank. I've never had one of those before. The boy who brought it wouldn't say anything. Not a word. And I don't even know who it came from, or what I'm supposed to do. Have you ever seen one before, Annabel?'

'I've heard of it,' said Annabel mysteriously, handing it back to her, 'but I don't know that I've ever seen one.'

'What does it mean?'

Annabel pursed her lips. 'Who's to say?' she said.

But Josephine could tell she knew more than she was letting on.

Annabel patted her on the arm, ushering her further into the house. 'Can I get you a drink?'

'No, thanks, Annabel, I've got the car.'

'Come and let me make you a cup of tea at least.'

Josephine gave her an agitated smile. 'No, really, Annabel, thank you, but I mustn't.'

26

Annabel's smile grew more serious. She stood very close to Josephine. Her hand slipped gently down from her arm to her hip, and came to rest lightly on her bottom.

'Is there anything else I can do for you?' she asked, very quietly.

Josephine closed her eyes and lifted her chin in pleasure. The touch of the other woman's hand was sensuous, comforting. 'That's nice,' she said huskily.

Annabel's hand explored Josephine's bottom, stroked the back of her thigh.

'You youngsters rush around too much these days, if you ask me,' she said with mock severity.

Josephine's eyes opened wide. 'Youngsters!' she echoed. 'You're teasing me.'

'You're not too old . . .' murmured Annabel, but didn't finish her remark.

'Well, I hope not,' said Josephine lightly. But Annabel was waiting for a signal of some kind, and Josephine wouldn't give it. She hugged the housekeeper and allowed her to fondle her a little more. The two women stood smiling at each other for a long moment in the cool hall; then Josephine gave a slight shiver. 'There is something you can do for me, Annabel.'

'What, miss?'

'Let me use your loo.'

'Go on with you, then,' Annabel said, releasing her.

Josephine darted for the stairs, favouring the housekeeper with a sweet smile as she hurried up to the bathroom on the landing. She went in, leaving the door ajar. Drinking coffee on the early morning flight from Edinburgh and then being interrupted in the middle of sex had put some demands on her bladder. Gratefully she plumped herself down on the oak seat of the great white pedestal and started to pee.

While she relieved herself, she looked around at the spotless white enamel of the elephantine bath and washbasin, the white tiles on the walls, the curtains of faded pink cretonne. The marbled lino was cold beneath her stockinged feet. A carafe of thick blown glass stood on the windowsill, holding a spray of teazles and dried grasses; a copy of the *Daily Telegraph* colour supplement lay, folded open to an article about Cartier Bresson, on the lid of the stool that doubled as a laundry basket.

Everything in this house seemed so peaceful and normal; yet it was here, in a sense in this very room, that Josephine had passed a few short years ago through the gateway from normality to the strange land of games. She remembered how frightened and nervous she had been, undressing for the first time in someone else's house; how she had lain in the the bath excitedly masturbating and wondering whether it was true that the two women really were the mistress and servant they appeared to be, or a clandestine couple of lesbian lovers. She gave a little silent chuckle of laughter to think how naïve she had been. Everything was true. Everything!

She looked up then, and saw the bathroom door had swung open wide without her noticing.

Annabel stood there, framed in the doorway. She had come silently upstairs and was standing there, watching her on the toilet.

Josephine was startled, then amused. You could never be alone in this house for long, whatever you were doing. You could never keep your clothes on for five minutes, either!

'Hello, Annabel.'

'Hello, miss.'

'Do come in.'

Quiet as a cat in her soft-soled shoes, Annabel came into the bathroom and stood in front of Josephine while she finished. She stood with her hands folded passively in front of her.

Josephine smiled. 'Could you pass me a piece of paper, please, Annabel?

Annabel indicated the roll, hanging from a holder right by Josephine's elbow. 'There it is, miss.'

Josephine batted her eyelids dreamily. 'Is it?' she said.

Annabel stepped forward. With steady hands she tore a few sheets from the roll, wadded them up and offered them to Josephine.

Josephine looked her in the eye and shifted back on the toilet seat, opening her legs.

Smoothly, lingeringly, Annabel wiped her crotch.

'I've got Dr Shepard on the phone,' she said.

'What?' laughed Josephine, outraged. 'Why didn't you say, you wicked girl?' And she sprang to her feet and hurried from the bathroom, leaving Annabel to pull the heavy chain on the toilet cistern.

In the hall, Josephine found the phone receiver lying on the top of the chest. She picked it up at once and held it to her ear, turning around and leaning her weight on the chest. The coiled receiver cord stretched tight across her bare stomach.

'Hello?'

'Josephine Morrow,' said Dr Shepard in her deep, brassy voice, 'what have you been doing this time?'

Josephine laughed. 'Nothing!' she protested.

'What's all this about mysterious messengers with blank dominoes?'

'I was hoping,' said Josephine, smiling at Annabel as she came slowly downstairs and passed her on the way back to the kitchen, 'that you would tell me.'

'You'd better tell me the whole story,' said her mentor.

'Well, I just got back from Edinburgh this morning, and took a man home with me —'

'Oh, yes?'

'— and we were getting to know each other a bit —'

'I can imagine,' said Dr Shepard, ponderously.

'Do you want to hear this or not?' demanded Josephine in mock annoyance.

'What, the story of you and your sordid Scottish toy boy? No, not particularly.'

'Of course you do, you old lech. Anyway, while we were busy, this boy broke in — just walked right in. Apparently he had a card for the lift, somehow he'd got my lock combination. I shall have to get that changed.'

'A boy?'

'Well, a young man. In what do you call it, livery, just like a pageboy in an old-fashioned hotel, you know? And he handed me a parcel, in fancy wrapping paper tied with a ribbon, and he walked out. Without a word.'

'And the domino was in the parcel?' ruminated Dr Shepard.

'That's right.'

'A double blank?'

'That's right. Hazel, what does it mean?'

'It means you're a very lucky girl,' Dr Shepard said. She sounded remarkably impressed, Josephine thought. That was unusual enough in itself. 'You've been selected,' said Dr Shepard.

A shiver of anticipation ran through Josephine's body. She pressed

29

her free hand to her groin, glancing down the hallway to see if Annabel was still spying on her.

'Selected? Selected for what?'

'Only they know that.'

'Who? Who do?'

'Whoever sent it to you.'

Josephine sensed at once that the doctor, like her housekeeper, knew rather more than that, but was unwilling – or forbidden, thought Josephine with another small thrill – to tell her anything more. 'You're a very lucky girl,' Dr Shepard said again.

Cradling the receiver between her cheek and her shoulder, Josephine reached her kimono down from the hallstand and pulled it on as they talked. She said goodbye to Dr Shepard. 'It's a whole new game, isn't it?' she said.

'A whole new game,' Dr Shepard echoed.

Josephine hung up the phone. 'Bye, Annabel!' she called, going out swiftly and shutting it behind her.

In the car she looked at herself in the rearview mirror for a couple of seconds before driving off.

Russell would have to wait. There was someone else she needed to talk to.

3

Coming down through Kilburn the traffic was quite a bit lighter, and she made good time. The sun came out briefly from the overcast sky as she accelerated under the booming Westway and took her usual short cut to Ladbroke Grove. It was nearly half-past one when she pulled in to the forecourt of a large self-contained house in Holland Park.

The house was old, perhaps two hundred years old, and large, four-storeyed. The grounds were small, immaculately kept, with beds of neat flowering shrubs around a plush lawn. Long curtains of fine white net guarded the privacy of the rooms behind the high windows.

An old man in a dark grey coat with a sleek fur collar-band was being helped down the broad front steps by a buxom young Indian nurse. He stared suspiciously at the slick red car as it wheeled to a stop behind the hedge, then his gaunt face broke into a smile of lascivious delight when Josephine came leaping out of the car and bounded past him up the steps, her kimono flapping. She'd got the obi tied in a secure knot around her waist now, but the breeze of her passing obliged the old man by whisking the skirt of the kimono high above her plump, bare bottom.

By the front door the engraved writing on a discreet brass plaque read LAMOUREUX CLINIC. Josephine turned the huge brass handle and went straight in. The student nurse on duty in reception looked up in surprise as she went striding across the foyer, breasts bouncing meatily beneath her kimono. Then she recognised her and smiled a greeting.

'Is she free?' Josephine asked her.

The nurse tucked a stray curl behind her ear as she glanced up at a large clock above the front door, then consulted her appointment book, running a finger down the page. 'Should be,' she said, smiling.

31

'Mr Mannenheim doesn't usually take very long.'

With a gesture Josephine indicated the door that led to the treatment rooms, raising her eyebrows to ask if she could go in.

'Upstairs, room 24. But please don't interrupt if she hasn't finished.'

'Of course not,' said Josephine. She reached across the desk and patted the nurse on the shoulder. The nurse smiled, warily.

She went along the hall to the tiny creaking lift, stepped in, slid the gate closed and pressed the button for the second floor.

The corridor was thickly carpeted with speckled grey wool. All the doors were closed and numbered. As Josephine strode silently by she heard from somewhere the sound of a female voice raised in tones of scolding derision. Instantly there came the crack of a whip, and a cry of glad agony.

It was business as usual at the Lamoureux.

The door to room 24 was ajar. Josephine listened a moment, but all was quiet inside. She knocked.

'Come in,' said a sweet clear voice.

Josephine pushed the door open and went in.

The room was a hospital cubicle of comfortable size. The walls were painted a spotless white, the floor was bare boards, stripped and sealed with a sheen the colour of golden syrup. Apart from a wheeled chromium rack that stood in the corner, hung with equipment, the main feature of the room was a large institutional bed with an ingenious metal frame that held numerous clips and pivots for apparatus of leather, cloth and steel, obviously for the restraint of restless patients. The bed was, as the receptionist had guessed, no longer occupied. The only person in the room, a tall slender nurse in a starched white uniform, was unfastening the press-studs at the corners of a large red rubber sheet.

'Josephine!' she cried.

'Hello, my sweet.' The two women embraced closely and shared a warm, lingering kiss. Josephine lifted a hand to the back of Jackie's head, stroking her fine red-gold hair, pressing their two heads closer together. Jackie's mouth tasted of something reeking and salty, a familiar, ammonia flavour. Her slim body was, as ever, prompt in response to Josephine's caress. She pressed her pelvis to Josephine's.

They interrupted their kiss to gaze at each other fondly. Jackie's eyes were green and sparkling beneath long curled lashes. Her skin looked scrubbed and shining, as if it had never heard of make-up. Freckles

32

of the very faintest tan lay across her sharp, straight nose like a sprinkling of soft sugar. Her lips were moist and pink, her teeth white and straight as her starched white cap.

Josephine kissed her again, riding a sudden surge of excitement at seeing her once more. She pushed her tongue into Jackie's open mouth and found her tongue quick and eager in response. It leapt and played about her own like a little lithe animal welcoming a mate into the warm moisture of its burrow. Jackie's lips closed gently on Josephine's tongue, sucking on it, drawing it in. Josephine's breathing quickened. She heard herself give vent to a whimper of impetuous desire. She pressed her hand to the front of Jackie's apron, feeling for the elusive contours of the little shell-shaped breast beneath.

Jackie slid her hands down Josephine's back, pressing and caressing. She ran her right hand down over Josephine's bottom and onto her thigh, then slipped it up beneath the skirt of her kimono. She fondled Josephine's bottom, slipping the tips of her fingers into her crotch from behind.

'I like the outfit,' she murmured as she nibbled Josephine's ear.

'This? Just a little thing I threw on.'

'You're not,' said Jackie distinctly, 'wearing any knickers.'

'That's right,' Josephine said, sighing with comfort at the warmth of Jackie's breath, the tenderness of her lips and tongue in the intricate portal of her ear. She threw back her head, feeling her hair slide back from her cheeks. Jackie kissed her arched throat.

'Didn't your ma tell you always to put knickers on?' Jackie persisted, gravely. Her hands roved over Josephine's body, her shoulders, the nape of her neck, her upper arms. 'What would happen if you got knocked down in an accident and had to go to the hospital?'

Josephine gripped the back of Jackie's neck with loving firmness and pressed swift, hard kisses on her mouth.

'I've got a card in my handbag, telling them to bring me here,' she said, surfacing.

Jackie gave an appreciative little laugh. With new urgency she wrestled with the knot of Josephine's obi until she had it untied. Impatiently she drew back the lapels of the kimono and fell upon Josephine's splendid breasts, caressing them with her hands. Josephine felt her womb thrill as Jackie's practised fingers found and teased her thick, dark nipples.

'Are you busy this afternoon?' asked Josephine.

33

Not ceasing to manipulate her friends's breasts, Jackie consulted her memory. 'Nothing one of the other girls can't handle,' she said, easily.

'Have you had lunch yet?'

'In a manner of speaking.' Reminiscently, the woman in the nurse's uniform licked her lips.

Josephine kissed her lips, that chin. 'What did you have?' she asked.

'Whatever it was, it was very salty.'

Josephine reached behind Jackie and smacked her on the starched white rump of her uniform. 'Naughty girl,' she said lightly, hugging her again. 'That's not a proper lunch. Didn't your mother tell you you should always eat properly in the middle of the day?'

'Oh, I did,' said Jackie innocently. 'I ate it very properly.'

'You're going to find yourself across my knee,' threatened Josephine softly, 'if you're not careful.'

'And if I am?'

For answer Josephine kissed her. 'There's something I want to show you,' she said. 'Why don't you come back with me? I've got the car outside.'

She spoke as if it was a perfectly ordinary conversation they were having, and Jackie responded in the same tone. 'All right,' she said, agreeably.

The two women broke off their embrace. Josephine helped Jackie to straighten the bed and check the facilities, ready for the next patient. Finding the huge sleeves a nuisance, Josephine slipped out of her kimono, bundled it up and threw it in the basket with the rest of the laundry.

'Going to drive like that, are you?' Jackie said.

'I'm sure you can lend me something,' said Josephine.

Jackie pursed her lips, putting her head on one side. She obviously preferred the view as it was. 'We can fix you up with a spare uniform, if you like,' she said.

Josephine smiled. 'One of the royal blue ones? With the frills on the apron?'

'That's only for sisters,' Jackie said.

'I'm very sisterly,' Josephine assured her.

'Let's see what we can find you.'

They carried the laundry to the lift, swinging the basket between them. A portly Nigerian put his head out of a door and ducked back hastily when he saw the nurse and her nude, black-stockinged companion strolling along the corridor towards him.

In a warm, dry room of sweet-smelling clothes and linen folded and piled on bare wooden racks, the Indian nurse Josephine had passed on her way in was standing on a chair reaching for something on a high shelf. Josephine noticed what wonderful hams she had. Jackie, meanwhile, put a friendly hand up her skirt and pinched her bottom.

'Hey, Sharlee, this is Josephine.'

Her hand pressed to her bottom, Sharlee looked down, suppressing an abashed grin as her eyes met Josephine's. Her eyes were huge and rimmed with kohl; her skin was a rich dark southern chestnut. She climbed down, murmuring a greeting to Josephine, her glance flicking rapidly back and forth from her to Jackie, as if she was too polite to stare at her bare body, but reluctant to look away completely.

'She wants to be a sister,' Jackie said. 'We need a sister's uniform.'

At this, Sharlee looked doubtful. 'Is she a client?' she asked in a murmur, as if Josephine wasn't there.

'No,' said Jackie. She leaned her hip on the racks and folded her arms. 'She's my friend.'

Now Sharlee looked wary, and even less willing. 'Will you sign for it?'

'Of course I will.'

Sharlee's expression became blank, passive. But she was still visibly hesitating.

'I'll let you measure her,' Jackie offered.

This convinced Sharlee. She gazed gratefully at Jackie, then glanced at Josephine. Her face was glowing with pleasure. She ducked away between the racks, into an adjoining room.

Eager to leave, Josephine said to Jackie: 'I know my size. So do you,' she added.

Jackie patted her hand, shushed her.

Quick footsteps announced the return of Sharlee, holding a tape measure tightly before her, bunched up in both hands. Though she was looking very happy, she became shy as she approached Josephine, and when she came close to her, lowered her eyes.

'Please lift your arms,' she murmured. Her voice was deep and rich, and tremulous with anticipation of joy.

Josephine gave Jackie a secret wink, then lifted her arms in a luxurious stretch, bringing them up over her head and thrusting out her chest. She imagined herself about to dive into warm water.

With a tiny flicker of her red tongue between full, sensuous lips, Sharlee came close. Josephine could feel her breath on her shoulder. Sharlee wrapped the tape delicately and precisely around Josephine's breasts.

The measurements took a while and included many that Josephine wouldn't have thought necessary at all for anything other than a tailor-made scuba suit. She bore them patiently, slipping out of her stockings and suspender belt when Sharlee asked, politely, and encouraging Sharlee to grow bolder as she ran her tape in and out of the more intimate curves and folds of her body. Jackie came forward and helped to guide her hand. 'Unfortunately Josephine's forgot to bring her undies too,' she pointed out. 'She'll need a full set, please, Sharlee, there's a pet. What about here?' she said, running a forefinger slowly down the crease from Josephine's hip to her groin. 'Have you measured here yet? No?' Her fingers trailed on Josephine's thigh. Soon Sharlee was accompanying her measuring with little pats and exploratory strokings. She had a wonderful touch. She could coo like a pigeon, beautifully. Josephine felt herself begin to rouse.

In the next room, a phone rang, and continued to ring. Sharlee jumped up at once and bustled off to answer it. Jackie went with her. She came back soon with a matron's uniform: plain dark blue bra and knickers, dress, frilled white apron, cap and gloves; even a pair of sensible black lace-ups. The dress had a stiff white collar that had to be fastened at the front with a brass stud.

'Where's Sharlee?' Josephine wanted to know as she got dressed up.

'Gone to an appointment,' Jackie said, pinning the cap to Josephine's thick, coarse hair with a hairgrip.

'Is she late?'

Jackie nodded, holding a second hairgrip in her mouth.

'Is she in trouble?'

Jackie took the hairgrip out, fixed it carefully in place. 'Sister Karlsen's getting her cane out. There now.'

Josephine looked at herself in the mirror on the back of the door. She was the very picture of a pillar of the caring profession. She smiled evilly, and gave Jackie a big wet kiss.

In the car, Josephine took her bag off the passenger seat as Jackie climbed in, and stuffed her gloves in the glove compartment. She started the engine.

'What's this you want to show me?' Jackie asked.

Josephine took the domino out of her bag and flipped it into Jackie's lap.

Jackie picked it up and examined it. She gave a happy cry and bounced up in her seat, kissing her friend on the cheek. 'You lucky thing!'

Josephine pulled out of the clinic and round the bend, heading back to the main road.

'Who gave it you?' Jackie asked. There was a definite wonder and envy in her voice.

'It came by messenger,' Josephine said, concentrating on the traffic. 'This morning. And he didn't ring the bell.'

'What?'

'He walked right in. I nearly had a heart attack. Just a kid, he was. He gave me that, all done up like a birthday present, then he turned round and walked right out again. Drove away in a big black Daimler. I chased him for a bit. Didn't catch him, needless to say.'

'And what did he say? Did he say anything?'

'Not a thing.' She noticed pedestrians glacing at them in surprise as they whizzed down Notting Hill. She supposed it must look a bit strange, two nurses in a bright red MR2. Not very medical.

'So you don't know who sent it?'

'No.'

'You will.'

Josephine glanced at her friend. 'Do *you* know?'

Jackie shook her head. 'It's the supreme masters,' she said. 'Only a supreme master sends you the double blank. It means –' She gave an odd little shiver. 'Total obedience,' she said simply.

Josephine felt her breath shorten, her pulse quicken. 'When? Where? How long for?'

'*Total* obedience,' said Jackie quietly. She reached out and put her hand on Josephine's thigh.

Suddenly, gesturing at a row of shops, she said excitedly, 'Oh, stop, stop here.'

'What for?'

'We've got to celebrate!'

There was a double yellow line. Josephine pulled in, braked. Jackie kissed her on the cheek, then jumped from the car. 'Lend us some

37

money,' she said as she went, and when Josephine handed out her handbag, ran back up the street with it. Josephine looked in her mirror and saw her going in an off-licence.

She sat waiting. Shopping women wandered by, smoking and trailing whining toddlers. A traffic warden appeared, sighted the car and came strolling purposefully towards it; then, seeing Josephine's uniform, changed her accusatory frown to a look of inquiry.

Josephine powered down her window and gave the warden a warm-hearted smile. 'It's a delivery, love,' she said. The hard lines of the warden's face softened. 'We'll be off in a minute,' Josephine promised her.

At that moment Jackie came running back from the shop clutching a very obvious champagne bottle protruding from pink tissue paper. Josephine started up. 'Thanks so much, dear,' she said, making eyes at the warden. Ignoring the warden completely Jackie jumped in and tugged the door shut after her. Josephine put her foot down and sped away, swinging aggressively into the traffic.

In the lift, they cuddled. Josephine could feel her friend's readiness. Where they touched, their bodies seemed to spark. Josephine wondered how much longer they would have together.

As they stepped out of the lift into the hall of her flat, an anxious voice called, 'Josephine?'

Jackie grabbed Josephine's arm. 'It's him!' she whispered. 'Your intruder!'

Josephine took her hand and squeezed it. She drew her into the kitchen, out of earshot. 'No it isn't,' she murmured, 'it's Russell. I found him this morning on a plane. I forgot he was here.'

Jackie smiled. Josephine understood that smile.

'What's his surname?' Jackie said.

Josephine was thinking. 'Harris,' she said.

Jackie straightened her uniform. 'How do I look?'

'Pristine,' said Josephine, and kissed her.

Jackie went and opened the bedroom door. Josephine tiptoed along the hall behind her, and when she went in, leaned against the wall to listen.

'Hello, Mr Harris,' she heard Jackie say breezily, 'and how are you today?'

Russell sounded alarmed and startled. 'Who are you? How did you get in here?' Josephine heard the creak of strained leather. 'Get me out of this!'

'One thing at a time, Mr Harris, one thing at a time. You mustn't excite yourself.'

There was a tiny pause then before Jackie said, concernedly: 'Hmm, your pulse is a bit weak, Mr Harris, do you know that? Tell me now, have you been having any problems with circulation lately, tingling feelings in your arms and legs, maybe?'

He sounded tired, and rather hoarse. He had missed his lunch. 'Of course I have!'

'Well, then,' Jackie said clearly, 'let's take a look at the ankles first, shall we? Let me just undo this strap here . . . and this one . . . There, now, can you bend your knees? That's good, Mr Harris, that's really very good indeed, you know. Can you bend them all the way up to your chest? That's fine, there's a good boy. Now then, can you lift your feet up in the air? Oh, well done, Mr Harris, gracious me, what a lovely view.'

Josephine grinned to herself. Russell's voice, sounding slightly muffled, said nervously: 'You're not a nurse at all, I know that.'

'Indeed I am, Mr Harris,' replied Jackie, managing to sound slightly scandalized. 'What sort of a woman do you take me for? No, no — keep your legs there now, please, I'm going to give you a little treatment here to see if we can't get your circulation up a bit, all right?'

There was another pregnant pause. Then Josephine heard the familiar crack of her black leather strap on naked flesh. She heard Russell shout out in protest and listened to Jackie's implacable reassurance as the strap rose and fell again and again and again.

In a little while it ceased. There were some indistinct rustling and moaning noises before Jackie said sympathetically, 'There now, Mr Harris, and my, that does look a lot better. But oh dear me, now, what's this? What have we got here?'

Josephine heard Russell mumble something. His voice was indistinct. He sounded breathless and embarrassed.

'What's that you say it is, Mr Harris, I can't quite hear you.'

'An erection.' The mixture of embarrassment and excitement in his voice told Josephine that Jackie was examining the offending member closely even as he named it.

They fell silent, but for some furtive creaking and squeaking noises, and gasps from Russell. Josephine pressed her hand to her crotch. She closed her eyes, seeing Russell waiting alone in a cold place,

39

chained to a post by his arms. He was wearing black sealskin trunks and she had a black leather basque and thigh boots. She would whip him with a martinet thonged with horsehide, with knotted tips.

She shivered and opened her eyes. She thought she could hear Jackie freeing Russell from his bonds. She heard her say: 'Where does she keep it now?' Then came the sound of rummaging in a drawer, rattling and clinking sounds as her equipment was all turned over. 'Ah, here we are.'

Josephine stepped quickly back into the lounge and looked around. The room was dull from the drab afternoon light. She touched on a Spruce Ferrier sidelight and angled it to pool on the floor and the plain white wall. She cleared up swiftly, sweeping some newspapers and faxes onto a pile by the Grundig and moving a glass fruit dish from the coffee table. Then she decided to move the coffee table as well. She made space in the middle of the room, and stood there, her arms folded.

Jackie emerged from the bedroom, smiling sweetly. She was leading Russell by a short black leash attached to the ring on his collar. He was following her along, rather red in the face, but not as red as he was in the bottom: Josephine looked and made sure. She was pleased to note he did indeed have a prominent erection. And his eyes bulged in his head when he saw her standing there, in her sister's uniform.

Jackie was looking slightly surprised, and rather worried. 'Oh, hello, sister,' she said, in a voice shining with assumed nonchalance. 'I was just taking Mr Harris here out for his afternoon exercise.'

'So I see, nurse,' said Josephine sternly, going over to them, 'but what do you call this?' She gestured imperiously in the direction of Russell's groin.

Apologetically Jackie said, 'Yes, I asked him that, sister, and he says it's an erection.'

'And are you responsible for this, nurse?' demanded Josephine.

Jackie was looking very humble and apprehensive now. 'I'm afraid I may be, sister, yes.'

'I don't remember that treatment for our patients includes giving them erections,' Josephine went on in a voice like cold wrath.

'No, sister,' said Jackie, looking at the floor. 'Sorry, sister,' she whispered.

'In fact it's shocking professional misconduct. I shall have to punish you, nurse. Go and fetch a chair.'

Jackie hesitated, holding up the end of Russell's leash.

'Leave Mr Harris with me.'

Jackie put the leash in Josephine's hand. She looked into her eyes an instant, her face perfectly blank and calm. Then she turned and bolted from the room, her head down.

Josephine heard her in the kitchen, moving the furniture about.

She held Russell at arm's length, glaring at him as if he was a particularly displeasing nuisance, and probably as culpable as the nurse.

'Turn around,' she said. 'Show me your marks.' Russell opened his mouth.

'*Don't speak*,' said Josephine tightly.

Russell's mouth closed with an audible snap. He turned round, winding the lead helplessly around his neck.

Josephine held on to it. She looked down at his buttocks. They were inflamed down almost to the backs of his knees. She felt a moment's weakness, felt herself losing control, yielding to desire.

'You may rub yourself with your hands, Mr Harris,' she said loudly. 'That also helps the circulation.'

Shakily, Russell lowered his hands to his bottom and pressed them there gingerly. He winced with pain and relief.

Jackie arrived, carrying a chunky upright chair in olive wood that had caught Josephine's fancy at a carpentry in Malta. She knew what sort of chair Josephine meant. She didn't mean one of the Kurt Schwesiger futon chairs of brushed steel with blown glass bearings. She meant a plain, sturdy kitchen chair. Without arms.

Josephine tried not to let her smile sound in her voice. 'Put it there,' she commanded, pointing with her free hand to the middle of the room. Jackie did, standing it to face Russell, who had half-turned back towards them. He was still rubbing his bottom. His eyes were a joy to behold.

Josephine tucked Russell's leash into his collar, handling it completely impersonally, pretending he was an animal or an inanimate object. Turning her back on him abruptly, she left him there and went over to sit on the chair, her chair. She sat down, straightening her uniform skirt under her with a sweep of her hand, then smoothing it over her lap. Jackie stood motionless beside her on the right, her hands clasped behind her back.

Russell had now turned completely back round to them. He stood

41

with his knees bent, staring at them helplessly, his hands pressed stiffly to his bottom. His erection stood at full salute.

Josephine looked up at Jackie. Jackie's eyes were staring too, icy and intense with love and longing.

'Now then,' said Josephine. 'Nurse. Across my knee, if you please.'

Jackie leaned forward, bending her knees, bending over to lie across Josephine's lap, her hands stretched out in front of her. They had performed this so many times the balance came to them in an instant. Jackie lifted her heels, held out her arms as though she was swimming. She lay still.

Josephine drew back her skirt.

Beneath her uniform Jackie was wearing white cotton knickers with a tiny stripe of orange, a lacy white suspender belt and seamed black stockings. Her bottom was towards Russell, who stood there, Josephine noticed in the reflected lamplight, with a shiny drip of moisture suspended from the tip of his quivering penis.

Josephine reached for Jackie's right hand with her left, took hold of it, and pinned it firmly in the middle of the helpless woman's back. With her right hand, she stretched out the elastic of Jackie's knickers. She looked up then, directly at the goggling Russell.

'Mr Harris,' she said. 'Turn your back.'

With a look of silent torment, he obeyed. He turned and faced the corner of the room.

Josephine pulled Jackie's knickers down, down past the bulge of her bottom to the top of her thighs. Her bottom was slender and white.

Keeping absolutely silent, Josephine bent her head and kissed Jackie's bottom. She felt Jackie wriggle a most undisciplined wriggle in reply.

She lifted her right hand and smacked it down, hard.

A quick blush rushed to fill her handprint.

She smacked her again.

A second handprint overlapped the first.

She smacked her again.

The three prints lay together in a blur. As she paused for a moment, watching, the stain began to spread across her friend's fair white skin.

But only on the right cheek.

The left cheek was as white as ever, if not whiter: unmarked, unspanked.

Josephine spanked it. She spanked it again; and again.

She felt Jackie moving, backwards and forwards, pressing her crotch against Josephine's thigh. Josephine spanked her quickly, repeatedly, catching her on the rhythm of her own little thrusts. Her hand grew warm.

She changed her position, wrapping her left arm around Jackie's waist, still clutching Jackie's right hand in her left, and leaning over the pinioned girl, tilting her bottom upwards. She smacked her until her hand was numb and Jackie was giving small despairing cries of excitement and distress. Her bare buttocks were now one large shapeless blotch of red. They looked quite hot and sore.

Josephine eased up, sat up, stopped. She looked round at Russell, still standing with his back to them. His hands were no longer on his bottom.

She put her right arm around Jackie's waist, steadying her. 'What is Mr Harris doing now, nurse?' she demanded loudly.

On Josephine's lap Jackie turned to look round, to her right, past the arm that was holding her down. 'Playing with himself, sister,' she said in a hushed tone, like a child gravely conscious of another's guilt.

'Well, I don't know! The filthy, disgusting beast! Get up at once nurse, and deal with it.'

With another secret kiss, Josephine let Jackie off her lap. She stood up readily enough, clasping her abused bottom with both hands and silently screwing up her face, grimacing in pain. Her cheeks were very pink; her eyes, when she opened them, sparkling.

She went across to where Russell was standing panting audibly and jerking frantically at his engorged penis. She smacked him sharply on his tender bottom, making him howl, and dragged his hands behind his back.

'Turn him round,' Josephine told her. 'Let him watch, if he wants to.' Now the young man's expression was pathetic with gratitude. 'But without touching himself,' Josephine pronounced. 'Go and get some handcuffs. And while you're in there,' she added, 'you can fetch me the hairbrush. Go on.'

Jackie left, her red bottom glowing.

Josephine stared expressionlessly at Russell, feeling the stinging in her palm tingle and begin to fade. She was remembering the young man who had propositioned her on the plane that morning, how self-possessed and cocksure he had been, convinced of his own excellent desirability. Now he stood there in a slave's collar and leash, gazing at her in apprehensive adoration. His penis was redder now than either his bottom or his face, and it was dribbling on the carpet.

'Lick that up,' said Josephine automatically.

While he was on his hands and knees obeying, his leash trailing beside him, Jackie came back.

Both Russell and Josephine looked at her in pleasure. She had almost stripped. Though Josephine had not instructed her to, she had taken off her uniform, both the apron and the dress. Her cap was still perched sweetly on her head — and her knickers were still down on her hips; but she was used to walking around like that. She moved with poise and grace across the floor in her black stockings and her white bra with a large star-shaped flower on either nipple. In one hand she held the handcuffs, in the other a long wooden brush.

She went straight over to the crouching Russell and, taking care not to overbalance, lifted her left leg over his back, straddling him. She leaned forward, quickly laid the brush on the floor one side of him and the handcuffs the other. Then Josephine saw her tug Russell's arms out from under him. His cheek hit the carpet, and he gave a piteous wail.

Swiftly Jackie crossed his wrists and locked the cuffs about them. Then she dragged him to his feet by hauling up on his leash and made him stand upright, swaying, facing Josephine in her chair.

She picked up the brush and brought it to Josephine. Josephine accepted it.

It was old, its bristles black and stiff. It looked more like a clothes brush than a hairbrush. It had been a present to Josephine from Annabel, a memento of the first spanking the doctor's housekeeper had ever given her, at Estwych.

'Take your knickers off,' Josephine told Jackie.

Jackie bent forward from the hips and bent her knees, loosening her knickers with her hands and drawing them down, down her thighs to her knees, and then to her feet. Bending to keep hold of them, she stepped out of them, then stood up and offered them to Josephine.

'Perhaps Mr Harris will look after them for you,' said Josephine.

Jackie went back to Russell, waving her dampened knickers in the air before his yearning face. She tucked them into the ring on his collar and left them dangling on his chest.

She patted him on his head and came back to Josephine.

'Across my knee again,' Josephine told her.

44

Jackie bent over.

Later, Russell Harris hung by his arms from the chandelier, which was industrial steel and bolted to the ceiling, while Jackie stood behind him, legs apart, spanking him for all she was worth with the black leather strap. His skin was white and sweaty. All the colour in his body seemed to have fled to his cock and the lurid, broad stripes across his back and bottom. His eyes were staring unfocused at the ceiling. His mouth was open, shaping inarticulate mutterings, cries and squeals. His chain was just long enough to allow him to sag at the knees, but never quite kneel down. He swung helplessly to and fro.

Josephine reclined on the floor between his floppy legs. She too had abandoned her uniform, but for the knickers and suspender belt, and one torn stocking. At the crotch of the knickers was a large stain, glistening darkly.

She caught Jackie's eye. 'Now,' she said.

Then she tilted her head back and took another mouthful of champagne. She reached up with one hand and took hold of Russell by his cock, pulling it towards her, popping it into her mouth.

He gave a strangled, sobbing cry as the effervescence enveloped him.

Jackie gave him a last crack with the strap. With an awful, bleating groan Russell ejaculated long and heavily into Josephine's mouth.

'How was it?' Jackie asked her a minute later, as she thoughtfully detached him from the chain.

'Not the best way to enjoy champagne,' Josephine declared.

She looked at her yuppie, lying there spent and collapsed, his legs across hers, his eyes closed, his penis still oozing. Gently she reached behind him and unlocked his cuffs. He gave her a look of pure, wet-eyed puppy love, then his eyes sagged closed again. He curled up in a foetal ball, hands clutched under his chin. He began to smile the smile of a sleeping baby.

Josephine's eyes met Jackie's. Jackie pulled a face.

'Shall we?'

'Let's.'

They left him there and retired together to the bedroom, their arms around each other.

45

|4|

September that year was chilly and damp. London was full of American and Japanese tourists in kagouls and ski jackets, trailing in hopeful herds from Buckingham Palace to Baker Street and back again. In wine bars and restaurants Josephine would find herself drifting out of the conversation, gazing around the clientèle or out of the plate-glass windows into the street. Shopping, she would stop and turn, staring at a passing head, a flash of colour from someone's coat. At home she flipped ceaselessly through the channels on TV. She was looking for a boy of twenty, blond, in a crimson uniform. She saw no one, everyone.

At her desk she toyed with the blank domino, pushing it around with the tip of her finger, squeezing it in her hand while she talked on the phone. Sometimes when being courted by clients of whom she had even the slightest suspicion, she would deliberately let them see it, holding it in one hand and stroking it with the other, turning it between her thumbs and fingers so they could see both sides were blank. 'My lucky charm,' she said, when anyone asked. Anyone who knew, wouldn't have had to ask.

They smiled indulgently. A glint in their eyes asked if the redoubtable Josephine Morrow was losing her edge. Their stupidity angered her and made her harsh. Secretaries at the coffee machine stopped talking when she went by.

She had Francis drive her one evening to a house in Wimbledon, where an elderly porter with silver hair, his face a riot of broken veins, asked politely to see her identification. Josephine unbuttoned her jacket and blouse and showed him her breasts, the tattoo between them. She got out the domino and showed him that. He raised his eyebrows, shook his head. She went in anyway.

In a lounge of marbled wallpaper and dark Symbolist canvases in heavy frames, an androgynous rock guitarist sat slumped in an armchair of worn purple velvet, toying with a Tequila Sunrise and chatting to a large black woman in a dark green suit by Azzedine Alaia. The woman sat with her legs apart. A naked man knelt between her legs with his head up her skirt.

Josephine passed into the billiard room. She played a game of snooker with a Swedish pilot she had encountered before at a place called Estwych. They were watched by two expressionless young women standing at attention either side of the curtained doorway. The women wore narrow collars of black leather and matching high-heeled shoes, nothing else. One had dark hair coiled up in a tight bun on the top of her head; the other, dull brown hair tied in a ponytail, and a large mole on her right breast. They had no tattoos. When commanded, they went without a word and fetched a tray of drinks and one of cocktail savouries, then resumed their posts as precisely as automatons.

Every time Josephine or her opponent failed to score, they removed an item of clothing. Josephine played badly, carelessly, and lost the game. Naked already, she was bent over the snooker table and spanked. The slaves stared unconcernedly into the middle distance as the tall Swede's large hand rose and fell on her plump buttocks.

When he had finished with her, Josephine got up and fetched the blank domino from her bag. She showed it to him. His mouth tightened, his pale eyes narrowed. He shook his head and left her immediately, snapping his fingers and pointing at his discarded clothes. The dark slave hurried to gather them up and ran after him, clutching them to her breasts.

Josephine went out after them into the hall, and wandered along to the bar. It was empty. The rock guitarist was sitting doodling Noel Coward melodies at the grand piano. He gazed at Josephine's nude form, offered her a line of cocaine, tried to give her a domino. Josephine showed him the double blank and he muttered a slurred oath of surprise and displeasure. She took the cocaine anyway.

At the weekend she drove to Scotland, to the highlands. Evening mist rolled down the hillsides and the air echoed with the anguished cry of an inconsolable bird. When the grey light failed Josephine was jolting slowly up a muddy winding track that led to a sombre castle on a cliff. Below, drab heather tumbled over rocks about a silent tarn. Admitted to the courtyard, she parked the Toyota in the stables.

47

There was a Jag she recognised, Tom Olav's old Range Rover, an Audi belonging to a prominent independent TV producer. There were half a dozen of them there, including Dora, an inquisitive middle-aged housewife from Durham, who had come with Sam to be initiated. Nobody knew who employed messengers in red uniforms; nobody wanted to get in the way of a supreme master's decree. Nobody would risk claiming Josephine while she was carrying someone else's domino. Josephine was out of the game.

They allowed her to sit on a stool in the corner and watch when Dora was hung up for her first whipping. The crack of the lash and Dora's high, gasping cries, the creak of harness and black leather and steel glinting in the torchlight, the shadows of rampant cocks and the heady scent of hot loins were too much for Josephine. She flung up her skirts and began to masturbate, there in front of them all, her legs stretched out in front of her. After that they came, all of them, masked, to her room in the deep of the night. They pulled her naked from her bed and took her in chains to the dungeon, where they made her endure a prolonged and painful caning. The rods had been steeped in pickle.

Abandoned, she lay on the floor of the cell, which stank of mouldered straw and ancient must. There were scratchings in the walls all night. Hard stone and aching flesh warred continually with sleep. It grew cold. A bell sounded somewhere, solemn and sad.

At first light the housekeeper brought Josephine her clothes. She gave her cream for her welts and a mug of strong, sweet tea. A baillie with an ancient shotgun and two tall hounds put her on the road back to England. Above his thick sandy moustache his eyes regarded her with stern, impersonal pity, as if she was the unfortunate bearer of some sinister and highly contagious disease.

All the way down the A68 it rained, a soft black drizzle that mired the windscreen. She had the headlights on before four. The radio was useless, a mixture of bad news and discouraging traffic reports interspersed with old pop songs that had been rubbish when they first polluted the airwaves, twenty years earlier. Josephine's bottom and thighs throbbed dully. Her head was thick, clotted with frustration and lack of sleep. She stopped for more coffee and painkillers, sat in the brash inhuman light of the Country Kitchen staring at the hessian-pattern formica, the brown plastic cruet. At the next table, three long-distance drivers were looking at her, talking about her in an undertone. She didn't feel in the least like sex, more like murder. She felt like letting one of them pick her up and then scarring him for life.

She went home.

She saw a lot of Jackie during this period.

Jackie took off her skirt and panties and came to sit on Josephine's lap. She sat sideways, twisting round from the waist to take Josephine's head firmly in both hands, tilting it backwards and kissing her hard, thrusting her tongue between Josephine's indifferent lips. Without looking, she took Josephine's hand, and spreading the fingers, pressed the palm to her crotch. She breathed a little snuffle of pleasure at the touch. She sucked Josephine's tongue as though she wanted to pull it out by the root. She nuzzled her ear, running her mouth through Josephine's thick blonde hair, kissing her temple and her eyelids, her cheek, her mouth again. She took Josephine's hand from her groin and sucked the fingers, slipping each one into her mouth and drawing on it as if she expected it to yield some sort of liquid sustenance, honey, milk.

Josephine felt Jackie's groin, stroking her flossy pubic hair, feeling the labia swell and open under her hand. Jackie wriggled on her lap, lifting her right leg and placing her foot on the seat of the chair between Josephine's knees, swinging her knee out and down, sliding a little lower to push her pelvis forward against Josephine's hand.

Josephine's fingers began to coax a heavy dew from Jackie's vagina. Jackie sighed and breathed in Josephine's hair, arching her throat, pressing Josephine's head to her breast.

'Oh love that's good. Oh it feels so good, Jesus it does, mmmm . . .'

She reached for Josephine's hand, gripping it by the wrist and forcing it deeper into her crotch, running Josephine's fingers back between her legs to probe her anus. Josephine twisted her hand and cocked her thumb, pressing it up between the moistening lips to dig for the clitoris under its tiny hood. Jackie made a guttural sound of satisfaction. 'Mm. Mm. Nn.'

Josephine was distracted, working on automatic. 'I'm sorry . . .'

'What are you sorry about?'

'It's not happening.'

'Speak for yourself.'

Jackie lay back across Josephine's lap, her thighs wide, abandoned to sensation.

'You'll fall.'

'I'm flying . . .'

49

Josephine thumbed her friend's clitoris, round and round, up and down. Jackie's eyes were closed, her long red-gold hair trailing. Her lips were parted as if for a cautious kiss. She was breathing out in a long continuous voiceless whistle of pleasure. Her body began to slide to the floor.

'I can't hold you!'

They were in Josephine's lounge. They went into the bedroom.

Josephine Morrow's bedroom was spacious and rather empty. The walls were painted the deep royal blue of a summer night, and there was a soft white wool carpet on the floor. The curtains were thick cream linen, drawn back either side of a window that looked out into the muddy sky. The bed was king-size, built low but standing on a raised platform. The platform had a ring-bolt at each corner. The bed was made, a pale mustard slub wool spread drawn tidily over it, top to bottom. Within reach of the bed, fitted units contained all the things Josephine might need – a drawer full of toys, another full of lingerie, a double wardrobe where all the clothes she could ever imagine wearing hung ready for her. There was a steel and canvas chair and a deco coffee table with a soapstone bowl of pot pourri. There were no clothes visible, no cosmetics, no clutter. A copy of *Oggi* magazine open at a photo of Tom Conti was the only casual sign of life.

Jackie tapped the switch and another steel chandelier, twin to the one in the lounge, lit up, its radiance doubled by the large mirror on the long wall by the door.

'No,' said Josephine. She turned the light off.

She took off the rest of Jackie's clothes, kissing the faint freckles on her chest before gently releasing her long breasts from their snowy brassière. Jackie pressed the length of her body against her, standing on one foot and lifting the other to caress Josephine's hip with the inside of her thigh.

She was wearing no lipstick. He teeth were clean and bright and her mouth tasted of mint. She was receptive. Josephine pressed her cupped hand to Jackie's crotch again, feeling her moistness undiminished, touching the tremulousness of her secret centre. She lifted her hand for Jackie to smell. Jackie took Josephine's hand in both of hers, licking her fingers again, slowly, savouring her own flavour.

Josephine arranged her on the bed, her legs wide.

'Touch yourself,' she said.

She felt distant, well-disposed, like a teacher meeting a former favourite pupil, or like the umpire at some strange, abstract sport, wishing to see fair play. Jackie extended two fingers, licking them unnecessarily, and stroked her clitoris with bold long strokes.

Josephine folded her arms. Her breasts felt heavy, slightly sore around the nipples. Her period was approaching. Usually at this time she was easily aroused, felt a sheen of eroticism on everything she touched and saw. A man in the lift. A woman on the underground, crossing her legs. Slogans in ads. Everything would promise to be a key to the dark, still cave of intensity where pleasure waited.

Today she felt dishevelled, neglected. All week she had kept finding that her jaw was tight, her teeth clenched for no reason.

Jackie raised her knees, lifted her feet off the bed. The soft hair in her cleft was dark ginger wetness. She rubbed herself, panting slowly in deep shaky gusts.

'Don't stop,' Josephine said.

She pulled off her loose Cardin top. She was naked under it. She shook out her hair, ran her fingers through it. It felt greasy, lank. She took out her stainless steel drop earrings and put them in a bowl in the vanity.

She untied her Peruvian wrap-round skirt and slipped off her panties, noticing a speck of blood. There was a wet spot too on her skirt, where Jackie had been writhing around.

On the bed, Jackie was on her back with her knees up by her ears. She was contracting her spine, lifting her pale white bottom off the bedspread. Josephine looked at it bobbing and thrusting arhythmically while her friend rubbed herself with the heel of her palm.

Josephine touched herself. She was dry, cold, closed. Her lips gave back a dull, irritable sensation to her questing fingers. She had not had an orgasm since the wretched trip to Scotland, when she had forced herself to come, quickly, mechanically, sitting on the stool in the corner at Dora's flagellation, knowing no one wanted her there, knowing they would punish her later for her insolence. She had spent the night with Jackie, last night and the night before, and slept innocently, one arm over Jackie's slender waist, her breasts against her back.

She took off her socks and knelt on the bed, bending to lick Jackie's genitals. Jackie arched her back with a guttural sound.

Josephine lifted her head. Jackie's fine long hair was down, spreading loose on the bed, across her face. One end of it was caught in the corner of her mouth. Josephine looked at her flushed pink face, kissed her on the mouth, and freed the hair, hooking it out with a fingertip. Jackie's eyes were wild, roving all about. Josephine knew Jackie could tell by her languid, calculated movements that she was exhausted, not really present. She stroked Jackie's cheek.

'I'm sorry,' she said again.

'Oh, love,' said Jackie sympathetically. She hugged her, rolling forward, sitting up. 'Is there anything I can do for you?' she asked.

'Lick me again,' she said, knowing there wasn't.

Josephine lowered her face to Jackie's crotch. She smelt of tamarinds. She tasted almost chemical, hot and sour. Her flesh seeped under Josephine's tongue. Josephine had soft curly hair in her mouth. She turned her head sideways, found the tight nub of the clitoris with her mouth, hearing Jackie gasp. She nibbled it lightly with her lips. Jackie had a leg over Josephine's shoulder. Josephine pressed her chin against Jackie's thigh, wrapping her left arm around it, kneeling beside her and slipping a finger into her hot quim.

As she licked, she saw pictures in her head. The deck of an ocean liner, passengers in 1930s clothes playing a game with quoits made of rope. A bank of ferns with black oil sprayed all over them. A school dormitory where she had once slept, a girl called Nina standing naked at the washbasins, her brown skin streaming. A man's genitals, pouched and hairy. A row of palm trees silhouetted against a bloody sky.

The entryphone buzzed.

'Damnation!' said Jackie.

Josephine lifted her head, got up wearily on her hands and knees, crawled across Jackie to the bedside phone.

Suddenly she thought, It could be him.

She pressed the button. She said, 'Hello?'

'Hello?' said a young man's voice. 'Josephine?'

Jackie was sitting up, pressing herself against Josephine's side, her hand on Josephine's shoulder. 'Is it him? Is it?'

'Who is it?' Josephine asked.

'Russell,' said the voice.

The two women sighed, deflated.

'What do you want?'

'I've got something for you.' He sounded cocky.

'Just a minute,' said Josephine. She took her finger off the button. She looked at Jackie.

'Tell him to piss off,' said Jackie mildly.

'He'll only come back,' Josephine said.

'Do you want him up?' said Jackie, curiously.

Josephine shrugged. She knew who she wanted to see and it wasn't Russell Harris.

She pressed the button again. 'Okay,' she said.

She got off the bed and pulled on her top, tied her skirt around her waist, slipped her bare feet into a pair of easy shoes. She looked in the mirror, tidying her hair with her fingers. Behind her, Jackie was mopping herself with a tissue and reaching for her bra.

'Stay in here,' Josephine said.

She went out into the hall and down to the lift.

With a soft chime, it arrived.

She thought about leaving him there for a minute or two, just to torment him. It was pointless, as pointless as everything had been today. She pressed the button.

The doors slid open and Russell stepped out.

'Hello, Josephine,' he said, and moved to kiss her.

She offered her cheek, accepted his embrace with cool neutrality. He smelt of the same aftershave as before, but it didn't disguise the fact that he'd been drinking. He was wearing a navy blue blazer with a golf club crest embroidered on the pocket, charcoal slacks and black brogues. He was carrying a parcel wrapped in brown paper, something two feet long and very thin.

'I've been trying to get hold of you,' he said, smiling.

'I know,' she said. Her answering machine was full of his suave, importunate messages.

'I've got something for you,' he said. His smile became ugly.

'You said,' said Josephine . She was regretting her decision already. She didn't want this idiotic young boy scout with his unco-ordinated lust. He wasn't even trained yet.

He took hold of her arm. She let his hand stay there, it was pointless telling him to take it away. She wondered, briefly, what had happened to his adoration. Had it turned to possessiveness so quickly?

She looked at the parcel in his other hand. He made as if to offer it to her, then seemed to change his mind. He let go of her arm and tore the paper off in a savage, vengeful gesture.

It was, as she'd guessed, a cane. A hook-handled length of wood, stained and polished.

She could tell by the way it sat in his hand that it was much too rigid, though at least it was as thin as she preferred.

She wondered then where he had got it. The Russell she had met on the plane would scarcely have known that shops for such things existed, let alone where to find one. He had obviously made some progress, then.

The cane had a little bow of black ribbon tied to its tip.

She put out her hand to take it.

Russell held it away from her, warding her off with his free hand.

She looked at him questioningly. Behind his tinted lenses, his eyes were unreadable. His mouth still wore that odd, malicious smile. She supposed he had been drinking to get up courage to come and ask her to beat him. He was wound up, excited, aggressive. He probably thought he despised her, but it was himself he despised.

Josephine could not raise any enthusiasm for this little boy who wanted her to play with his stick. It was a good job Jackie was here. Jackie was a kind-hearted soul, she wouldn't turn him down.

Josephine said, 'You'd better come in.' She turned and led him down the hall.

'You don't understand, do you?' he said, following behind her. His voice was nasty, gloating. She could hear the drink on his tongue.

She stood in the lounge, her hands on her hips. 'What do you want, Russell?'

He ignored her question. 'You made a fool of me,' he said. 'You must have thought I was a right twerp, didn't you?'

She didn't answer.

He lifted the cane.

'This is for you,' he said. He obviously thought he was brilliant. 'I've come to see if you can take it as well as you dish it out.'

Josephine sighed. He understood nothing; himself least of all. Still, it was her fault. She was responsible for starting him off.

She saw him notice Jackie's skirt and panties lying discarded on the floor. 'Is your friend here too?' he said, with a sneering emphasis. 'Jolly good. I've got plenty of medicine to go round.'

He swished the cane through the air.

He really was quite drunk, she realised. And she was very tired.

'Russell,' she said, heavily.

'Don't patronise me, Josephine,' he snapped.

He stabbed the cane into the carpet at the side of his foot and struck a pose.

'What's it to be?' he demanded.

'Come on, then,' she said.

His smile was triumphant.

She led him in the bedroom. Jackie was sitting on the bed in her bra and a pair of exercise tights.

'Oh very nice,' said Russell.

'Hello, Mr Harris, have you come for your tea?' she asked, her voice light and inoffensive.

'I've come to teach you a lesson,' he said. 'Both of you. Your perverted little games.'

'My oh my,' said Jackie, pertly.

'You had your fun with me,' Russell went on. 'Now we'll see how you like being on the receiving end, shall we?'

Jackie looked at Josephine. Josephine was past caring. 'You don't have to stay, love,' she told her.

'Silence!' he commanded. He grinned wolfishly.

He unfastened the middle button of his blazer. Then he took his glasses off, folded them precisely, and put them in his breast pocket. He looked around the room.

Josephine thought of the dishwasher waiting to be unloaded, the kitchen floor that needed washing. She wondered how Russell would look in a little frilly black dress and apron.

Russell pointed with his cane.

'Get those pillows,' he said. 'Put them here.' He pointed to the foot of the bed.

Jackie turned round where she sat and pulled two of the pillows out from under the crumpled bedspread.

'You too, Jo,' Russell commanded.

Josephine went round the bed and took the pillows from the other side, brought them to him. They laid them in two piles, side by side.

'Take those off,' said Russell curtly, pointing the cane at Jackie's groin, twiddling the beribboned end in a little circle in the air.

She got up and stood beside the bed. 'What about my tits?' she asked, pleasantly.

'Silence!' he said thickly. 'Take your bra off too,' he said. He swung round to address Josephine. 'And you. Take everything off.'

55

Jackie slipped her hands behind her, unhooked her bra and slipped it off her shoulders, putting it on the bed. Her breasts swung forward like pears on a branch as she bent at the waist to pull down her tights.

Josephine took off her top. Russell's eyes swivelled greedily back and forth. He didn't know which to look at first.

Josephine slipped off her shoes and pushed them aside with foot. She untied her skirt and gathered it up in a loose bundle, tossing it into the chair.

'There, that was easy, wasn't it?' said Russell. 'I notice you're neither of you wearing any knickers,' he commented, insinuatingly.

They didn't speak. He had told them not to. But he seemed to be having difficulty sustaining the conversation alone.

'I know what you've been doing,' he said raggedly. 'I can smell it in here,' he said.

The front of his trousers was bulging, his erection spoiling the expensive line of their cut. Josephine caught Jackie's eye. She could tell Jackie had noticed it too.

'Well, seeing as you like each other's company so much, I'll do you both together,' Russell decided. 'Side by side. Come on, bend over.'

Josephine turned to the bed and bent over for him. The pillows were to raise their buttocks to a convenient height and prominence. She supposed Russell had been reading some books, or at least studying pictures in a magazine. Her sore breasts flattened against the soft ridges of the bedspread. She folded her arms and laid her head on them, face down. At the same time she felt the mattress give, felt skin slide against her skin, down over her hip and then her shoulder, as Jackie lay down beside her. Their arms touched.

Josephine adjusted her position, brought her knees in to the bed, stretched her feet out on the floor so her toes were not cramped under her. She kept her legs together, expecting any second that he would tell her to open them. She thought he would be eager to arrange them himself, to handle their hips and their bottoms, bringing them properly into line. But all he said was, 'Back a bit, you.' Josephine felt Jackie shift herself backwards, supposed he was prodding her in the buttocks with the tip of the cane. 'Now sideways. To your right.'

Jackie's bottom nestled alongside hers.

There was the quick buzz of a zip being opened.

Josephine turned her head a fraction and saw Jackie looking at her. She remembered the first time they had been punished together, in the attic at Estwych. The group had chained them naked face to face, breast to breast, and given them what they said was a hundred strokes of the strap. She wondered if anyone had really been keeping count.

Russell also knew enough to lay the cane across their bottoms, to measure his stroke.

He had fallen silent.

Jackie's pretty eyes closed. Josephine could hear her, feel her breathing.

The cane left their buttocks, lifting up above them.

There was a long, empty moment.

'Damn you,' said Russell. 'Bitches. Bitches!' He shouted it. His voice was congested.

They waited.

Josephine imagined him standing over them, legs apart, his prick quivering, brandishing his new toy above his head.

Silent and still they waited, their bare bottoms raised on pillows, offered to him.

'Damn you,' he muttered. 'Damn you! I c – I c-c- . . .'

Stuttering, he choked and sobbed.

Josephine drew a deep breath. It was no less than she'd expected.

She got to her feet, climbing backwards off the bed, patting Jackie's back as she rose.

'No!' said Russell, anguish in his voice. 'Bend over!'

Josephine ignored him. She turned and looked him in the eye.

His shining red prick was sticking out of his fly. It appeared to be wilting. His face convulsed with guilt and misery and he burst into tears.

At once Jackie was on her feet, making consoling noises, taking him in her arms and kissing his brow, smoothing his hair, stroking his penis. Josephine reached out and gently relieved him of the cane.

At that Russell struggled. He shoved Jackie away, viciously, sending her sprawling against the bed. He came at Josephine, his hand outstretched, shaking.

'Give me that!'

She slapped his face hard. He recoiled, snivelling, clapping his hand to the place.

Josephine put her foot up on the bed, gripped the cane in both hands and brought it straight down across her knee. It snapped with a small, dry crunch. She tossed the two ends into the corner.

Jackie was up again, hugging Russell, who was quite as broken as his cane, sobbing and bleating incoherently into her tangled hair. She looked at Josephine over his shoulder. 'Shall I take him away?' she asked.

'Sure.' Josephine hardly cared. She knew she should care, she even wanted to care. All she felt was the small guilt of being relieved of a tiresome responsibility. She reached out and patted Jackie's shoulder, ran the back of her hand gently over her face. Jackie kissed it as it passed.

'Come along, now, Mr Harris,' said Jackie. 'I'm going to take you to a nice place where you'll be very happy.'

He raised his head, looking suspiciously, warily at both of them. His eyes were red with tears. Josephine wondered when he had last wept, this hard man of the city, and how much more he would weep before he was trained and ready, in the quiet, patient rooms of Estwych.

Jackie was tucking her breasts into her bra, fastening a suspender belt around her hips. 'I'll have to wear my uniform,' she said happily. 'Would you do me a favour and call the clinic for me, tell them I shan't be in for a few days?'

Looking away to conceal a smile, Josephine put on her Charnier dressing gown and went quickly from the room.

She made the call and left the message. All the while she was on the phone she could hear Jackie chatting nonchalantly to Russell, hear his sullen monosyllabic replies. She was glad now she'd asked him up. Everything was working out for the best. She hummed as she poured them out a cup of coffee.

Josephine's period came and went. She didn't miss Jackie while she was away. She knew she'd call when she was back in town and ready to see her again. Rain lashed down across the patio, on the roof of the penthouse. Aeroplanes sliced slowly across the grey sky, and wet pigeons sought shelter under her eaves. At the office one Wednesday morning they had a meeting with the Swiss branch of a pharmaceutical multinational. There had been a crisis over the closure of a research lab.

A black American woman with a sultry Southern accent made a presentation, leading them sardonically but knowledgably through professionally-prepared flowcharts, picking incriminating figures out of laser-printed spreadsheets, marshalling the evidence for obsessive overspending that the accountants had attempted to disperse and disguise. She leaned towards them across the table, balancing on her wrists, her fingers raised and curled. She paused, as if giving them a moment to consider her cleavage, then made a delicately obscene joke and lowered her eyelids, distancing herself from the murmur of appreciative chuckles.

Josephine sat back, watching the performance as though it was something on TV that she had just happened to tune in, following the story with half an ear, waiting for the hook. A management buyout had failed, courteous overtures were being made.

The door opened suddenly, surprising everyone. A short young man in a peaked cap came striding in. He looked like an old-fashioned pageboy in his crimson jacket with its mandarin collar, its brass buttons and black frogging. His hair was curly, blond, as fine as a baby's.

There was a fuss in the corridor behind him. 'You can't go in there!' called a woman's voice. The boy was taking no notice. He scanned the faces around the conference table, and fixed his eyes on Josephine.

'You're wanted,' he said. His voice was quiet. It anticipated no refusal.

Josephine's secretary came running in after him, trying to apologise. 'I'm terribly sorry, Ms Morrow,' she said forcefully. 'He just walked in. I couldn't stop him.'

Josephine picked up her handbag and pushed back her chair.

Ignoring the secretary, the security man hurrying along the corridor, the Swiss representatives and the rest of the meeting, the messenger turned smartly round and left the room.

To the consternation of everyone, Josephine followed.

'Ms Morrow! Josephine! Where are you going?'

'Good heavens!'

'Do you want us to carry on?'

But Josephine was already gone, brushing past her astounded secretary and the belligerent security man without a murmur, following the boy into the lift.

The doors closed.

Josephine looked at the boy. He was not looking at her. He stood passive, with his arms at his sides.

'Can you tell me anything?' she asked him.

He didn't reply. He didn't even acknowledge that she'd spoken.

Her heart was racing in her chest.

She looked at the indicator, the numbers of the floors flipping by.

The lift stopped in the basement. The doors opened. The boy walked smartly out of the lift and down the ramp into the car park.

Josephine followed. Her heels tapped a brisk tattoo on the grey tarmac. She heard them distantly, as if they were someone else's. Her breasts felt tight, her breathing loud and shallow.

The messenger led her to the black Daimler. It was spotless, gleaming, freshly waxed. The messenger opened the rear nearside door and stood to attention, looking indifferently over Josephine's head as he indicated she should get in.

Josephine ducked her head and stepped into the Daimler.

Inside was a dark woman in her forties, in a French suit and large dark glasses. Her mouth was wide, her lips magenta, expressionless. The suit was black, a masculine cut with padded shoulders and a flared skirt. She sat well back in her seat, her hands on her thighs. On her left index finger she wore a thick ring of black lacquer with a large square-cut ruby, and a creamy silk neckscarf tied like a cravat. The car was fragrant with L'Elegance. The upholstery was black leather. Something by Schubert was playing very softly.

The woman glanced at Josephine as she sat down beside her and the boy shut the door. She did not speak.

The boy got into the driver's seat.

'Go,' said the woman.

The boy started the car.

|5|

Excited as she was, at first, it was no different from Francis's days off, when someone else drove her around. The woman beside her was placid, composed as any phlegmatic broker. She did not look at Josephine. She looked straight ahead.

They pulled out into the street. There was a policewoman there to see them out. She held up the traffic for them.

Who was this woman?

Josephine knew that of all things, that was the one that didn't matter. She took a deep breath, and turned in her seat to face her.

Unbidden, she opened the second button of her blouse. With two fingers she spread the opening, revealing the domino tattoo.

The woman took no notice.

Of course, Josephine thought.

She opened the next button down.

She reached in between her breasts, where the domino itself, the double blank, was resting. She took it out and showed it to the woman, offering it to her.

The woman paid no attention.

Gently, Josephine put the domino on her thigh.

The woman ignored it.

'You were not told to open your blouse,' she said quietly.

Swiftly Josephine took the domino off the woman's leg and slipped it back in its place. 'I'm sorry,' she said.

'You were not told to apologise.'

Josephine started to do up her blouse. Her hands paused on the buttons. She wondered if she could be seen at all from outside. She wondered if there were any more traffic lights on this road.

Her mouth was dry.

She licked her lips.

61

'Mistress,' she said.

She knew the boy was listening.

'Your slave begs to display herself to you,' she said.

'If you speak again,' said the woman mildly, 'it will be the worse for you.'

Josephine put her hands down.

She closed her eyes and tried to still her clamouring heart. Her blood was up. But she had to be quiet, be obedient.

The woman had a foreign accent, almost anglicized but still audible. Josephine remembered Vienna, a solicitor who had been a pig across the conference table but extremely keen in bed. He had looked good too, in harness.

Discreetly, she stroked the seat either side of her. It felt sleek, firm, supple. Sitting back, she breathed in its aroma, the perfume of her captress. She willed herself to be soothed by the Schubert.

The Daimler cornered sharply, accelerating. Fine hydraulics cushioned Josephine as she was pressed into the armrest. She opened her eyes, unsatisfied.

They were travelling through back streets. The traffic was light. Josephine had no idea where they were. Closed warehouses slipped by on either side, a grimy brick Victorian school behind a high wire fence.

That would do, thought Josephine as they passed it. A classroom. An old classroom. An old-fashioned teacher.

She gave the woman a glance. Perhaps if she took off her sunglasses, and put a long black gown on over that suit.

No, thought Josephine then. I don't need to go back to school.

I know what I need to know.

Her excitement subsided.

Forever, she suddenly thought. It might be forever.

At that she felt a surge of panic and horror; and a moment later, a quiet thrill of pure delight.

She was going all the way.

All the way, they had said to each other when she was a girl. This summer, say, with that boy — might one go all the way? Whispering in the dorm, after lights out. Sometimes, lying in one bed together, cuddling, whispering the most exciting things of all.

All the way. Meaning something quite different now; and yet, in fact, not so different at all. To seek the passion that transforms, that exhilarates, that exalts.

Forever. For real.

And what was real now? How could you tell?

Would she ever see her parents again? Her friends? Would she ever go to the office again?

Perhaps everything would continue exactly the same as before, but on new terms. Terrifying terms.

Perhaps everything was going horribly wrong.

Perhaps they were going to kill her.

Perhaps they would let her live, but put a stop to all her pleasures. Perhaps this woman was not one of them at all. Perhaps she was a policewoman, on some sort of horrific Euro vice squad.

Suddenly Josephine recognised where they were. They were passing her local tube station. She saw the dry cleaner's on the corner, people beginning to converge on the sandwich bar.

The boy certainly knew his London. He'd brought her home by a route she didn't even know existed, and cut ten minutes off the journey.

He pulled up outside the building and stepped around swiftly to open the kerbside door. Josephine got out. The woman followed. 'Park it,' she said to the boy as she emerged. He saluted and slammed the door.

Josephine led the way into the building, nodding to the receptionist and walking smartly across the lobby and into the lift.

In the lift, neither of them spoke. Josephine stared at the door. She glanced at her captress. Her perfume filled the lift. Her eyes were invisible behind her dark glasses. The set of her lipsticked mouth promised strength and torments. Josephine lowered her head. She stared unseeing at the floor.

The woman strode straight into the flat, noticing nothing around her. She took off her sunglasses and stood in the lounge, facing Josephine, scrutinizing her. She stood with her feet apart. Beneath the black skirt her legs were firm and strong. Without looking she closed the glasses and slipped them into her breast pocket.

Her eyes were slender as leaves, the irises smoky grey. Her nose was large and strong, the planes of her face taut and refined. It was the face of a pianist, a ballerina. Her eyebrows were plucked and trained into a formidable arch. She did not look pleased.

Josephine ached, thrilled.

She kept her hands at her sides, gazed at the floor, at a spot five inches in front of the woman's feet. 'This slave begs permission to speak,' she said.

'Refused,' said the woman distantly.

The carpet shimmered before Josephine's eyes,

Now she knew she would be punished. Whatever else was true, that was certain.

She tried to empty her mind. She thought of nothing. She thought of the woman's tone, running things she had said through her mind, over and over, caressing the words.

They stood like that, mistress and slave, for some long minutes. Josephine thought her legs would give way. Her will came and went. She felt exhausted. She was in suspense, longing for resolution.

In the silence she heard the tiny noise of the lift starting down.

Another eternity passed.

The messenger came in, and closed the door behind him.

The woman barely glanced at him.

The boy walked straight past Josephine, into the bedroom.

Josephine heard the sound of a drawer opening, the merest rattle of a chain, the links sliding against one another.

The boy came back. He came straight up behind her and took hold of her wrists.

He cuffed her hands together behind her back. His touch was swift, impersonally sure.

Josephine lifted her head then. She looked at the ceiling; at the steel chandelier.

The boy's hands went to her side. He unfastened the waistband of her skirt. He unfastened the zip. He let the skirt fall around her ankles.

He hoisted her slip, bundling it up above her hips and tucking it inside her blouse.

She was wearing tights. He gave the briefest glance at the woman, who gave the curtest nod.

Brutally fast, he hauled down her tights and panties together. Josephine gasped with shock and discomfort, feeling her bottom squeezed and released, surging out of the elastic. She wobbled on her feet, off-balance because of the handcuffs.

The boy exposed her, pulling her panties clear of her crotch, not even glancing at it, or at the woman.

'Turn her,' the woman said.

With a firm hand he supported Josephine's elbow, turning her to face the bedroom door, with her back to the room.

Then he let go of her.

For a while, they left her there like that.

Josephine heard one of them, surely the woman, go to the cupboard and pour herself a drink.

Then there was no sound for a while.

She tried not to shiver, but she did.

She screwed her eyes tight shut.

Any second now, the lash would fall, igniting her with pain.

Nothing happened.

She stood there, her slip tucked up around her waist, her tights pulled down around her thighs. The metal of the handcuffs was cool against her hands and against the small of her back until the heat of her body warmed them up. She found herself swallowing convulsively, the muscles of her neck taut with tension. She wanted to beg for the whip, but they had left her nothing, not even that.

Her knees shook.

She felt a slow drip begin to seep from her vagina onto her thigh.

It was as if they were all killing time, waiting for an appointed moment. They were looking round the flat, searching it in a cursory way. Josephine heard sounds of the woman taking things from shelves, putting them down carelessly. The boy had gone back in the bedroom. She heard him rummaging through her drawer again, sliding the wardrobe open. Clothes hangers clinked together as he slid things about on the rail.

Inside Josephine's head, voices clamoured. Her home was being invaded! Everything was in danger. It was not what she desired. She was subjected. They exposed her body, then disregarded her. What she desired was no longer important.

She felt her bare bottom with her fingers, reassuring herself. She pressed her thighs together, and trembled.

'Turn,' said the woman after a while.

Josephine turned and faced her again. She was sitting in a chair holding her glass at a careless angle. There were a couple of books on the table, CDs on the floor. The woman was showing no interest in them.

'Who punished you last?' she asked. 'And what with?'

Josephine swallowed again, hard. She felt her jaw trembling.

'You may answer,' said the woman lazily, and sipped her drink.

Josephine's memory had gone blank. Her mind raced. Who? When?

'At Gair Clovulin,' she said. 'Tom Olav. Some other masters. With – canes.' The word wouldn't come out. She stumbled over it.

The woman did not react visibly to this information.

Josephine could hear the pigeons, pattering on the gutters. Outside, a patch of weak blue opened in the grey sky.

She shifted her weight. Her thighs parted stickily. She felt herself sagging.

'Stand up straight,' the woman commanded.

Josephine brought her legs together and stiffened her spine. Her shoulders were tired, her forearms aching from tension, from being held awkwardly behind her back. She lifted her chin. Her breasts felt constricted. She longed for the woman to fondle them, knead them, pinch and squeeze them.

Behind her, the boy came out of the bedroom. He passed her, carrying her black leather attaché case.

He brought it to the woman. She moved her head for the first time since Josephine had turned round, glancing at the case with a faint but undeniable flicker of interest. The boy held it up. She gave a nod.

He set the case on the table, turning it towards the woman. He snapped the catches open and lifted the lid, presenting the case for her inspection. She leaned forward a little in her chair, looking impassively into it.

Reaching delicately in with her index finger and thumb, as if to select a flower from a vase, she took out a magazine Josephine had been sent by an admirer in Chicago. She sat back in the chair, turning the pages indifferently, glancing at the particular arrangements of flesh, steel and leather that had been thoughtfully disposed for the photographer. Josephine could have sworn she saw the twitch of a smile.

Then the mistress looked up and nodded to the boy again. She gestured slightly and indirectly at the case.

Swivelling it around on the tabletop, he began quickly but methodically examining the implements that nestled in its cushioned interior. He took something out and showed it to the woman, who had discarded her magazine, letting it slide off her lap to the floor.

When he held up the thing he had taken out of the case Josephine could see what it was. It was a slim black collar with a silver buckle, and a silver ring set in the middle.

The woman nodded.

'Strip her,' she said.

The boy reached into his trouser pocket and produced a short shaped rod of matte black plastic. He held it up, his hand closed around it. There was a soft *snick*. Suddenly a shiny blade was sticking out of his fist.

He came to Josephine and cut the clothes from her.

His hand moved everywhere with arrogant speed and precision. The knife was obviously very sharp. He slashed her jacket from the lapels diagonally down each sleeve. She felt the point of the knife, moving fast, cut through the blouse beneath and whisper past her skin.

He tugged the remnants of the jacket from her.

Then he slashed her blouse, straight down the front, and horizontally straight across from arm to arm, the blade passing across the slope of her breasts, never touching her.

She closed her eyes, frozen with fear.

She felt nothing. She heard the knife hiss again through the silk down each arm and the blouse fell from her in shreds, her slip peeling away beneath it in long petals. He cut that from her with lazy, unspecific strokes, as if cutting the wrapping from a misshapen parcel.

She felt him hook a finger in her bra at the back. His finger was warm. There was a sound of elastic parting. He leaned towards her, inserting his finger up between her breasts, pulling the ruined bra toward him; and he cut the shoulder straps.

Her breasts fell free, and the master domino tumbled to the floor.

The boy knelt at her feet.

For a moment, she thought he was going to pick the domino up. Instead, he ignored it. He was turning his attention to her legs.

She looked straight out in front of her, above his head.

The woman was watching them, incurious as ever.

Josephine, trying not to tremble, felt the boy snag her tights on the point of the knife and twist. The sheer fabric laddered at once. He helped it on its way, cutting and chopping. For the first time she felt the point of his knife prick her, just below her knee. Despite herself she shuddered.

She wondered if he had meant to cut her then, there.

He spent a long time carving away her panties in bits, as if he enjoyed doing something badly and flippantly once in a while. His blond head bobbed at the level of her groin. She would not look down at him, would not. She stared at the wall beyond. There was a print there, just out of the line of her sight, a Chinese painting of a heron, five pure lines of black ink and a grey wash. She thought of the boy as a Zen artist of the knife, able to encase a living subject in a deadly shell of flickering steel while never — never unintentionally — harming a hair of her body.

A supreme master, one like her new mistress, would have only supreme servants.

There was another click. The knife was back in the boy's pocket.

Josephine stood naked in a pile of rags. She faced the mistress, breathing hard, trying to still the tremors of apprehension and excitement jagging like lightning through her body.

The woman nodded again, as if what she had just watched was perfectly acceptable but nothing out of the ordinary.

'Dress her,' she said.

Josephine caught her breath. She wanted to swoon. There was red behind her eyelids.

The boy reached into his jacket pocket and pulled out her collar.

As he fastened it around her throat, lifting the hair from the nape of the neck to buckle it at the back, then straightening the ring in front, she wondered what his marvellous hands might do under her command. She wondered what he did for his mistress when they were alone together. She hoped, one day, she might be privileged enough to find out.

He fetched her things from the bedroom: a suspender belt; a fresh pair of seamed black stockings; a pair of shiny ankle boots with needle heels.

He dressed her. He hooked the suspender belt around her hips, straightened the suspenders against her thighs. He broke the cellophane on the packet of stockings. The noise sounded very loud in the silent room, angry and sharp. He made her lie down on the floor. Wedged under her, her arms and hands hurt. The cuffs dug into the base of her spine.

Leaning down he parted her legs, opening her wet crotch.

It was clear that it didn't interest him.

He knelt down between her feet.

Gently he pulled on her stockings, rolling each methodically and slipping it over her foot, up over her heel, drawing it gradually along her leg, smoothing it and straightening it as he went. He was a servant but she was a slave, she was nothing to him. One day, if circumstances changed, if he gave their mistress displeasure while she continued in perfect obedience, perhaps the roles might be reversed, and she be called on in her turn, to punish him. She look at his crimson trousers, straining up over her haunches as he reached forward. It would be a pleasure, Josephine thought, to spank his beautiful bottom until it matched the colour of those trousers.

Now he grasped her thigh with both hands, as if it were a rope. His fingers were hard and unfeeling. He pulled her along the floor towards him, hurting her shoulders. She lifted her head involuntarily, stifling a gasp as the carpet rasped her back.

He bent her knee, tucked her toe into his groin.

She felt his genitals, soft and yielding beneath her toes.

If she should kick out now.

Not voluntarily. Nothing she did now could be voluntary. But reflexively, her body testing this servitude, struggling against her will. In fear. There was fear. There was very much fear. That refined, high, vibrant fear that sings like the string of a harp, that says, Soon it will hurt. There is no other future. You know it. You have already submitted to it.

The fear. The fear that releases. The fear that is extinguished in the realisation of the fear, which is when it hurts. It will hurt. Oh God how it will hurt.

When will that be?

When we choose, said the eyes of the boy.

He turned over the tops of her stockings and fastened them to her suspenders. His knuckles came an inch from her oozing quim. They did not touch it. Did not so much as brush it.

Finished, he ran his hands down her legs, as a painter runs a hand down a painted post, automatically, without thinking, to ensure perfection. He sat back on his haunches and slipped on her boots.

Then he got hold of her hips and helped her stand, with great difficulty, balancing on the heels without the aid of her hands.

This, Josephine thought, was the way she had been made to dress, as a slave, an object of subjection and perpetual open regard, when she had begun. When her life had begun again. When she had first entered the mystery, and kissed the rod. Her obedience justified their

69

domination; her disobedience animated it, incurred the pleasure of their displeasure. By not yielding, she yielded, and they went deeper in together, into the place where they could punish her.

There would be pain. But it would be *that* pain. And afterwards, there would be pleasure.

When they chose.

If they chose.

'Turn her around,' said the mistress to the boy. 'All the way.'

The boy's hand was on her elbow, turning her about like a farmer turning a pony. Wobbling, she obeyed.

'Hm,' said the mistress, considering what she saw.

Unexpectedly she got up. Josephine heard her, felt her, come up behind her. There was a long pause. Josephine could feel her eyes examining her bottom, appraising it, coming to a decision.

It was made, and communicated in silence. There was the sound of the implements in the case being disturbed. Something suitable was being selected. Suddenly the boy was standing in front of her, holding up her martinet, hefting it, dangling its tails on the palm of his other hand.

Josephine closed her eyes.

She hoped he would not whip her in front. At least, not at first.

She sensed rather than heard him step behind her, and she was grateful.

Then the whip whistled to her, and she was on fire once more.

From the first, she never knew when the martinet was falling and when it was not. The strokes fell so fast and so prolifically the stinging was constant. Yet she knew from his movements, and from the quality of the pain, that the boy was laying it on quite lazily, with little force. Adrenalin was exploding through her. Still she had not made a sound. She was holding her breath, hunching forward with her hands behind her, willing her knees to hold, willing herself to remain upright, to present her bottom properly to the whip.

At once a thong caught the heel of her hand, a horrid pain like the blow of a hammer. She slipped, tottered on the heels, and fell, banging her head on the floor. Pitiless, he continued to whip her. She jerked and writhed, fighting to keep her legs together and her bottom towards him. The thongs caught her on the hip and she squealed, squirming and thrusting out her bottom. The thongs fell again and again.

Enough, she wanted to call. Enough!

Let them drag it out of her.

She panted, struggled. Endured.

'Enough,' called the mistress. 'Stand her up. Bring her here.'

Josephine did not think she could stand. She really thought she was unable. Her bottom felt grilled, her legs were shocked and dead. When she tried to move her hips spasmed, reacting to the blaze of pain. Somehow the boy pulled her up, held her up while she coped with the high heels collapsing under her. Her face felt cold, then very hot. She panted, jerkily. She willed herself to remain upright.

She looked down at her mistress in the chair. The woman was sitting back in the futon sling with one leg thrown across the other, her arms on the chair arms. Her voice, when she spoke, was throaty and slow.

'How is your tongue, eh?' the woman asked her. 'Is it busy? Is it active?'

She took her sunglasses out of the breast pocket of her suit, unfolded them, and put them back on.

Then she uncrossed her legs, and set both feet flat on the floor, her skirt stretched between her thighs.

'On your knees,' she said to Josephine.

The boy lashed Josephine once more across the bottom with the martinet, and she toppled forward, sliding somehow onto her knees, her head lolling against the inside of the mistress's knee.

She looked directly up the woman's skirt.

Beneath it, her new mistress was naked.

In her crotch there grew a great bush of hair, very dark and very tightly curled. She smelt of L'Elegance, and earth, and heaven.

'Proceed,' she said to Josephine.

Awkwardly, painfully, Josephine edged forward, riding on the pain raging in her bottom. She slid her head, face first, up the mistress's black skirt. She shut her eyes and opened her mouth.

The mistress slid down in the chair, pressing her quim into Josephine's face.

It stirred, moistly, against her; engorged under her; opened to envelop her.

The whip fell.

Josephine jerked, losing her position, her chin jerking up and hitting the woman on the pelvis. At once the whip landed again, making her arch her back and shout in pain and desperation.

The whipping ceased.

71

She resumed her place.

The woman's labia filled her nose and mouth. Her clitoris was a small nub against her tongue. She thought of it as the head of a flower. She slavered it with everything in her stinging, swollen body.

The mistress's thighs closed on her head, scissoring, clamping her tight.

Now, thought Josephine, sucking hard and slow, now the boy will abuse me. Now that I can't see him, can't defend myself against him, he will unfasten his smart red trousers and ram his thick blond cock inside me. He has seen me. Oozing. He knows I am ready for him. Our mistress will tell him to penetrate me, at once, now, to amuse her, to arouse her while I pleasure her with my mouth. I shall scream into her vagina as his stiff flesh pummels my blazing backside.

It did not happen.

Josephine plied her mistress with her mouth. As she kissed her, the woman became wet and soft. Her flavour was strong, gamey. Josephine believed she could get used to it, in time.

She believed she would have time.

Josephine found herself lost in a world of darkness and fire. She forgot the city, the office, the building, the flat, the bedroom, even the lounge where she knelt on the coarse carpet. She was back where the human world begins, between the thighs of a woman. Space had been taken away from her, and now time was measured by the pulsating of the pain receding in her bottom, the steady lapping of her tongue. She tasted salt, the pungent liquors of pleasure. She could feel the arousal of the mistress, the intensity of concentration in the fierce flesh squeezing her head.

Inside her head, fantastic images blossomed and changed. She thought she was looking down from her patio into the street. Then she was swimming weightless, high above a black whirlpool of stars that drew her down. She saw a French boudoir in powder blue and pink, rococo decorations of gold and silken tassels: a manservant in a peruke, naked from the waist down, his bottom fresh from the whip, scored with a tracery of red. His erect penis was decorated with a little black ribbon, tied in a bow. He had a pointed nose and a curious, impish smile.

The woman sighed, sank still lower in the chair. The grip of her thighs loosened, and Josephine kissed them. Her mouth was full of hair. The fire of her abused flesh had fallen quickly to a tingling irritation. She longed to pull her hands from the cuffs and clasp them to her bottom. She took a breath.

Earnestly she nuzzled her way back through the hairy thicket, between the complicated folds of flesh and skin, moving lower down the inner mouth with its bony rim. She tried to press the tip of her tongue into it, licked it all around, then slid her tongue up between the engorged lips, up the channel to the shaft of the questing clitoris. She turned her head and sucked. She licked her more slowly, feeling for the rhythm. She felt the mistress's pelvis thrust against her cheeks and her tongue was there to meet the tiny blind head of passion. Again and again they pushed together, groin to mouth. Josephine could hear the woman breathing deeply, above her, all around her. This was the way it would be, from now on.

'Stop,' said the woman. Her voice was deep.

Josephine withdrew, her mouth from her crotch, her head from her skirt. She blinked as she emerged, and sat back on her haunches, sending darts of pain lancing through her body.

The mistress's face was calm: no flush, no pallor or sheen; no sign there of stirring in her loins. Behind her dark glasses her eyes were unreadable, invisible.

She rose from her chair.

'Follow,' she said.

Josephine rose, without the help of the boy, who stood apart, by the window. His arms were folded, his fair face passive with unconcern. The martinet lay on the table, the magazine neglected on the floor. From its open pages, spreadeagled devotees offered their flesh as silent invitations to a sweeter, simpler world. Josephine wondered if the boy cared at all for any of this, if he simply worked for pay and asked no questions, made no judgements. He was beautiful. She wanted to press her mouth to his blond curls.

Her hands pinned behind her, she followed her mistress into the bedroom.

Faint sunlight bloomed and faded in the room. The drawers had been ransacked. Black leather and steel, satin and lace, were strewn and tangled across the top of the unit, spilling onto the floor. He had turned out the wardrobe too. Her Courrèges suit, black padded shoulders and a pencil skirt, had taken his fancy for some reason. He had laid it out, still on its hanger, on the bed.

The mistress picked it up and threw it on the floor.

73

She walked around the bed platform, sizing up the room, taking possession. She snatched up a bridle from the vanity, twisting it between her hands, as if she wanted to crush and break it. She dropped it, kicked it aside with the toe of her Italian shoe. She sat on the bed, her hands wide, her fingers clutching the yellow bedspread, pulling it up in two peaks. She lifted her feet, pressed the toe of one foot behind the heel of the other, kicked off her shoes. They thumped to the floor, fell on their side, lay still.

She stood up again then, and unfastened her skirt.

From the lounge, Josephine heard the sound of a Telemann minuet, precise and clear.

The mistress stepped out of her skirt and laid it neatly across the back of the chair, straightening the pleats with her hand. She removed her half-slip. Her legs were white above the tops of her black stockings, white flesh sharply bisected by narrow black suspenders. Her bottom was broad and bare beneath the tail of her blouse. She did not remove her jacket.

She sat on the edge of the bed and unfastened her suspenders. Precisely, carefully, she rolled her stockings down to the knee. Her thighs were smooth, shaved.

She lay back on the bed. The sunlight came and lit her closed face, her raised chin, the swell of her brassière beneath her formal clothes. She spread her legs.

'Continue,' she said.

Elegantly the music rose and fell. Josephine wondered if the boy were behind her, watching them through the doorway. She was not permitted to turn round. She knelt on the white wool carpet and shuffled forward on her knees to the bed. The soft portal of her mistress's flesh was closing, drying, cooling. She set her mouth to it again.

The mistress lowered her legs around Josephine's neck, caressing her black leather collar with her heels. She pressed her heels into Josephine's shoulder blades, pulling her forward, pulling her in.

Josephine's lips teased the mistress's lips. Her tongue probed down, seeking the warm mouth. Crisp, wet hair pressed hard into her nose and cheeks. She breathed again the breath of her mistress, the scent of perfume, the winy, fecund scent of woman. She ran her moist lips down the inside of the thigh to the knee. The skin was smooth and cool, hot only as she slid her mouth back up again, into the wet crease of the groin, kissing the fringes of her hair up over the pubic arch, rubbing her lips across the line of the pelvis; then dipping down again to circle above the spreading vulva. She licked, she sipped. The mistress lifted her bottom from the bed, mashing her crotch into Josephine's face. She inched backwards, pulling Josephine after her with her feet. They crawled towards the top of the bed, spilling a dribble of bright juices beneath them that settled on the corrugations of the bedspread, then soaked in, darkening in pools and spots.

The sunlight came again. Josephine felt it on her back, her throbbing bottom. Her breasts were pressed into a ruck of coverlet, her tongue was in her mistress's vagina. Behind her back her arms ached, distracting her.

There was a cool hand on her back suddenly. The boy was there, leaning over her, resting his left hand on her back, his right hand on her bottom. Josephine writhed, shouted in surprise, and he smacked her hard. He put his hand behind her head, pushing her face into the mistress's crotch. She gasped and sucked, lost in the folds of flesh. With his other hand, brutally, deliberately, the boy parted the cheeks of her bottom. Reluctantly she felt him press with his thumb and finger.

Perhaps he was not allowed to fuck the slaves, she thought. Perhaps it was beneath him. Perhaps, on dark nights on their mistress's vast estate, miles from all other habitation, he coupled with other boys, other servants, forcing his white seed into their mouths, their anuses.

Helplessly she opened and he thrust his thumb and finger into her, burning, both ways at once.

|6|

'Stop,' the mistress commanded her again.

Josephine lifted her head, surprised. Stop? Why stop? What was wrong?

She cried aloud in pain as the boy tightened his grip on her vagina and pulled her off the bed. She struggled to obey, scrambling backwards without the use of her hands. He let go. She fell to her knees on the floor again. She felt she had been torn, split. There were tears in her eyes as the boy pressed her face to the floor.

She crouched there, stunned. There were sounds of busyness, quick and precise. After a minute the mistress handed the boy a leash, and he squatted down to clip it to the ring on Josephine's collar. Then he pulled her to her feet.

The mistress was dressed again, as if the interlude on the bed had never happened. She was standing in the doorway with her skirt drawn up to her hip, fastening a suspender. She let her skirt fall and twitched the pleats with her hand. She touched her fingers to her neckscarf and walked back into the lounge.

'Fetch a chair,' she said.

Josephine's heart sank.

The boy left the room. Josephine stood, blinking back sudden tears of frustration and despair. Her crotch still burned where the boy had gripped her. Her leash dangled between her breasts. The mistress could save her, but she would not. She stood now in the lounge, fists on her hips, ignoring her new slave.

The boy came back, carrying before him one of the olive wood chairs from the kitchen.

He stood it in the centre of the room, where Josephine always did. She felt at once that they knew this, that the mistress had told him to put it there to make a point.

The mistress took off her jacket.

The boy stood by her, attending. He helped her off with her jacket, hung it on the back of the wooden chair.

The mistress smoothed her skirt under her and sat down on the chair he had brought, placing her feet flat on the floor. She took off her sunglasses once more, and slipped them back in her breast pocket. Her face gave no sign that Josephine's attentions had meant anything to her at all. She looked sullen rather than stern, as though what she was about to do was a chore, neither pleasant or unpleasant.

She made another minute adjustment to the lie of her neckscarf and tugged sharply at the cuffs of her crisp white blouse. Her breasts were large and rounded, like melons beneath her blouse. Josephine found herself wishing she would unwrap them suddenly and present them to her view, to her lips. The taste of the woman's cunt was salty on her tongue.

The mistress looked at the boy.

'Bring her in,' she said, and taking hold of her black ruby ring with the strong fingers of her left hand, she began to pull it off.

The boy came into the bedroom. He picked up the end of Josephine's leash and led her into the lounge, across the floor to the mistress in her chair.

Josephine stood there looking down at the seated woman. The smooth lap of the black skirt concealed the powerful thighs that moments ago had been gripping her head. She felt a pang of loss, of sudden disappointment.

The mistress took the leash from the boy. She pulled on it, and the boy clasped the back of Josephine's neck, pushing her down across the mistress's lap. As she overbalanced and fell, his hands supported her, seizing her hips and propelling her forwards with a practised shove.

Josephine lay across her mistress's thighs, her hands a dead weight cramped behind her, her legs stretched out straight, her toes on the floor. Her bottom was still aching from the whip. Her eyes were wide open. She stared at the carpet.

The spanking was brisk and cruel and impersonal as only a mistress could give. No man, Josephine thought as she lay there crying and jerking, flailing her legs and displaying herself heedlessly as she ground her pelvis against the woman's thigh; no man had ever punished her so fiercely and abased her so completely, using just his hands. It was more humiliating, far more, to be spanked across her mistress's knee than to be whipped by the boy. She was aware, all the time that the hard and unforgiving hand belaboured her sore cheeks, all the time that she begged and squealed and wept, that the boy stood there a little way apart, at attention, his hands behind his back.

She knew how a bottom could be tenderized with the martinet, brought to a peak of agonized sensitivity all over, without force, without a weal to show for it, so that afterwards even the touch of a hand would provoke a yelp of distress.

That was how they had prepared her, waking every nerve end in her buttocks to anguish, then allowing her to think it was over. Permitting her to lap at her mistress's quim, as though she had been forgiven.

To be punished for giving pleasure. To be torn away from giving pleasure and punished instead. That was more humiliating even than the punishment itself. She cried aloud, hectically trying to throw herself off the mistress's lap, until the boy was commanded to hold her down.

Punishment she knew. But punishment with gratification, punishment and afterwards reward, release, the gift of the penis, the vibrator, the rousing tongue. She thought of Jackie's nimble fingers. She thought of the mistress's fingers, held rigid and unyielding now as they came smacking down on her frantic bottom. She knew they would not curl afterwards, gently, coaxing her to pleasure. These fingers would give her nothing but punishment.

No one had treated her like this, like a rag doll to be whipped and thrown aside, since the first tempestuous week at Estwych, where she had been initiated, where she had been trained and earned her tattoo. Her tears ran over her forehead into her hair, dripped on the carpet. They were tears of shame. They had taught her, they had instructed her, and she had forgotten.

The punishment ceased at last. Dimly, while she lay slumped across the mistress's knee, lost in a storm of pain, she heard the boy being tersely dispatched to fetch the car.

They were leaving.

They had come and looked her over. And now they were going again, as abruptly as they had come.

The woman allowed her to kneel on the floor by her chair. Graciously she ignored the red-eyed, snivelling mess of her face. She put her ruby ring back on, pushing it hard over the knuckle of her powerful hand. Josephine saw that the hand was red from punishing her. Crawling feebly within the tiny compass of the handcuffs, her locked hands tried to clutch her bottom, straining hopelessly to give her that minimal relief.

Josephine lifted her pounding head. She looked up beseechingly into the woman's eyes. They were calm, grey, utterly indifferent.

The mistress regarded her silently for a long time.

Then she said, 'Do you wish to speak? You may speak.'

'This slave . . .'

Her voice came out as a croak. Her vocal cords were not her own. She swallowed tightly, tried again.

'. . . slave begs to go with . . . mistress.'

Unexpectedly, the woman laughed.

'With me, you mean? Oh, no,' she said softly, with terrible condescending humour, as if speaking to a child who had said something amusingly ridiculous. 'Not with me.'

She shook out her heavy dark hair, fluffed it out with her fingers. The room seemed to fill with the scent of her perfume. Briskly she untied the scarf from her neck.

Beneath was a black leather collar scarcely different from Josephine's own.

'I hardly think he would allow us that.'

She leaned forward, the scarf between her hands. Quickly, firmly, she knotted it around Josephine's eyes.

After that, all was darkness, dejection and confusion. The boy returned, or perhaps it was someone else. She didn't hear them speak. Josephine lay on the bed. Her hands were freed. Her crotch was wiped. She was dressed in a clean bra and panties, a fresh pair of stockings put on her by neat, deft hands. She lifted her arms and felt a dress slid expertly over her head, suffocating her an instant, then being tugged quickly into place and buttoned at the back. Flat shoes were slipped on her feet.

Throughout she remained as limp and passive as the doll she had thought of.

To be abased by a servant was humiliating enough. To be abased by another slave was inconceivable. There was nothing she was capable of any more, nothing she could cling to.

They knew it. They collared her, but did not bother with the leash. They didn't even cuff her hands again. They knew she had no will left.

She understood dimly, in the way that a songbird understands, perhaps, when it is caught and put in a cage, that it is no longer free to fly and sing and mate in the forest. It was why they had come. Why he had sent them. To reduce her to this.

They took her arms and marched her to the lift. Together they rode down in silence to the basement garage. Josephine could smell the cars, the petrol; hear the baffled acoustics of the confined space; feel the tarmac beneath her feet. They hurried her to a car and put her in the back. She recognised the scent of the Daimler. The doors slammed.

The car started. Josephine fell forward, steadied herself against the seatback. She lay back in her seat as they went up the ramp to the street. Traffic noise enveloped her, muted, like television in another room.

'Where are you taking me?' she asked, heedless now she knew it didn't matter.

'You're going on a little journey,' said the woman. Until she spoke Josephine had not been sure she was in the car.

'Will he be there?'

'Who can say?'

Unsatisfied, she felt the car drive on. The city roared past, dimly. She had no idea which direction they were driving.

'Can't you tell me *anything* about him?' she said.

She heard the woman shift round in the passenger seat to address her.

'If you don't keep silent I'll have you flogged until you're hoarse.'

Her bottom and back still ached. Her skin felt tight, her muscles seized. She felt the blood rise to her face. That she had allowed herself to be whipped and spanked by a servant and another slave, without a master even being present. She felt ashamed, mortified that she had made the mistake of thinking the woman her new mistress. All her desire for her hand had vanished the instant she had seen the collar she wore.

Now she was determined no one should lay a finger on her unless it was her master. She knew he was a man, at least she knew that now. She hugged this knowledge to her secret heart.

Her blindfold smelt of L'Elégance. How did he keep his slaves, this man? In luxury, she hoped. Perhaps it would be Daimlers all the way now. Private apartments, accounts for particular purchases, phone calls in the middle of the night. '*Prepare yourself.*' Making haste to place herself ready for him before his key turns in the door. Hearing him enter the room, not turning on the light. Feeling the weight of him, the presence of him. Hearing the soft, swift whirr of an opened zip, the heavy whisper of trousers lowered. His hands, suddenly, cool on her hips. The moist tip of his penis probing into her crotch.

Lying face down across a heap of pillows, naked under his hands or with her nightdress rucked up to the waist. Waiting for his pleasure.

She knew what he wanted. She knew already what he would be like. Very dark, with heavy-lidded eyes and diamond studs in his earlobes. Or middle-aged, with iron-grey hair and perfect manners.

He would not find her wanting. She would show him there was no need to treat her like this, like the least of slaves, like nothing.

Only in private would she let him treat her as if she was nothing, worth nothing. And only because afterwards, after whatever ordeal he saw fit to put her through, then the slick head of his penis, gorged with blood, would come to rest in the wet tight clutch of her vagina.

Where it belonged.

She was sure of that. If someone so powerful had sought her out from a distance, if he knew the layout of her office and flat, the way to send his messengers into either and out again with impunity — then he knew everything about her. She had been selected, Hazel had said. Prized. However he tried to disguise it, to throw her off her guard.

It was her he wanted, not anyone else. Which must be the reason the woman was so cold, so vindictive to her. The reason she had sampled her caresses so callously, rousing her and then rejecting her.

She was escorting her replacement to her master's bed.

Josephine remembered being taken to Estwych the first time by the redheaded man in the taxi. She had forgotten his name. She had liked him then, and remembered him fondly. At the time he had had her very confused. She had been blindfolded then too, and he had spanked her in a field. She had thought he was the mysterious Dr Hazel.

In a moment of panic Josephine lost control of her thoughts. She knew she knew none of this, nothing at all.

All she knew was herself.

She wished she had had time to say goodbye to Jackie. Properly.

They drove for a long time. Josephine fell asleep. In her sleep she dreamed she was out at sea on a long wooden ship: so long you

81

couldn't see the end. It was like a Viking ship. She was trying to walk along it towards the stern, where she felt sure the receding land was. But the gunwales were full of dead animals, animals with thick fur coats. They were heavy and soft, and appeared to have no bones; they had been taken out to build the ship. She kept kicking one of the animals, and feeling her foot thud into its rubbery and unresponsive flesh.

She woke to find herself slumped sideways in her seat, her head at an uncomfortable angle against the door. Her blindfold had come off one eye. Through the window she glimpsed a brick gatepost, grass. The ground beneath the car was uneven. Josephine jolted away from the door — and her blindfold fell off altogether.

She could see a cracked concrete roadway, grass growing through the cracks. The ground was flat. They drove across old tarmac, towards a squat wooden tower. On the roof was an array of aerials and meteorological gear. An anemometer spun slowly.

Josephine wondered if she would be punished for losing her blindfold.

It was an airfield. Turning to look out of the back of the car as they took a corner, she saw a small plane out on the runway. There were trees on the horizon.

The car stopped at the tower. The boy put on the handbrake.

'The papers,' said the woman.

The boy reached into the glove compartment and pulled out a slim sheaf of printed papers. He gave them to the woman. The woman gave them to Josephine.

'Hurry up,' she said.

Bemused, still half asleep, Josephine took the papers. She made to unfold them, to see what they were.

The boy was getting out of the car, coming round to open her door.

'They're not for you,' said the woman sharply. She was not looking at her, had dismissed her already. 'Give them to the controller.'

Josephine got out of the car. She was stiff and aching, trembling in every limb. The autumn wind was fresh and chilly on her face. The boy climbed back into the car and started the engine. Josephine looked at them a moment, the woman and the boy sitting there behind the smoked glass, driving away, denizens of a separate world. She knew she would not see them again.

She opened the door and went into the tower.

There were two rooms, one either side of the stairs. The door on the left was open. Inside was a low counter. Behind it sat a young woman in a grey uniform, her hair tightly permed, her face innocent of make-up.

Josephine went in.

Seeing the papers, the woman held her hand out.

Josephine asked, 'Are you the controller?'

'No,' said the woman. She smiled slightly, amused by Josephine's mistake. She nodded to the papers.

'Will you give them to him?' Josephine asked.

'That depends,' she said. An archness in her tone belied the primness of her appearance. She took the papers sharply, unfolded them and began to read.

Before she had read more than a line or two, she picked up an old brown bakelite telephone. She listened a moment. Josephine could hear a tinny voice on the other end.

'She's arrived,' the woman stated. She listened again.

Josephine watched her. The wall behind her was full of charts stuck with pins and webs of coloured thread. Faded notices in violet duplicator ink curled on rusty drawing pins.

Overhead a door opened and closed. Footsteps passed along as booming wooden landing, came downstairs.

A man came into the room. He was in his mid-thirties, slightly built, with fair hair falling across his forehead. His eyes were tawny and his mouth boyish and amused, as if he shared the joke the woman saw. He wore a brown jacket of distressed leather, wool trousers in the same grey as the woman's uniform, an open-necked shirt of light blue, and black riding boots, their tops hidden beneath his trouser-legs.

He looked at Josephine. His eyes focused on her slim black collar.

The woman held the papers out to him. He took them, barely glancing at them. Was he the controller?

'Come,' he said.

She followed him outside, and onto the runway.

The plane was unfamiliar, an anonymous two-seater business jet, painted white. She climbed in, sat down with some care, and fastened her seatbelt. The plane was not new. The cockpit smelt of stale pipe tobacco and fuel. The autumn sun lit a web of invisible scratches on the windscreen.

The pilot climbed in and started the engine. He spoke briefly on

83

the radio as they began to move. Josephine looked out of the window, glimpsed a fluttering windsock, a gull flapping heavily away from the grass beside the runway. She looked down and saw their wheels lift and bounce, lift again. They were flying.

She was glad she had lost her blindfold.

Flying in commercial aircraft, even cabin class, was boring: no different from a bus, she had always thought. Small planes really gave you the sense of precarious insecurity, the thrill and mystery of flying, as though gravity were being cheated. The green airfield tilted up and flowed away beneath their wings. She felt at the mercy of the air.

Especially since she had no idea who the pilot was or where he was taking her.

She saw woods, the sea, a dull glaucous bay cluttered with harsh tall rocks.

The pilot turned to her. 'Champagne?' he said.

Josephine remembered Jackie, the champagne she had bought to celebrate the arrival of the wonderful domino. 'What are we celebrating?' she asked.

'A beautiful woman in my cockpit,' he said, with a mocking touch of old-world gallantry. 'It's cause enough for celebration, don't you think?'

Josephine wondered how freely she could speak. 'I imagined you did this all the time,' she said.

'Perhaps,' he said.

They climbed steadily. Josephine's ears popped. The engines throbbed loudly. She hoped they would not be flying for too long.

'Am I allowed to ask where we're going?'

'You're going to school,' he said, with a slight emphasis.

'Is it far?'

'Far enough.'

She had to be content with that.

He told her where the champagne and two flutes were stowed. When she took them out she found they were made of plastic.

'Your first test,' he said, 'is to open that without making a mess. Can you do that?'

'If you can hold her steady I will,' she said.

He held her steady. They were levelling off now, three thousand feet, he said on the radio. They flew over the sea. With care she eased the cork from the bottle without an explosion, poured the foam without

84

an overflow. He commended her, raised his glass to her in a toast. The controls tilted and turned without his hand.

Josephine looked down. She saw islands.

'Drink up,' he said.

She drank the champagne quickly. Her head felt light. She became detached from her sore body. She was unsurprised when he said: 'Take off your blouse.'

She obeyed. She folded the blouse and put it in the pocket on the door where the bottle and glasses had been.

'And your bra,' he said.

She bared her breasts for him. She wondered if he just wanted to check her tattoo, if he would comment on it. She looked at him, but he was looking ahead, flying the plane. She sat back, her eyes closed, expecting to feel his hands come exploring. He didn't touch her.

Clouds curled by below like spun semen.

He told her to refill her glass.

Thinking of Jackie, Josephine suddenly thought of the story she had told her, about the doctor who had driven her to Estwych in an old sports car. He had made her undress, then had not touched her. What if this were the same man? She stole a look at his hands. They were soft, feminine, more like a surgeon's than a pilot's.

Perhaps he was the master.

Then she decided the drink was making her irrational. Who said Jackie's story was true? Or any of her stories? She never told the same one twice.

Anyway, Josephine had wonderful breasts. Men liked to look at them. Men like to suck and squeeze them. One man had whipped them with a rod of gutta-percha. The pain had been horrible, completely inappropriate. She had curled up in pain, and begged him not to do it again. Her refusal had earned her a prolonged session spreadeagled over a table. With every blow that fell on her bottom and thighs she had shouted, silently, inside, Not my breasts! Oh, not my breasts! In relief and gratitude.

Afterwards he had turned her over and teased her with a feather, so delicately and precisely that she had come off fast and hard. She thought her heart had stopped. It had, for a moment, she was sure. It had stopped.

'Isn't this exciting?' asked the pilot. 'To be drinking champagne in an aeroplane, naked, with an unknown man? Your nipples should be erect. Fondle yourself.'

Lazily she complied. It was easy enough. The desire the whip had kindled in her reawoke, leaping in her womb. Her nerves came alight, her stripes prickled, demanding to be bathed and soothed. Her breasts felt heavy; her diaphragm rose on a swell of longing. She wanted to touch her crotch but he had not commanded that. She felt her panties moisten.

The pilot reached out and slipped a finger through the ring of her collar. He tugged lightly. She gasped.

He pulled her face down to his crotch, unzipped his fly with his free hand. He stroked her back.

She wished he could see the stripes on her bottom. Delicately she reached into his fly and slipped out his penis. It was soft and white, with a rosy ring around the foreskin. She lifted it with her finger and thumb and kissed it on the underside, nibbling with her lips until it grew fierce and hard. She reached in again and gently freed his balls, easing them out over the teeth of the zip.

He was dry. She manipulated him with her lips and fingers until a bead of clear moisture welled from the eye of his glans. She looked up at him. He was smiling distantly, not looking down at her. The plane, or her heart, bobbed in a sea of turbulence.

Josephine remembered Russell.

She sat up and took a mouthful of champagne. Then carefully, holding it in, she bowed down and slipped her mouth over the head of the pilot's penis, and down the shaft.

She was gratified when he cried aloud.

Champagne dribbled down his penis, fizzing, wetting his pants and trousers. She wondered if she would be punished for that.

She sucked him slowly and deliberately, easing into a rhythm, then breaking it suddenly; slipping his foreskin down and up and down and mumbling her lips around behind his glans, then suddenly thrusting him deep in her mouth, as far as she could take him without gagging. His thighs trembled with tension beneath her breasts. He made a small noise in the back of his throat, then fell silent again as she worked on him. He stroked her back abstractedly, his touch soft and dreaming.

The plane flew on.

When he came he surprised her. She was shifting position, easing her uncomfortable sprawl to bear down on him and he came suddenly, flipping out of her mouth, his semen half in her mouth, half splashing down her chin. He jerked back in his seat, still throbbing, and his seed splashed into the cool air of the cockpit. She reached for his penis, to draw it back to her mouth, but he pushed her hand away.

She wiped up with a paper tissue from a wooden dispenser. His erection cooled and shrank. He did not speak. She scanned his face for signs of pleasure or displeasure. He zipped himself up again, looking at her with his mild eyes. They were very bright now in the white cloudlight.

'I'm sorry,' said Josephine; then, apologetically: 'I shouldn't say that, should I.' She didn't know what she was saying. The taste of him was acrid and strong in her mouth and in her nose. She dabbed at a splash on her breasts. Her longing was stronger than ever, but she knew he would not relieve her now, or allow her to relieve herself. She passed into a light depression, just as she'd used to after unsuccessful sex with Larry, her husband.

She sat up and looked out of the windscreen for the first time in several minutes. They were over land again, drab green fields, tiny villages. A tanker lorry flared with sunlight, crawling up a country road. Then the clouds closed in again.

The radio crackled. A voice spoke in French. The pilot answered in the same language. His voice was calm, measured. Josephine drank the last of the champagne, swilling her mouth with it. She was getting cold now.

'May I get dressed?' she asked.

'Of course,' he said. 'We must have you properly presented for your first day at school.'

She put on her bra, hating the constriction of her breasts that still tingled with unsatisfied desire. She pulled on her blouse and buttoned it.

He flew her into the mountains. There was a high meadow, a pinnacled château perched above a dark valley. A tiny river glinted below, blue as diamonds.

He landed the plane in the meadow, carelessly, it seemed to Josephine, as though impatient to be done with the journey. They jolted and bumped to a stop. She felt ill, apprehensive. Three young men all in black jumpers and slacks and calf-boots, came running to

87

the plane. They ran in step, like soldiers. When one of them opened the door for her to disembark, she saw he wore, as they all did, a black leather collar like her own.

She turned to the pilot, but he was on the radio again, speaking rapid French in a dialect she couldn't follow. Perhaps it was code. She felt alone. One of the young slaves was taking Josephine's papers from him, holding a clipboard up for him to sign. The other two hustled her to the ground. As one slammed the door of the plane, Josephine noticed an insignia on it: the domino mask, painted in elegant lines of glossy black. Had that been there when she had climbed aboard? How could she have missed it?

The air was cold and clean and moist as dew. There was snow on the rocks above the meadow. Her ears were popping, her legs reluctant to move. 'I need to piss,' she told the men. They said nothing, gave no indication whether they understood, whether they could understand.

They hurried her from the field, jogging either side of her like a police escort. Worn stone steps led down into a courtyard. Their hurrying feet echoed from flagstones where gritty traces of trodden snow lay about. They went down again, into a quadrangle of the château. Dark walls rose up around her, fanciful Alpine tracery of finial and crocket. The windows were tall and narrow, without lights behind them. Two masters, one in a high-collared cloak, stood chatting in a corner of the quad. They fell silent, their breath pluming in the air, watching Josephine and her escort trot by.

The young men took her down steps to a thick oak door with a square barred window. One opened the door, the other pushed her firmly over the threshold.

She found herself in a small cell, twelve feet by twelve. There was a low broad wooden bench, a wooden folding bed made up with sheets of unbleached cotton and coarse grey blankets, and a metal bucket of galvanised iron, with a lid, in the corner. There was no other furniture. The floors and walls were stone, bare but for a pair of hooks with iron chains looped from them, and a heavy staple in the wall above the bed. There was a window too high to see out of. It was barred like the window in the door.

Josephine looked around, bewildered, frightened. The door was open, but one of the slaves stood in her way, his arms folded. His head had been shaved. The other had gone, she knew not where. 'I have to piss!' she said again.

His eyes indicated the bucket in the corner. Uncertainly, unwillingly, she went to it and stooped, lifted the lid. The stink was sharp, unpleasant. In discomfort under the eyes of the silent slave, she raised her skirt, lowered her panties and squatted.

As the stream of her piss mingled with the remains in the bucket, the second slave returned, bringing with him a stout woman in a dress of plain black serge and button boots. Her skin was coarse and cheesey, and she had a distinct moustache on her broad upper lip. She glared at Josephine as if she had no right to be squatting in her presence. Josephine felt her urethra close; she willed herself to finish and empty her bladder.

The woman spoke, impatiently. Her voice was low, her language the same as Josephine had heard on the radio in the plane. The slave who had fetched her went out again and returned immediately with a tin bath which he put down in the only space, the middle of the cell. He went out again at once.

The châtelaine spoke again, grimly. 'I don't understand!' cried Josephine. The woman gestured heavily and the remaining slave came over and hauled Josephine off the bucket by one arm. She struggled, dismayed, as he pulled her upright. The last of the piss ran down her leg.

The man began to undress her. His breath smelt unpleasantly of onions.

The other slave came back, struggling with two buckets of water. He stood one down on the floor and slopped the other into the bath. He looked on approvingly as his companion stripped Josephine naked. Noticing her wince as he pulled her dress off, he turned her round by one arm, revealing the stripes on her buttocks and thighs. The woman came and leaned across the bath to finger them appraisingly. Josephine tried not to cry out again. She failed. The horny thumbs of the châtelaine seared her maltreated flesh.

The woman commanded the slaves to put her on the bed and leave. They shut the door behind them. Weeping, Josephine submitted to a thorough examination. This was not the treatment she had expected from the sign of the double blank, the master domino. It was not what Jackie had led her to expect, not at all. She had been dreaming of luxury and privilege, a separate world where pleasure was the only law. She shivered and gasped as the wardress probed her quim with an imperious finger, smiling a cheerless smile. Her teeth were ancient and bad.

Josephine allowed herself to be put in the bath. The water was thawed mountain snow, icy cold and pure. The woman sponged her charge down, scrubbing between her legs, mopping only slightly more gently at her stripes. They began to ache again.

She talked to Josephine for a while, incomprehensibly. Josephine wondered if she was mad, or stupid. 'I can't understand!' she said. '*Comprends pas!*' She shook her head. The woman scrubbed her face, soaking her hair. She was hauled out, dried off on a harsh, thin towel and her arms strapped behind her back. The wardress took a short chain from one of the hooks and looped it through the staple above the bed, padlocking it there and fixing the shackle at the other end to the ring on Josephine's collar. It was just long enough for her to lie down or kneel up on the bed. The cell was cold. Shivering, she crept between the sheets.

The woman left, slamming the door behind her. The deep echo seemed to linger for an age in the vaults of thick stone.

Josephine lay there, hungry, exhausted from her journey, her fright and mishandling, the fatigue of her alcohol haze quite worn off. A slave returned for the bath, throwing the buckets into it and splashing the water around noisily as he dragged it to the door. He ignored her. Josephine tried to sleep.

It grew dark. There was no sound from the castle. She heard an owl hooting in the silence. She dozed and woke. She smelt fire, saw a confusing light. She sat up, her back against the wall, the chain cold where it hung on her bare breast. The door was open. A man stood there, a burning lantern in his hand. It was the pilot. He was wearing a domino mask.

He shoved the door closed and hung the lantern on a hook. He stood at her bedside. He was wearing black leather gloves, and beneath his jacket his chest was bare. The light of the lantern fell on his tattoo.

He held a riding crop, a shank of bone or steel sheathed in leather, with a whip tassel at the end. Josephine opened her mouth and a low moan escaped her.

He reached down to poke her breasts with his crop, and play the tassel across her nipples. Despite herself, she felt a shiver of longing. Her nipples rose again for him.

'You were wilful this afternoon,' he said.

'No —'

'Wilful and clumsy. An obedient slave swallows and says thank you, hm?'

He raised her chin with his crop. She looked fearfully into his lion-coloured eyes.

'A good slave laps up the cream with her tongue. She does not *wipe* it with a *tissue*.'

He lashed her breasts twice with the tassel of his crop. She felt its tiny sting, her hands jerking involuntarily, as if they had forgotten they were confined. Cramped from lack of circulation, they prickled horribly.

'Well, now, Josephine. You will learn!'

He raised the crop as if to cut her across the face. But the blow did not fall.

He put one knee on the bed, brought his face down close to hers.

'You will learn,' he said, soberly. 'Kiss me.'

Trembling, she brought her face to his, pressed her mouth to his mouth. He tasted of brandy and chocolate cream. He thrust his tongue into her mouth. She kissed him willingly, sucking his tongue, sliding her own over it. Her tongue begged him not to use his whip.

He released her, disdainfully. He wiped his mouth with the back of his hand. She glared at him, insulted.

He gestured again with the crop. 'Come on, now. Out of that bed. Turn over.'

With difficulty and dread, she obeyed.

'Crouch down. Your bottom up. Well up.'

She struggled into position.

'Spread your knees so.' His hands taught her, positioned her. 'Keep your back dipped. Stretch your spine, Josephine.'

She tried.

'You have a beautiful bottom, Josephine,' he said.

She pressed her cheek against the rough blanket, waiting.

His hands traced the marks the chauffeur had left there with her martinet. 'Did they punish you, Josephine?'

'Yes,' she said, stammering. Was it nervousness, fear, shame?

'Why did they punish you?' His voice was as gentle as a priest's, inquiring after her sins.

She was confused. 'I don't — don't know.'

91

'Indeed you do, Josephine,' he said sternly.

'To — to — humble me,' she said. Her knees and hips shook. She had not spoken so since the earliest days, at the mercy of her tormentors at Estwych.

'Then why pretend you don't know?' he asked, gently again, as if in sorrow for her fault, his obligation to chastise her for it. The end of the crop tickled her slit. She hissed through her teeth.

'Beg for forgiveness,' he told her.

'Forgive me, master!'

He laughed. He had tricked her.

'Beg for punishment,' he said.

'Please punish me, master! Punish me as I deserve!' Her voice echoed from the high ceiling and bare walls. It astonished her with its sincerity.

The crop fell. She screamed. It fell high on the crown of her left buttock, biting her with teeth of fire. She heard it swish back, up into the air, then heard him exhale with a grunt as it fell again, in the same place on the right. She jerked against her chain, she bit her pillow, she pulled and pulled at her bonds. The crop rose and fell, dancing on her flesh. It laced her hips, her thighs. She pulsated and moaned, white-hot with pain. She thrust her bottom at him, crying inarticulately.

The beating stopped. She heard the sound of a zip fastener opening. Then his hands found her hips. He was on the bed behind her. He leaned on her back, put his face over her shoulder, close to her face.

She felt tears running from her nose, mingling and flowing from her mouth. A last sob escaped her, like a convulsion.

'What do you want, Josephine?' he asked. His voice was lazy, ironical.

She did not speak.

Everything, she thought.

But she would not tell him.

The ram of his prick thrust hard, deep, into her quivering loins. She screamed again as the rough fabric of his trousers abraded her blazing bottom. She was invaded, impaled, destroyed. He worked her to a blinding, choking orgasm, another, and another. His balls were tight, slapping against her crotch. She drooled on the pillow, her eyes popping, her haunches ablaze. She gripped and slid and tugged him to a loud, wet climax.

Pleasure filled her, hot as her haunches, hot as his seed in her loins. She turned her head on the pillow to see his face.

'Master?'

'Not I,' he said, chuckling. He smacked her bottom contemptuously and withdrew his wilting prick.

|7|

S he woke. The high window of the cell was bright with grey daylight. A woman was looking down at her, a brown pottery beaker in her hand.

The woman was another slave, wearing the black collar. Her hair was long, thick and dark brown, almost black. It was kept off her face by a simple band of black plastic. She wore a full skirt, almost to her ankles, of gauzy black tulle, layer upon layer of it. Her feet were bare. The skirt was held up by a wide belt of black leather; between the collar and the belt, she was naked. Her breasts were not large, but heavy and pointed, her areolae large and purple as the skin of a beetroot. Between them was the tattoo of the domino mask, going blurred and blue with age.

Startled from her sleep, Josephine said nothing. There was something in the woman's posture that enjoined her to silence. She was determined not to speak, not to give any of them anything until they forced her to. But shifting on the bed she felt an agonized jolt in her fettered arms, and she moaned aloud despite herself.

'You're awake, then,' said the the woman in a precise, educated English accent. She squatted down beside the cot, set the beaker on the floor, and leaned over to unbuckle the straps that restrained Josephine's arms. When she moved, the shape of her legs showed clearly through the skirt, though they remained veiled, shadowed.

Her face was white, without make-up, and rather broad. Her nose was snub, her eyes brown, round and very lustrous. Her lower lip was full and fleshy; her teeth grazed it, as she concentrated on opening Josephine's straps. She was older than she looked, Josephine supposed, now that she was close up: thirty, thirty-two. She moved, leaning further over. Her breasts dangled above Josephine's face. Her flesh smelt of wheat, fields of wheat in summer. Her armpits were shaven.

Josephine stifled a cry as her arms came free. She sat up, leaning against the wall, hugging her dead arms in front of her, squeezing and kneading to get some feeling back into them. The chain that held her to the wall dangled down behind her, cold at her back. She hoped her visitor would undo that too, but she wouldn't ask, for that or anything else.

The slave sat back on her heels, picked up the beaker and offered it to Josephine. Willing her prickling hands to obey her, Josephine took it carefully and brought it to her mouth. Confused, she was expecting coffee or tea, but it was some kind of flower cordial, very sweet and fragrant. Taking another sip, she at once felt its effect, soothing, but at the same time invigorating.

The slave's eyes were on her, appraising her: her face, her body, her posture. Josephine was careless that her breasts were bare, and that she was naked under the sheets. Something about the other woman's proximity, the circumstances, a sense of enforced conspiracy in their movements, a certain air of being on the alert for approaching foot-steps that the woman had at the corners of her eyes – Josephine remembered what the pilot had said. It was all like being back at boarding school.

Still she would not trust her. She was self-sufficient. She would survive.

Solicitous, the woman took the beaker from her as soon as she had emptied it. 'This is your first time, isn't it?' she said, quietly.

Josephine had to answer to that. She nodded.

'They will be along to inspect you soon,' she said. 'They will decide what course of instruction to give you. It will be menial work at first – the laundry, the kitchens, that sort of thing. Can you sew?'

Josephine gave the smallest possible shake of her head, meant to indicate lack of interest as much as lack of ability.

'Don't be surly with them,' her visitor said, more sharply. 'It all takes longer and gets much more painful.' She spoke with authority, her great eyes regarding Josephine solemnly. 'If you take my advice you'll speak modestly and obediently. There are advantages to that, even here.'

She cocked her head a degree, as though thinking she'd heard something. She brushed her fingers over the back of Josephine's hand, as though expressing sympathy for a hospital patient.

'Who was it?' she asked.

Josephine looked blank. She had no idea what she meant.

'Your husband? Your lover? Not your father, surely?'

Who had put her there, she apparently meant. Josephine shook her head again. The chain clinked lightly at her neck. 'I don't know,' she said.

This seemed to impress her visitor greatly. 'You don't?'

'He sent me a domino,' Josephine said. 'A double blank.'

The slave raised her expressive eyebrows, turning her head slightly and looking at Josephine askance, as if with recalculated admiration.

At that moment a door slammed somewhere in the distance, echoing in the corridor.

The slave got to her feet at once. Her body was tensed, poised for flight; but she paused, still hovering at Josephine's bedside, unwilling to leave. When no further sound came, she turned back to her, moving lithely with new purpose.

'They'll come and inspect you first,' she said again, even more quietly than before. 'Are you clean? Did she bathe you last night?'

Without asking permission or signalling what she was about to do, she took hold of Josephine's covers with both hands and whisked them down. Her eyes darted here and there across Josephine's body. Automatically, Josephine closed her legs and drew her knees aside.

The slave smacked her on the thigh. 'Don't be silly,' she said simply. 'Show.'

Reluctantly, feeling more foolish because she'd flinched than embarrassed to be complying, Josephine let her legs fall open. She lay back on her elbows with her knees raised while the slave examined her.

'What's this?'

The slave touched her lightly on the inside of her left thigh, a couple of inches above the knee.

Josephine glanced down. She had found a dried smear of the pilot's semen, splashed down her leg as he withdrew. There was more around her quim, crusty peaks in her pubic hair.

At the slave's bidding Josephine slid down on the cot as far as her tether would allow, and lifted her knees. The slave looked concerned about the cruel purple marks of the pilot's crop. She stroked them with her fingertips.

'I wish I could get you something for these,' she said. She seemed even more distracted. Voices could be heard, echoing from what sounded like a stairwell. She leaped up again.

'I've got to go,' she muttered, intensely. 'My name's Prudence, what's yours?'

'Josephine,' said Josephine. She lowered her legs stiffly.

Prudence nodded, as if that was at least an acceptable name. 'We'll have the same keeper,' she said, as though she expected Josephine to understand something by that. Her glance fell again unhappily on Josephine's exposed bottom and crotch. 'See if you can't – ' she gestured to her own crotch, made a scrubbing motion with her fingers, ' – clean yourself up,' she said.

Then she was gone.

Josephine picked desultorily at the encrustation in her pubic hair, but it was hopeless. She sighed and pulled the sheet back over her. She felt sore from her punishments, and tired from a poor night's sleep. A bell tolled the hours, somewhere in the château, and every hour had seemed to inaugurate or interrupt another bad dream.

The door of her cell opened and the moustached châtelaine entered, fingering a ring of black iron keys at her belt. With her was a small elderly man in a black satin frock coat and tight black velvet trews. He wore a white shirt with a high stock and a crimson waistcoat over it. His hair was long and white, coiffed perfectly in waves back from the shining dome of his forehead. His eyes were grandfatherly and kind. He smiled Josephine a grave smile, meeting her eyes an instant only, then turned to the stout wardress and spoke to her in rapid French.

His French Josephine could understand, partially. He was asking her age, where she came from, what she did, how far she had been trained. The name of Hazel Shepard was mentioned. She noticed the man was wearing a large square-cut black ring, very like the one the woman who had come to her flat had taken off to spank her.

The châtelaine knew all the answers to the questions, or seemed to. She spoke gruffly, as though constrained by some embarrassment or sense of impropriety, though in such a woman that was hard to imagine. While she spoke her gaze roved over the cell. She took in the empty beaker on the floor, the harness that Prudence had taken off Josephine's arms. She didn't seem put out by either.

'Good morning, my dear,' said the man suddenly, in perfect English.

97

Josephine stared at him. 'Good morning,' she said, a trifle belatedly.

'Welcome to the Château des Aiguilles,' he said, cordially, as though she were a tourist come to look over a stately home. 'I cannot promise that you will be happy here with us,' he said, with a gentle, apologetic smile, 'because your happiness, of course, is in your own hands. I can only say that I *hope* you will be happy,' he said, a little pedantically, 'and that you have it within you to be happy. Oh yes, you do,' he went on, as if she had made some sign of contradiction, though she hadn't moved a muscle or even framed the thought of a denial. 'Are you obedient? Are you considerate and dutiful? Not always, I think.'

It depends who's giving the orders, she thought to herself; but her face remained as passive as ever.

The old man spoke to the châtelaine again, and she replied in muttered polysyllables. She looked sour. Josephine wondered if she had any other expression.

The man turned to address Josephine again. 'Let's have a look at you, then, shall we?'

The woman stepped forward and for the second time that morning, the covers were snatched away from Josephine's nudity without even a by-your-leave. There was alcohol, gin or jenever, on the breath of the grunting châtelaine, mixed with garlic and cheese. Josephine turned her face away. The woman's callused fingers, poking and probing her flesh, were far less welcome than Prudence's delicate, abstracted touch. She bore the indignity. She had no choice.

The old man had flapped the tails of his coat and clasped his hands behind his back, inclining his head at an attentive angle. He reminded Josephine of an antique priest or pedagogue, his role here a mere happy extension of his professional capacity. As his lapels drew back, the sight of his crimson waistcoat reminded Josephine of the boy in his red messenger's livery.

Was this dried-up old pedant her new master?

Involuntarily she shut her eyes and gave a shudder.

The woman said something sharp. She had found the semen stains.

The man spoke precisely to her, and she bustled heavily to the door of the cell. She opened it and went outside. Josephine heard her shouting for someone.

'Someone has been using you already, apparently,' said the man, smiling. 'I can see you are going to be popular, my dear.'

Josephine would not reply.

98

The châtelaine came back inside, followed shortly by a slave. It was Prudence. She looked blank-faced, as if she had never seen Josephine before. She was carrying a double handful of snow.

The old man smiled gently. The châtelaine muttered an order.

Prudence came to the cot and knelt down again, just as she had a few minutes previously. Her eyes betrayed nothing, no sympathy or silent message. She looked perfectly serene. She pressed the snow into Josephine's crotch.

The chill of it was electrifying. She gasped, backing up against the wall again, though it was only her body moving, there was no escape. Her heart stopped and the blood clamoured in her ears as Prudence methodically scrubbed her with the melting snow. Her crotch was wet, and icy water was trickling down between her legs, soaking into the thin sheet.

Silently the old man stepped forward to watch the operation.

Prudence bowed low over Josephine, wiping the smears from her thighs. As she finished, she ducked her head as if checking closely for any remaining pollution. Her full lips brushed Josephine's pubis in a secret kiss.

Josephine was startled. Life thudded back into her shocked limbs.

But the old man had seen. Before Prudence could get to her feet, his skinny hand flashed out and snagged her by the collar. He spoke to the châtelaine in French. 'Call Simon,' he told her.

The woman was at the door, shouting along the corridor again.

Josephine lay back against the wall, trembling from the cold. She rubbed at herself, trying to wipe the water away. Prudence stood docile in the master's grip, her head hanging down. The last of the snow dripped off her reddened fingers onto the floor.

A young man came in. He was of middle height, muscular and swarthy. He wore a featureless black sweater and black trousers tucked into polished black knee-boots. From the black leather belt around his waist hung keys, a silver whistle, a coiled whip. His stern eyes were framed by a black domino mask.

The cell was crowded. The châtelaine stood in the doorway, her arms folded, her face solid and resentful as ever. No one spoke. The old man held Prudence facing the bed where Josephine lay. He pushed her forward and briskly whisked up her lacy skirts at the back. As he stepped aside to give the young man room, Josephine saw that Prudence wasn't wearing anything under her skirt. Her chubby

99

bottom and thighs bore the fading purple marks of previous chastisements.

Simon drew his whip and the master nodded.

Simon raised the whip to his shoulder and lashed Prudence across the bottom. Josephine saw her eyes close, her lips and nostrils tighten. At the second blow, the blood drained from her face. Three, and she had not made a sound. She clasped her hands in front of her tightly, tighter as the whip came down again.

Violent red streaks laced her pale flesh. Josephine thought then how well she marked, how much the masters must take pleasure in punishing her. As the fifth and sixth strokes fell, still she made no sound. Prudence was obviously habituated to the ways of discipline. Josephine began to wonder if perhaps she had called this down upon herself deliberately, to demonstrate her prowess to Josephine herself, her ready affection, that she would kiss her though it meant a whipping.

Simon had lowered the whip. The master released his grip. Prudence did not move or sway. She stood pale and stiff as a doll, leaning over the cot. Her skirts slithered softly back down over her abused bottom. Josephine saw her struggle to control her breath, saw her jaw trembling, her bare breasts quivering. Her eyes were still closed. Then they snapped open and fastened on Josephine with a look of pure drama. They were reddened, and wet, though no tears fell from them. Their pupils were wide with shock. They seemed to convey a warning – no, a challenge. Then she was gone, walking straight and erect, her hair flowing behind her, stepping stiffly past the châtelaine and out of the cell as if she had received nothing more than a reprimand.

Simon was looking down at Josephine. His eyes behind the mask were golden brown, very like the pilot's. His black hair fell in a curl over his forehead. He was a Greek, she thought, or an Arab. She remembered the beaches of Evvoia, the naked houseboys laughing and brawling on the sand, tugging themselves erect then strutting to and fro, eyeing her slyly, parading themselves for her favour.

'This one too?' said Simon.

Josephine caught her breath. She had done nothing.

The old man nodded, crooking a finger and holding it to his lips as if making a very precise decision. He patted Simon on the arm. 'Her first day,' he said. 'Go easy on her.'

Simon reached down with his left hand, pulling Josephine away from the wall and turning her around by her shoulder. Out of the corner of her eye she glimpsed the whip as it snaked through the air. Then a violent blow struck her across the buttocks, driving her into the wall. Josephine screamed, rising up on her knees and pressing herself against the wall, grinding her face and breasts and hips against the stone as though the pain of that would keep away the pain of the lash now biting again in the underhang of her bottom.

But that was the end of it. Two fierce strokes and no more. Her bottom pounded as though Simon's whip had merely revivified all her punishments from yesterday. She felt their eyes on her, watching her writhe, approving the obscene tracery that marked her buttocks. She was panting, her breasts heaving. She would not look round. Water dripped from her pubic hair onto her thigh.

The master's hand was on her shoulder, turning her back to face them. 'Simon is your keeper,' he said. 'He will see to your work, your exercise and discipline.'

Simon coiled his whip and returned it to the loop on his belt. His eyes regarded Josephine indifferently. To judge by his implacable expression, beautiful naked women in distress meant nothing to him. She gave him a level, unyielding look. 'Keepers' meant nothing to her either. They were merely obstacles between her and her master. When she found him, she would be exalted. Then perhaps a man like Simon would interest her, when she could have him at her disposal, performing his work for her pleasure.

She was convinced now that the old man was not her master. He had shown no interest in her, no evidence that she was one he had sought out particularly and brought to this place. To him, she was just another slave.

She knelt on the bed, her thighs apart, her hands on her aching bottom. She bowed her head for the châtelaine to unfasten the chain that held her to the wall, seeming as subservient as Prudence had been. But in her heart she ignored them. She had been called to go beyond them. She would endure.

It was the beginning of a long and dreary time for Josephine Morrow. She was taken from the cell and put into a dormitory with five other women. Prudence was one. At night they slept with their hands bound, chained to the wall at the head of their beds. But sometimes, particularly when Simon was called away, or during rest periods in the day, they would be left unlocked and unguarded. Then they would creep into one another's beds and kiss one another's breasts, bring relief to moist and swollen quims with skilful tongues and fingers.

As the nights went by, the population of the room changed. One woman disappeared, then another, and others came to replace them. Strange passionate love affairs and rivalries would ebb and flow in the dark, silent desperate games that frequently ended in fierce tussles and spankings. When Simon discovered them, the indiscretions of one or two would be paid for by all, queuing up to be spanked across his knee on a chair in the middle of the dormitory. Josephine would accept these injustices silently, never doing anything to incur them herself. She would receive visitors to her bed, but never go to another's. In this way she quickly became the most desired and hated woman in the room.

By day it was as Prudence had told her. They were woken by shouts, and ordered to dress in the long gauze skirts, or sometimes in ugly black shifts of coarse cotton. They were not permitted underwear, for no one wanted to look at them. They scrubbed vegetables in the kitchen, swept snow in the thousand courtyards of the château, cleaned windows and polished silver. Simon would deliver them, manacled and chained together, to the supervisor of their work. For the least infraction, or often it seemed none, their skirts were raised and punishment applied with vigour and without mercy.

Sometimes their work would bring them into contact with the male slaves, whose conditions seemed to be very similar. Despite the winter, they were often dressed in revealing clothes. Some wore tiny chains around their ankles, or dramatic scars, signifying some kind of ownership or allegiance. They seemed more sullen than the women, less resigned to the drudgery and indignity imposed on them. They ate in a separate hall, and slept in a wing far from the women's quarters. Prudence seemed to know all about them, or pretended to. There was one she fancied, a tall blond youth with an air of perpetual surprise. She claimed she had spoken to him once, when they had been left alone together at some task, and that on another occasion she had stolen a kiss as they passed in a dark corridor. Cleaning windows in a high room, she paused to look down into the quadrangle. 'There goes Eduardo,' she whispered to Josephine, dusting close by. 'If I weren't married –' She broke off, in a little laugh. The women were forbidden to speak of their lives outside the château, but Prudence had told Josephine her husband brought her to the château every year. He was among the masters somewhere. Josephine never saw him, or Prudence never identified him if she did.

The masters were mostly men, dressed as Josephine had observed, in cloaks or suits of black leather, and always in domino masks. They were of all ages, and all races. They lived for skiing and dancing, music, banquets that went on till dawn. On fine days they rode out to hunt in the black pine forest that climbed the walls of the valley behind the château, laughing and calling to each other. Hanging out washed white sheets in a high walled area, her red, numb hands fumbling with the clothespegs, Josephine heard the sound of the horn echoing through the chilly air. She wondered what it was they hunted with such gusto.

For the most part the masters ignored the lowly domestic slaves, though some took occasional perverse pleasure in degrading themselves to enjoy the body of a drudge or skivvy. Dusting one day in a library of hundreds, thousands of ancient books of all languages, bound in leather, Josephine was called upon by a short fat man wearing brass spectacles over his mask, who directed her in a high, hoarse, asthmatic voice to kneel between his legs and take his penis in her mouth. His ascent to orgasm was laboured and prolonged. He shouted confusing directions as he wheezed and panted. His hands roamed up and down her back and over her breasts. When he came she swallowed every drop. You are not my master, she thought, as the acrid flavour suffused her throat and tongue.

Another man who made use of her at this time was black and tall, very handsome. She longed for him to remove his mask, so she could see his face properly. His hands were large, his penis too. He sat in a large chair and took her standing, between his legs. She flowed for him as she had not since arriving here, days, weeks ago, was it? Time moved strangely in the Château des Aiguilles. Days stretched out until the morning seemed a week past or disappeared altogether as the slaves worked in underground chambers, out of sight of the winter sun.

Life went on all day and all night too, in the château. Then suddenly everyone would vanish at once, and the whole place lie shuttered and deserted for days. Tattered cobwebs would hang in rooms where Josephine would have sworn she had recently swept, or eaten, or been whipped, or used. Days turned into dreams, and dreams into reality that found her weeping, or panting, or bleeding, crying aloud.

Forgetting who and where she was, she caressed the close, tight curls of the black master's head, hugging him to her in desire. His eyes flashed at her in cold anger. He spent in a furious rush; then, summoning a nearby keeper, he had her flogged at his feet for her presumption.

In the dormitory that night he came to her, enjoyed her again in her bondage. The other women watched in oppressed silence. Few masters ever came to the dormitories, with their air of domestic decrepitude, the smell of the sleep of generations of unkempt women. Josephine's status rose again. She was moved to the bed by the door and required to keep a whip, a martinet of stiffened leather, under her pillow. Sometimes, at night, Simon would come and use it on her, by candlelight. Once Josephine saw the tall black man standing in the doorway, motionless, watching them. You are my master, she thought at him. You are mine. And she wished fervently it could be so; but after that night he left, or lost interest in her, and she never saw him again.

'How long does this go on?' she asked Prudence, in an outburst of passionate frustration. The masters used their bodies, or ignored them, and at night they were chained, their hands behind their backs. She lay on her face in the afterglow of the whipping, aroused, yet permitted no release. She ground her pubis into the mattress, but it was not enough.

'It's like the winter,' Prudence said. 'It goes on until you can't believe there ever was a summer.' She stirred, her chain rattling in its staple. 'It's always winter here.'

Simon took Prudence and Josephine to a dim high-ceilinged drawing room lit by oil-lamps in brass sockets above the mantelpiece. The walls were panelled, the windows covered by heavy dusty curtains that trailed on the floor. The carpet was thick, an oriental design. The women were made to strip and kneel in front of the fireplace, their backs to the flames. Three masters, one of them the old man who had inspected Josephine on her first morning, sat in front of them in high-backed Jacobean chairs. They spoke in French, though one of the masters, a woman, had an accent Josephine recognised as Italian, Neapolitan. There was a disagreement. Josephine followed it a while, as best she could, then let it wash over her. The masters were discussing a question of promotion, of someone's readiness for initiation into the realm of pleasure. She felt drugged, stupefied by labour and discomfort, long nights sweating without release. She was

104

too exhausted to pay attention, even though she knew it was her they were talking about. She drowsed as she knelt, her eyes open. She felt the heat of the fire on her naked bottom and back, the soles of her feet. Draughts fluttered ceaselessly around the old room.

A servant in a green velvet doublet brought the masters a decanter of wine and a plate of small biscuits. They pushed back their chairs out of the lamplight, leaving space on the carpet in front of the fire. The old man beckoned Simon, who had been standing in the shadows all the while, at ease, staring into infinity. To demonstrate some point, or perhaps simply as entertainment, the slaves were to be instructed to make love, there on the carpet.

'Take her in your arms, Prudence,' said the old man. His voice was small and dry, like the whispering of autumn leaves against an attic window. 'She is lovely, isn't she? Kiss her. Take her for your own.'

Limbs aching from alternating toil and immobility, Josephine found herself lying down on the floor facing Prudence. Prudence hugged her to her breast. She pressed her mouth against Josephine's. She stroked her hair. She leaned up on one arm, stroking her with the other. She kissed her cheek, her neck, ran her lips lightly around the lower edge of her collar.

Josephine felt inert, entirely unresponsive. What she longed for at night, in chains, she did not want when it was required of her. Prudence was a foolish, impulsive, big-hearted woman. It was no wonder her husband found her a trial and needed to bring her to the château every year for a season under the whip. Her breasts sagged. She was sweaty from kneeling in front of the burning logs. Josephine, on the other hand, was dry, dry as an ancient Egyptian mummy, dry as dust. Prudence's questing fingers irritated her. Josephine kissed her again and again, as if she didn't know what else one was supposed to do. When Prudence ran her hand across Josephine's immobile flank and curled her fingertips into the cleft of her bottom, she jerked her hips and wriggled away.

There was a curt murmur from the masters, and Simon's hand fell on Josephine's shoulder. He pulled the women apart, signalling them both to rise, unfastening the whip from his belt. Gripping Josephine hard by the upper arm, he walked her across the room, into a corner out of the lamplight, and pulled her down, twisting her arm until she was bending, touching her toes. He gave her six swift cuts, low on her bottom and curling generously around her hips, where Prudence's

105

caressing hand had passed only seconds before. The pain was a dream of pain. Josephine did not cry out, not because she was determined not to, but because when she opened her mouth no sound emerged. Her posture did not waver because she could not move.

When she clutched her bottom, Simon curtly knocked her hands down. He walked her back to the hearth. She moved awkwardly, feeling the eyes of the masters on her red-streaked bottom.

Prudence was standing there with her eyes cast down, her hands clasped behind her. Simon took her into the corner now and bent her over. Josephine saw him give her four strokes. Prudence held her pose, her back well stretched, legs straight, showing him the dark cleft of her bottom and the purse of her vulva, revealed between her thighs, as though it was her pride, and the cut of the whip a tribute of admiration to do her honour.

'Do you think it unjust that your partner should suffer for your reluctance, Josephine?' asked the old man, his face in shadow. 'Ah, no, my dear. That is your mistake. The whip is her spur, do you see, to make her try harder. It gives her heat to melt the snow that lies between your thighs. Do you feel its heat, Josephine? Have you forgotten? Touch yourself, my dear.'

Standing before them, Josephine slipped a hand between her legs. She was amazed to find herself moist and opening. She felt nothing, nothing at all. She was like a spectator at her own dissipation. She lay down again on the carpet as Prudence was brought back to her. She parted her legs and Prudence lay on top of her.

Prudence kissed her face, her forehead, her eyelids. Josephine reached up and pulled off Prudence's headband, letting her hair cascade darkly down around them, curtaining them from the flickering light, the steady eyes of the masters and the keeper. Prudence kissed her mouth. Their tongues moved together, Prudence's keenly, as though the whip had warmed her indeed, as though she was grateful for Josephine, for this wonderful treat. Josephine's tongue moved too, slowly, abstractedly, like a limb whose use has been forgotten during months of confinement.

'Use your hands, Josephine,' commanded the old man. 'Feel her breasts. She is naked for your pleasure, Josephine.'

Sluggishly Josephine obeyed. She put her hands between their bodies and cupped the soft weight of Prudence's breasts, squeezing them, rubbing her nipples with the sides of her thumbs. Prudence

106

gasped, nuzzling her ear.

'Feel her bottom too,' continued the unrelenting director. 'She was whipped for your fault. Feel where the whip kissed her.'

Her own sore bottom pressed into the carpet by the weight of Prudence's hips, Josephine spread her hands across the width of Prudence's buttocks. Prudence flinched as her fingers found the marks the lash had scored into her. Cruelly, Josephine's fingers did not relent. She pressed and stroked those marks until Prudence squealed in her arms, burying her face in her hair and grinding her hips against her. Still she felt nothing, nothing save a faint surprise that she had come to this, come from her life in a city whose name she could no longer quite be sure of, to lie on the floor and arouse another woman's body to pleasure with her hands and thighs and tongue, for the entertainment of a panel of watching strangers.

Prudence moved, thrusting a sure hand between Josephine's legs, pressing a finger against her anus. Josephine bucked and whimpered. Prudence drew her finger forward until it touched the lips of Josephine's vagina, then slipped it between them and forced it into her.

Josephine was still tight, slippery but unyielding. Prudence's finger was a rod of fire. She threw back her head, banging it on the floor and yelling in objection; but Prudence's mouth was on her right breast, nuzzling and sucking, biting at her nipples, as if trying to suck up something, some life force she was striving to push through Josephine's body from below.

They rolled over. Prudence's finger twisted, was torn out of her. Josephine bit down on another cry. She hung her hands and knees over Prudence's recumbent form, her head low, not meeting Prudence's eyes.

'Use your mouth, Josephine . . .'

They were told to set themselves head to tail now, and bury their faces in each other's crotch. Prudence was mushy, wet and soft. Josephine couldn't find Prudence's clitoris with her lips or tongue. Everything was in shadow.

The château bell sounded the hour, on and on. It was lounder up here. What hour was that? More than twelve, surely. Would it never stop tolling?

Prudence arched her back suddenly, losing the grip of her mouth on Josephine's vulva. Her thighs braced around Josephine's cheeks as she thrust her pelvis up, grinding herself against her face. She smelt of growing things, things of earth, mealy and ripe. Her fingers dug into Josephine's back, each fingernail like a steel tack. Distracted, Josephine's rhythm failed. They collapsed together.

Simon was standing over them, a sharp goad in his hand. Josephine did not want to see him, did not want to acknowledge that he was there. She plunged her face between Prudence's thighs, licking messily and indiscriminately around the folds of her flesh.

Prudence was crying and groaning, rising heavily and unevenly towards orgasm. They were on their sides again, Josephine leaning up on one elbow, forcing her head through the arch of Prudence's leg. Hearing Prudence puff and grunt with exertion, toiling towards release, Josephine lifted her free hand and grabbed her partner's left breast, kneading it spitefully. Then she reached over her head, blind, across Prudence's hip, and slapped her bottom hard.

Prudence came at once, shuddering and sliding, falling on her back, her heels banging on the floor.

Reaching down, Simon seized Josephine by the thigh and pulled her away from her companion. He forced open her legs and tested her crotch with an unkind hand. He stood over her, rubbing his fingers and sniffing them. He shook his head at the members of the tribunal.

'You see?' Josephine heard the old master say, distantly. 'She is too powerful for her. Too powerful for herself. Her body is locked away from her.' He sounded sad, sorry to have his judgment proved.

'Then we must lock her away from us a little longer,' said the woman, throatily, in French.

Simon took Josephine away, down to a solitary cell in the dungeons, where he chained her upright to the wall by a short chain. He had her fold her arms behind her back and fastened them there. Then he beat her long and thoroughly with a leather strap.

She was kept in solitary confinement for a long time. Her meals were brought by the châtelaine, whose bad opinion of her and of the world in general had not improved. She was given sordid, demeaning tasks, washing out sanitary napkins, emptying buckets of excrement. Every night she was brought Simon's boots to clean and polish. One day while she was on her knees, poking a wire down a blocked drain in a quadrangle near the workshops, a party of male slaves went past along the cloister. One of them was the boy, the chauffeur.

She rose to her feet, staring. It was him, she was sure of it, without his crimson jacket or his peaked cap. He wore the collar, the black singlet, the tight black trousers with the flap at the back. She knew his fine blonde curls. In the cold morning light his profile was as sensuous and youthful as ever.

She called out. Her breath steamed in the air. What had she called? She couldn't have said. What was his name? What was hers? Six pairs of male eyes turned involuntarily to her. It was him, it was. There was no recognition in his puzzled gaze.

The keeper shouted a peremptory command to his gang, lashing at shoulders and buttocks with his crop. In a moment, they were marched away, out of sight. In another, two keepers came and hauled the slave who had shouted into the cloister, tore off her shift and punished her severely.

8

The slave is woken from a dream of a city, of helicopters hovering outside her window, their pilots, goggled and reptilian, gesturing to her, mouthing incomprehensible instructions. She finds herself in solitary, lying in bondage. Her chains are unlocked and she is pulled from her bunk, handed clothes to put on. Shivering, she dresses in suspender belt and stockings, shiny black slippers, pants of sheer black gauze that do not conceal her crotch. She is handcuffed, a gag of stale leather forced into her mouth and fastened behind her neck.

Her keeper walks her on a leash for a long time through empty vaulted corridors where torches burn low in sconces of brass; down staircases of blood-red oilcloth on time-blackened wood; between ranked sculptures of naked women covering their eyes, gazing beseechingly upwards at some unseen tormentor. If she has ever been down this way before, the slave does not remember it.

He takes her to a room where a pale young man with a domino mask and a domino tattoo lies naked and listless on a four-poster bed. His sheets are tossed, his long hair tousled. There is an overpowering smell of rosewater.

The recumbent master gives a condescending command in a language the slave does not know, if she ever did, and she is bent for him over a low wooden bar at one side of the room. The bar is waxed, and bowed in the middle from an accumulated weight of successive bodies. Her hands are uncuffed, and she is told to reach down in front of her and grasp another bar at ankle level. Her keeper then squats in front of her, and fastens her hands in place, locking each of them in a manacle bolted to the bar.

The keeper leaves. She hears the door bang hollowly behind him. She is alone with a master. This is not customary for a lowly domestic slave at the Château des Aiguilles, but she thinks nothing of it. She thinks of nothing.

The languid young master stands behind her. He runs his hands over her bottom and down her legs. He parts her legs, replanting her feet. When she drops her head and looks backwards between her feet, she sees his bare legs, his bare feet. His feet are white as porcelain, as smooth as the feet of young girls.

She feels him stretch the elastic waistband of the black gauze pants and lower them to her thighs. They rest, stretched lightly, around the tops of her stockings.

The master probes her quim with his finger. He speaks to her, asking her a question in the language she does not understand. She is gagged, and makes no attempt to reply.

He leans across her, putting his weight on her back, pressing her hips painfully down onto the wooden bar. He toys with her hair, which is long now and hangs down around her face. His other hand at her crotch is firmly insistent.

His cock is erect. She feels it nestling between her open thighs. He rubs it up against her quim with his hand.

After a while of this, he steps away from her again, grunting to himself, an incomprehensible mutter. He goes and fetches something. She hears behind her the sound of a lid being screwed from a glass jar.

The master slathers her anus with cold greasy ointment. He prods and pokes it in through the sphincter, rubbing it into the skin and into the flesh within, then applying more. The impersonal pressure of his finger in her tender passage stirs her. She pushes against it, driving it deeper. She feels the other fingers of the master's hand curl up under her vulva, milking her juices. She smells herself. She sighs into her leather gag.

His prick, when it comes to her again, is firm and wet. For all the effete appearance of his frame, his long, shapeless hair, his erection is sturdy, and he presses the tip of it into her greased anus and pauses a moment; then taking hold of her hips, he thrusts himself inside, quickly and hard.

The slave moans into her gag. Her head swings, rolling from side to side. Her arms are stretched down in front of her, firmly anchored to the bar, her legs stretched behind her, the master stands between them. The skin of his legs is smooth, hairless or shaven, against the inside of her thighs. His thighs rub back and forth between hers as he thrusts into her.

The feel of his penis inside her is hot, almost painful. She feels herself squeezing tight around it, as though her rectum thinks it is a turd and needs to be expelled. When penetrated like this she always feels for the first second or two that she is going to shit, to foul the master's genitals and thighs with her excrement. This never happens, but always feels as if it is about to. The slave has no feelings about this, neither anxious or eager. She thinks of nothing as the young man in the mask grinds his pelvis against her buttocks, pressing her up against the bar.

He reaches beneath himself again, fondling her quim peremptorily. His touch is unsure and careless. He finds her clitoris and slicks it with the creamy mixture their own secretions have made with his lubricating ointment. The smell of roses stupefies the slave. Her body is full of glands and valves, releasing and relaxing themselves into the hard, sure grasp of pleasure. The poker heat in her anus turns to moist, slippery warmth. She feels the head of the master's prick knock against the seat of her clitoris from within. She gasps, gagging. She wishes there were another prick in her mouth, instead of this stinking gag, and yet another in her vagina. She wishes to be pierced, to be extinguished, to be invaded at every orifice. She feels the master's fingers clutch her hips hard, scoring her with his nails.

Shouting in his foreign tongue, he wrenches himself out of her and panting loudly, leaning down over her back and licking her shoulder, her neck, inserts himself in her vagina. Her pleasure blossoms out and around her suddenly, like a tree, like a jolt of cocaine, lighting her nerves. If she were not strapped across this bar, she could reach behind her and stroke his balls.

He begins, more slowly and seriously, to thrust himself in and out of her. He makes an earnest snuffling noise. She takes her weight on the bar and on her right leg, and lifts her left leg at the knee, raising her left hip and angling her pelvis around toward him to take him easier and deeper. Her foot rises in the air, her shin slides down his leg and the heel of her slipper comes up against his bare bottom. He snarls and slaps her bottom, twice. She lowers her left foot back to the floor. Her bottom stings where he smacked her. The stinging feeds into the tingling of her loins, the blooming of her pleasure.

He gasps and cries out hoarsely. He grinds into the slave until she thinks he is surely about to climax; but in time he jerks himself free again. She hears him standing behind her, panting. He wipes his hands clumsily around her crotch, smearing all the grease and fluids there together, wiping them on her bottom and into her pubic hair. He drags her pants down to her ankles, pulls her feet free. Then he leaves her and goes elsewhere in the room. Looking back through the arch of her legs, she cannot see him.

She hears his bare feet pad back towards her, out of sight. Then his hand rests in the small of her back, and there comes an excruciating pain in her anus. He is forcing something, not himself, something cold and hard, glass or metal, into her rectum.

For an instant, it is the same as when he penetrated her with himself. She feels a blaze of fire, a reflex spasm of evacuation, then a deep, choking surge of desire. Her knees shake. Her head hangs down. His weight is off her, his feet padding away again. He says something to her, something cold and ironic, from across the room. He returns to her with a whip.

She sees the lash dangling between her legs. Then it is gone, and pain flashes through her, slamming her hips against the wooden bar. The master stands, panting, as though to give her one blow with the whip took all his strength. But he whips her again, clumsily, the tip of the lash looping back and catching her low on the left thigh. Inside, she squeals. The noise is a hoarse, voiceless sucking against the wet leather of her gag.

He whips her twice in quick succession, catching her high on the upper slope of her right buttock with a slamming stroke that feels as if it will leave her a bruise; and then, before the pain of that can even register, giving her a stroke that finishes long on her left flank with a sting like the sting of a hornet.

The slave is unused to being whipped so carelessly. Her keeper's strokes are more precise, more expertly laid on. This young master may be unskilled; he may be incapacitated with drink or drugs. He may be simply wishing to show her his contempt, to punish her ineptly and make her a present of it. Perhaps she is worth no more than that. None of these reflections occurs to her. She is in pain, deep in a river of pain that runs from her stuffed anus into the room, and through the cellars of the Château des Aiguilles like a conduit of oily water, thick with blood. She smells blood. She smells fire. She smells roses, and leather.

The master is in front of her, reaching down, pulling up her head by the hair. He is unbuckling her gag, drawing it from her mouth. Strings of saliva trail after it from her mouth. The ram in her rectum is warm and makes her shiver as she arches her spine.

The master squats again, holding her head up between his hands. His palms are hot and slippery against her cheeks. He bends her neck backwards until it hurts. He puts his cock in her mouth.

She salivates around it, sucking on it as if it could give her life and nourishment, as if it were a breast and she a baby. He stutters and snarls with pleasure. His voice is high and tense. He wipes his hands in her hair, smearing it this way and that. The taste of his cock is the taste of her shit, and her cunt, and his own musk. He is salty as the herring she ate for supper. She runs her tongue beneath the rim of his glans and he shouts with joy. She does it again.

Her hips and legs are stiff, turned to wood by the whip. Her weals crawl with fire, subsiding, then suddenly breaking through again. She sucks urgently on the master's prick. The ache of the whip spirals around the fierce obstruction in her anus. When she grinds herself against the wooden bar, the object pounds the base of her clitoris through the wall of her vagina. She gasps around her mouthful of cock, then closes her lips around it more firmly.

He pulses once, twice, and pauses, rigid; then jerks a third time, weakly. His ejaculate splashes her throat and she swallows hard. There is no more. His orgasm was feeble after all, his passion roused and spent too many times today, perhaps; or else he came too soon, unready. The slave does not speculate. She hangs her head, knowing she will be whipped again now.

She is. Then she is taken back to her cell in chains.

Another day she thinks has been selected for promotion.

The slaves are brought into the long room in a line. They are led by their keeper, who holds the leash of the first. There are six of them. They are blindfolded; their hands are buckled in tight leather cuffs and chained behind their backs. They wear sandals and collars; nothing else.

The masters stand or sit around the fireplace, smoking and drinking. There are no other slaves or servants present. The masters ignore what is happening at the other end of the room, where a high bench and a number of hassocks have been set in place. There is an atmosphere of custom and peaceful expectation. One of the younger masters flexes a crop experimentally and taps it against the side of his

A master takes off his gloves to spank a slave. He stands sideways on to her, her left hip against his leg. The bench supports her bottom at a convenient height for him. He places his left hand lightly on her right hip and runs a finger down the cleft between her buttocks. The slave shivers, but makes no sound. The master begins to spank her slowly.

The second master now signals to a keeper. A strap is brought to him. He walks up and down the line. He has decided to test all of the slaves, to give each one the strap, in no particular order. He awards the second slave one stroke, then the fifth two, one on each of her buttocks. The third slave, her bottom now growing quite red from the spanking she is undergoing, receives two strokes with the strap. She cries out, her voice clear in the hush. The master who has chosen her waits a moment or two for the strokes to flare and burn down in her flesh before resuming her spanking. His colleague takes the strap to the sixth in line. He spends some time on her.

The other masters stand looking on. The young master lingers his crop. He has not yet made up his mind. Any of these blotched and glowing bottoms might be the first.

No slave knows when a blow will fall on her. She can hear the sounds of smacks, regular or sudden, to either side of her along the bench. No matter how well trained she is, no matter how she wills herself to silence, it is difficult to keep from crying out when her own bottom is suddenly smacked or whipped. Now involuntary gasps, the scuffing of sandals on bare floorboards, are becoming more frequent. So also is the clink of chain. She has no way of knowing when the chain will be attached swiftly to her collar, pulled tight and attached to her cuffs; when she will be drawn quickly and quietly from her place on the bench and the end of her chain secured to the belt of a master who has selected her. Either side of her, her sister slaves are being selected and removed. Perhaps new slaves are being brought in and lowered into place. She has no way of knowing.

There is a pull on her collar. She is being raised to her feet, turned to face the door, required to walk. She leaves the room, walks the corridors, seeing no one. She has already forgotten the discipline she has undergone.

Behind her, in the long room, the testing continues.

The slave is brought up long flights of stairs, into a low bedroom. As the door is closed behind her, she hears the castle bell ring sonorously past another hour of her captivity.

She is unlocked, uncuffed, unchained.

'You will not be restrained again until I put you there,' says a low voice.

Master, she thinks.

Her eyes are still covered. She feels warm, sure hands on her, turning her this way and that, palpating her buttocks, testing the heft of her breasts. Her thighs are parted, her hidden folds parted and probed. She thinks of nothing. The bell ceases, there is silence in the room, but in her head is a high singing of excitement, as if something wonderful is about to happen to her, some Christmas, some birthday, some cracking of the chrysalis, like remembering her name.

The next thing she feels is water. A sponge has been dipped in warm soapy water and is being passed up the cleft of her bottom. She is washed thoroughly below and above, the water sluiced away into a tub. She is rubbed and patted dry with a thick towel. She smells the body and breath of the fat châtelaine, the smell of face powder, oil and garlic. The hands that make her toilet are not gentle.

No words are spoken. There is a grunting as the châtelaine withdraws, carrying her basin with her. The door closes and the loose, heavy footsteps slump away down the corridor into silence.

The slave stands naked in the warm room. A hand, one of the warm, dry hands, takes her by the shoulder and guides her to the bed. It lays her down on her face. The hands part the cheeks of her bottom. There is a brief pause, then a whistle in the air, and a crack of appalling pain across her bottom.

Despite her discipline, she yells aloud in shock and anguish and claps her hands to the place.

The blow is not repeated.

Slowly she removes her hands, thinking she has been tested again, and she has failed.

She lies there with her hands at her sides, waiting for the second cut. It was a crop, she knows it was, she can tell them all now by the pain they leave and the way they leave it.

There is no second cut.

One of the hands lifts her shoulder, guides her up on her feet, then presses her down until she kneels on the floor. It is thickly carpeted. Thumbs and fingers prise her lips open. An erect penis is inserted in her mouth.

Very near her ear, a husky voice says: 'Caress me with your lips and tongue.' Does she know this voice? She does not know.

The slave obeys.

Her mouth is dry, but she sucks and draws on the penis until they make moisture between them. She moves her head around and lifts her hands to steady herself, holding on to the thighs of her master. He is wearing tight trousers of some kind of cotton drill. He does not forbid her to hold on to his thighs while she sucks his prick.

His prick is curved, circumcised, shiny smooth on the underside. It tastes clean. His fly is buttoned, holding his balls tight back inside his trousers. She strokes them through the cloth with the knuckles of her right fore and middle finger. His prick jumps in her mouth. His hand strokes her hair, which has fallen into her eyes. She sucks with energy and faith, sucking the saliva to a froth by whipping her tongue back and forth beneath his cock, drawing in air. She squeezes their combined juices back and forth as she circles her head about, rubbing the glans of his cock against the inside of her cheeks, her tongue, the roof of her mouth. He is still swelling, growing still stiffer, under her attentions. His hand leaves her hair and grasps her right breast, squeezing it.

Master, she thinks.

She sucks with renewed vigour. She opens her mouth and runs the tip of her tongue over the tip of his cock, curling it around to slip the underside up over the tiny oozing eye of the glans. In her mind's eye, she can see it. She can recognise a cock by its feel between her lips and on her tongue now. She knows this cock, a cock like this. She has felt it here, since coming to the château, more than once. She can remember this, though she no longer remembers her life before the château as any more than a series of improbable dreams.

She knows it is of no consequence to her, yet she wonders who her master is.

She reaches up and boldly clasps him around the bottom, angling her head for him to thrust himself deep into her; and he does so. He is breathing harshly, snorting between clenched teeth. She knows that sound. She runs her tongue up and down the length of the underside of his cock once, twice, three times, then clamps her lips fiercely around the shaft as far up as she can reach, and flicks her tongue rapidly back and forth, back and forth across the underside of his glans until he comes.

Just as he does, he tugs his prick out of her mouth and ejaculates on her upturned face.

She feels the splatter on the fabric of the blindfold, on her cheeks and in her hair. Semen splashes on her eyes and nose. It runs down beside her right nostril onto her upper lip.

It feels copious, hot, wet and good. She opens her mouth a little and tilts her head to let it trickle in over her protruding lower lip, between her teeth.

It tastes rank and fine.

There is a deep chuckle in the room.

Her blindfold is removed.

She is kneeling on a deep pile carpet beside the bed in a large, luxurious chamber. The bed is a four-poster, canopied in gold and blue cloth that looks very heavy and ancient. The room is lit by a chandelier. The ceiling is stained with black smoke overhead. The man in front of her is masked. He wears a black tunic with the hood up, the front unfastened down to groin level. There is curly black hair on his chest. It has completely overgrown the tattoo there. His erection, beginning to subside, is dribbling on the carpet..

The young man wears a supercilious smile on his good-looking face. His nose, the planes of his cheeks, the sallow colour of his skin, all make him look like a Mediterranean playboy, she thinks. He wears a gold ring on the hand that dangles the riding crop. His boots are thigh-length, and perfectly polished. He is her keeper. His semen cools on her cheeks and chin.

Confused, she looks right and left.

There is someone else in the room. It is a woman. She steps forward from the corner behind the door. She is not very old, about twenty-two, twenty-three. She has a mop of curly red hair, a green velvet dress with a deep décolletage. Her breasts are pronounced and high, though not large. She laughs softly. Her voice is deep. She has freckles on her face, and on the hands she clasps theatrically before her.

'Thank you, Simon,' she says in her deep and husky voice, 'that will be all.'

Simon tosses the riding crop on the bed. He bows to the woman, to them both, slipping his flaccid prick back inside his clothes. Smirking openly, he strides from the room. The door bangs softly closed behind him.

'Do you know why you've been sent to me?' asks the woman.

The slave remains silent, her head bowed again.

The woman comes over to her, tilts her chin up with one finger. The slave looks reluctantly up into stern, smiling eyes. The mistress has freckles. 'Do you?' she repeats.

'No, mistress,' admits the slave. Her heart is sunk already.

'Perhaps you have been unsatisfactory,' says the woman, relishing the words. There is a light of gaiety in her eyes. In other circumstances, she seems to be a woman who might have been amusing to know as a friend. But there are no other circumstances. There is only the Château des Aiguilles, the eternal bell, the eternal winter. There are only dim rooms panelled in dark wood or draped with dusty velvet hangings, corridors where slaves with ancient besoms of twigs sweep up clots of dried mud from the heels of the masters' riding boots, spilt tobacco, scraps of blood-stained cloth. Each room is seen once, then never again. The slave had once begun to think that there were ten thousand rooms in the château, and a torment waiting for her in every room. When she had visited them all, then she would be free.

Such thoughts no longer trouble her. No thoughts do.

'Have you?' demands her new mistress, holding up her chin to make her stare into her eyes. They are brownish green, not as bright as the green of her dress. Her cheeks are a ripe and healthy pink. 'Have you been unsatisfactory?'

The slave licks her lips. 'Not willingly, mistress.'

The woman laughs, shortly, as though she has caught the slave out. 'Slaves do nothing *willingly*,' she says. 'Slaves have no will. They do everything obediently. Have you been disobedient?'

The word 'disobedient' she gives the same rolling emphasis she gives the word 'unsatisfactory'. She scans the slave's face, looking for signs of weakness, unreadiness, failure.

The slave tastes the acrid, salty savour of her keeper's semen. She thinks it is clinging to the back of her throat.

'No, mistress,' she says.

The young woman drops hold of her chin and steps back from her. 'Then why on earth are you here?' she asks. Her voice is light and pleasant. Her incomprehension might be genuine. Only a slight undertone of archness indicates that she is playing.

The slave says something bold. 'Because you sent for me, mistress,' she says.

'Did I indeed,' the woman replies. She sounds truly bored now,

121

talking at random with a slave to pass the time in this high and dreary place. The windows of her chamber are tall, slender and pointed, glazed with small panes of glass, some of them stained glass. She looks towards one now, patting her curls with her hand as though the window were a mirror.

'And why would I do that?'

The slave crouches lower to her knees.

'It is your pleasure, mistress,' she murmurs.

'My pleasure,' says the woman, who seems to have nothing better to do than echo and repeat the slave's words with a sarcastic, slighting tone, as if she found them somehow quaint and muddle-headed. 'Because it is my will,' she says, as if correcting the slave's misapprehension.

The slave bows her head.

'Or because you have deserved it,' the woman goes on. 'My punishment. Or reward. Perhaps it is your supreme reward, to be sent to me. Have you considered that?'

The slave touches her forehead to the carpet. The carpet smells of wool and dust. It prickles the cold skin of the slave's forehead.

The woman's tone changes completely. It is as though she has been merely toying with the slave until now, and now she has decided to do whatever was in her mind when she sent for her. 'Get up,' she says. 'Turn your back.'

The slave stands, her haunches still stinging dully from the keeper's crop. She turns and faces the bed.

The blindfold appears in front of her face, and is tied deftly behind her head.

'Put your hands on your hips,' the woman instructs her. 'Pull your elbows together.'

The slave obeys. She feels her shoulderblades contract, her breasts lift and separate before her.

Through the crooks of her elbows the woman slides a length of light, cold metal. Leather and metal laces are fastened around her elbows, drawing them together and tying them to the metal rod.

Something round and smooth, like a glass egg, is pressed into her mouth and tied in place with what feel like leather thongs.

The slave settles into herself.

In her heart is a feeling of lightness, like a small light in a dark space, a candle in the niche of her cell. She breathes more deeply, feeling her heart expand, the darkness and the small flame at the centre, which is very luminous and white.

'Turn.'

The slave turns to face the voice.

She feels cold steel bracelets locked around her wrists, hears a length of chain rattle and clink softly as it is drawn tight between them and locked in place.

Then her collar is unbuckled and removed, and replaced again at once the other way round, with the buckle at the front.

'Turn again.'

A chain slithers through the metal ring on her collar, knocks against the metal rod pinning her arms. Sure, practised hands feed it between the rod and her bare back, and a moment later pull it taut. Her head is dragged backwards until her neck hurts and she begins to breathe faster, trying not to make a sound against her gag.

She feels the small white light is burning in a large dark space now, like a cave underground. It rocks and bobs, as though it were afloat.

Obedience keeps the flame afloat, keeps it from toppling into the dark water and drowning.

The slave is pushed forward. She falls on her stomach on the bed. Her head is dragged so far back on its chain that her face and breasts are lifted off the eiderdown.

The woman takes hold of her feet.

She shackles them together at the ankle.

The slave feels the soft silk of the eiderdown against her nipples. She can still see the small white light, though it is a long way below her now; she has risen above it into the effortless air. The rock has almost closed around the light. There remains only a small gap, a cleft through which she can still see it shining brightly below.

There is the clinking of another chain, and a tug on her ankles where they are joined.

The chain is attached to the rod through her arms. It is pulled tight.

The slave bends her knees, feels her feet drawn up behind her. The edges of the shackles press hard against her ankles. Her buttocks ache where they have been spanked and strapped and cropped. Her body is bent into the shape of a bow.

She cannot move. She cannot move a muscle.

The dark closes over the flame.

123

The light is not extinguished. It continues to burn, undisturbed now, deep within.

The slave is extinguished. She is gone. She is a standing wave of invisible fire.

A long time, or a short time, later, the mistress, or someone, rolls the slave onto her side. They take hold of her breasts with firm hands, fingers spread.

The slave feels a surge within her wave. Desire aggravates her annihilation. Her mistress rubs and squeezes her nipples.

Her hands are gone, then, for a moment. There comes the sound of the woman breathing, handling something that creaks softly, like leather. It sounds heavy.

Sharp points press into the underside of the slave's breasts, like the teeth of metal combs ranked one in front of the other. She draws a breath and tastes glass and leather. She feels the gag is suffocating her. Her breasts are being manipulated into an apparatus of leather straps and sharp teeth.

She is rolled back onto her belly. Their very weight impales her breasts on a thousand spikes. She swallows a wail of distress, forbidding it to rise up her throat.

Where her crotch presses into it, the eiderdown is soaking wet.

She is left like that for one minute, two.

Then the gag is suddenly drawn from her mouth.

She gasps in surprise, relief, dismay. Drool runs down her chin.

'What are you feeling?' demands the mistress. Her voice, her face, feel very close. Her question is urgent, intense. 'I order you to tell me.'

'*What do you want?*' she remembers the pilot asking her. '*What do you want?*'

She had not answered.

The slave's lips work, freeze. Her breath comes short and ragged, clutching at her chest as though it threatened to stop altogether.

'You *will* tell me.' The mistress is merciless.

Blind, immobilized, the slave swallows. Her word chokes her.

'Nothing –'

It is not true.

She feels hunger, fatigue, excitement, pain, pleasure, longing, trust, hope, despair –

'Everything!' she gasps. She is panting from the overwhelming intensity of it all. 'Everything!'

She smells again, suddenly, the sickening scent of roses. Nothing, no one moves. Everything is silent and still. The room and all its luxuries and torments have dropped into oblivion. The standing wave slumps, the huge dark cave contracts to nothing, the little white light goes out.

|9|

Josephine woke. She did not know where she was. She knew only that she was no longer where she had been, and that where she was now she had never been before.

She was alone, in a large double bed, between crisp sheets of printed cotton. The print was a bold design of huge orchids silk-screened in flaming oranges and mustard yellows. There were no other bedclothes. The bed was firm and comfortable, and she felt astoundingly, wonderfully, warm. She did not remember when she had last woken in warmth.

The bed was in a large, low room. The walls were stone, built of large stone blocks painted white. There was an old wooden electric fan mounted on the ceiling; an antique bureau and mirrored chest of drawers in plantation style.

A venetian blind was lowered over one wall, with slats of golden wood. The slats were closed. Nevertheless, brilliant sunshine leaked into the room through the blind, through every crack and crevice of it. The shape of the sunlight through the slats showed an arched dooway in the wall. The air smelled of salt, and pineapple, and sun.

She could hear a subdued sound of people talking, walking slowly past below, laughing merrily. She could hear the sound of seabirds.

Josephine flung back the sheet, damp from perspiration, and jumped out of bed. She was completely naked.

She spent a useless few minutes of complete disorientation, turning this way and that about the room, looking for anything she recognised. There was nothing. There was a plaited straw rug, a large peacock chair in wicker and an even larger swivel chair in leather, a majestic slab wardrobe, a full-length looking-glass on a swivel stand, an enormous television, a bamboo cocktail cabinet and a crescent-shaped coffee table, also of bamboo.

On the coffee table was a small pile of printed papers, a key on a large circular plastic tag, and a square glass ashtray large and thick enough to bash someone's brains out with. In the ashtray was a white matchbox.

Josephine went over and picked up the matchbox. It rattled. It was full of matches, white-tipped ones. It was completely unused.

On the cover it said, in gold script with flourishes, *Concord Reef*; and under this, in very small capitals, also gold, *DOMINICA*.

The pile of papers proved to consist of a magazine, several tourist information leaflets, and a map of an island shaped like a snowman tilting over sideways. Dominica. 'Welcome to Concord Reef. Our business is your pleasure.' A hotel. She was in a hotel. On Dominica.

She sat down suddenly on the foot of the bed and looked at herself. She looked thin, undernourished, and very pale. She looked in the mirror. Her eyes were dull, her hair too. But she did not look unhealthy, or feel it. There were no wounds or bruises on her anywhere. She ran her fingers through her hair. It had been cut while she slept, cut professionally and well.

She wondered what the hell had happened to her.

She looked in the wardrobe. There were T-shirts, swimsuits, frocks, shorts, a pair of slacks, and two pairs of sandals, one plain, one fancy.

She recognised none of them.

She found a lightweight cotton robe and put it on, belting it around her. The feel of it against her skin reminded her of her kimono, back at home, in London. Back – before.

Cautiously she raised the blind.

The arch opened onto a tiled balcony, with a red railing all around. Beyond, several yards away, she could see a white wall with arches like the one she was standing in. Above the wall was a red tiled roof; and above that a sky as rich and dense as cobalt.

Stepping out through the arch, Josephine found herself in the open air, three or four storeys up. She stood beside a bleached sun-lounger, looking down into an explosion of lush green foliage, the branches of trees confused with greenery sprouting and spilling from ledges and balconies around and below.

She went and leaned on the railing, and looked straight down. Through the branches she could make out red and white striped awnings below; and over to the left, blue as a kingfisher, the sea.

Dominica.

127

People passing along the arcade below, strollers, invisible beneath the awnings. A pulse of distant reggae mingling with the seabirds. Hot sunlight pouring out of the sky, glaring off the white walls. Smells of cooking food; sweet smells of cinnamon and coconut, of rich, lush greenery. A man's voice raised in excitement, laughing. A car horn, or was it a trumpet?

She went back into the room and sat on the bed.

After a moment, she got up and lowered the blind again.

There were two doors in the room.

Josephine went and opened the one on the opposite side of the room from the balcony.

It opened onto a broad stairway leading down to the floor below, and thence to an inner courtyard.

Josephine closed the door and locked it. It seemed important. It seemed to have been a long time since she had had the freedom to lock a door between herself and — other people.

She tried the other door.

On the other side of it was a large, well-appointed bathroom, with apricot fittings and an apricot streak in the fake marble tiling.

Josephine went in and took a long shower. First she had the water hot, then turned it cold. After that she ran it pleasantly warm, and stayed under it for a long time.

While she showered, she tried to remember what the hell had happened to her.

She remembered the plane flight to the Alps, the château. She remembered a dormitory, the weight of chains on her neck and hands. She remembered faces: a young Arab in a domino mask; an Indian in tight breeches and buckle boots, who had a pet monkey on a leash; a fat woman with a moustache. She remembered snow on a stunted thorn tree; hanging out washing that froze, crackling, on the wet black line. It all seemed like a strange, elongated dream; or like the sensations of someone who lies a long time in fever; and misconstrues all that happens around her. Josephine's body, aching faintly in the cascade of warm, reassuring water, felt as if it had recovered from a terrible accident. She supposed her mind would follow.

She turned off the shower and climbed out. She sat on the loo and stared at her feet. She had no inclination to get dressed and go downstairs, but the room had neither telephone nor bell-push.

In a while, hunger overcame her. She wondered what they had been feeding her, wherever it was.

In a drawer she found clean, white underwear. It seemed to be brand new. Doubtfully she put on bra and panties. They were her size. She pulled on a long-sleeved cheesecloth blouse, the slacks and the plain sandals: more clothes than the weather required, but she felt an imperative need to cover herself up as much as possible. It was like the need that had made her lock the door of the room. She unlocked it now, and went out, locking it again from the outside.

Walking carefully downstairs, she realised how weak she was. Her head started to spin. Leaning most of her weight on the banister, she coped with the rest of the journey down. At the bottom she entered a spacious lobby with planters full of palms and scarlet tropical flowers. There were couches and chairs, a cigarette machine, an aquarium of blue and silver fish, and a desk with a young woman sitting behind it, busy with a pile of filing cards.

Josephine approached. The woman greeted her civilly in Spanish, by name. There was nothing in her manner to indicate whether she had ever seen Josephine before or not.

Josephine leaned towards her, bracing herself with both hands on the desk. She asked, 'Do you speak English?' The woman said she did. Josephine said, 'Will you answer a strange question for me?'

The woman looked charmed, as though Josephine had offered to tell her a funny joke.

'Do you know how long I've been here?'

The woman nodded, regarding her steadily. 'You arrived last night, Señora Morrow. I hope your room is to your liking.'

Josephine nodded sombrely.

She took a deep breath. The lobby seemed to surge around her, as if everything swept into giddy motion the moment she stopped looking at it.

'This is the Concord Reef Hotel?'

'Si, señora.'

'Dominica?'

The woman smiled, as if this was going to be a funny joke after all. 'Si, señora.'

'And can you tell me the date?'

It was the middle of June. But yesterday, in the mountains, there had been snow. In fact, there had always been snow. At the château, everything had been wintry. Perpetual winter.

129

Perhaps it had been a dream.

Josephine sat at a table on a covered terrace with an arched whitestone loggia on one side and, behind a bank of greenery, the swimming pool on the other. She ordered coffee, a meal. She ordered at random and didn't notice what they brought her. She ate a few mouthfuls, then put her down her fork. She drank quantities of coffee, which seemed to have no effect. There was a clinging, muffling film between her and the world, like shrink-wrap. She picked at some fruit. Then, abruptly, she went back to her room.

The bed had been made, the towels replaced, the leaflets on the coffee table tidied back into a neat, square pile. Josephine leafed through them again, trying to orient herself, trying to understand. Only after several futile minutes did her eye fall on a date; only then did she realise how long the winter had lasted.

She had lost a year. She had been away, wherever they had taken her, whatever they had done to her, for more than a year, nearly two years.

Josephine sat down on the floor. Her lips moved silently for a while as she tried to explain it all to herself. She failed. She undressed and crept back into bed. She slept for several hours. Then, waking suddenly, she lay back against the pillows and listened to the people walking in the street below, unaware of her, unaware of the significance of dominoes, unaware of a château in the mountains where it was always winter.

Her eyes filled with tears.

Josephine had never been to the Caribbean before. She had always wanted to go there. She remembered lying in bed with Jackie, drowsily after sex, fantasizing about a holiday they would take together, away from the depression and grime and noise of the city. Away to Dominica.

She wondered who else she had told. A hundred people, probably, over the years. Her Caribbean holiday had always been her fantasy, back from when she was just a lowly departmental assistant: the supreme holiday she never quite got around to taking, even after she could afford to.

Now it was spoilt.

They had abandoned her here, like a child in an unfamiliar playground among children she didn't know, children who came here daily, whose playground it was. They had rejected her, taken her into

130

their castle and thrown her out again. She had been tested and failed, tested and failed, tested and failed.

Time and again she wondered whether any of it had ever really happened. Her memory was confused, mostly blank, but sometimes, in the middle of the night awash with swirling, disconnected images, faces, masks, naked bodies. She heard screams, the crack of the lash. She was weak but unharmed. The castle had had a name, but she couldn't remember it. Places like that didn't exist, couldn't exist, not now, even if they ever had.

Places like the Concord Reef Hotel, on the other hand, were only too real, only too banal.

This was where the idle rich came to play. American lawyers, German industrialists, English stockbrokers – all the incidental characters of her previous existence, all the types she met on business, on planes, at meetings and conferences: they were all here, all hiking and snorkelling and drinking and lazing to their rich and idle hearts' content. Some of them were charming. Some of them were very beautiful. Josephine wanted nothing to do with any of them.

She put on a Gottex sun-top and frilled skirt in marmalade orange and dove grey. It looked good in the mirror, though it was nothing she would ever have bought for herself. Would she? Who was she, anyway? The woman in the mirror had her breasts, her eyes. The hotel manager, a tubby native in a sky blue linen suit and white patent leather shoes, bowed and kissed her hand when they met. The barman called her Miss Morrow, and sent her new cocktails at all hours with his compliments, a pale blossom at the rim of the glass. They treated her like a great man's widow; like a convalescent child; like a film star dying slowly of some incurable disease.

Soon she came to understand she was a prisoner here, in this prison of luxury. She had no passport, no money, only unlimited credit at Concord Reef. Whatever she asked for they put on her bill, it was already paid for, there was no bill, instructions had been given to the manager from the owner, which was to say the company, it was offshore, it was in Europe, it was multi-national – her enquiries, laconic enough to begin with, soon ceased. She did not care. She had failed. She deserved their pity.

At first she was always tired. She slept on her balcony in the sun, or in the shade. She knew no one, she received no visitors. She ate at the same table, a table laid for one, or alone in her room. When she grew sick of four walls, of the unchanging view from her balcony, she sat in the casino, watching the wheel, the cards, the red and black, changing places, changing back again; but she did not play. When rich men, seeking to impress their companions, or unaccompanied themselves, pressed chips upon her, 'for luck', she left them on the table. Invitations to parties arrived in her pigeonhole, or came sliding under her door. She did not reply; she did not go. After a while, they ceased to pester her with their attention. The barman protected her, the croupier, the waiters at the restaurant on the terrace. She sat in the bar, looking down at the swimmers in the hotel pool; but she did not swim. She looked, still, on all that bronzed and gleaming skin, for a familiar tattoo, and despised herself for looking. She never saw it.

Later, a conversation with a waiter persuaded her to stroll into town one day, if only to prove to herself that she still could. It was as she had imagined, hot, noisy, crowded. If the visitors were rich and idle, the natives were poor and overworked, mostly at selling exotic rubbish to visitors. Taking an ill-judged turn from a district of dingy prefabs, Josephine found herself committed to pushing through the throng at a street market. The smell of sweat and suntan lotion assaulted her, mingled with the reek of frying, the stink of donkeys. Flies crawled on her face, her bare arms. Hands grabbed at her, voices shouted at her, demanding she buy their sugarcane, their hats of plaited straw, fans of parrot feathers, their lumpy figurines and garish jewellery. 'No money!' she shouted back, excusing herself. 'No money!' The stallholders didn't believe her, or didn't care. They ran after her, jostling her with their pans of bread and painted drums.

Feeling a rising hysteria, as if she was suffocating in flesh and dust, she ran between the stalls down an alley where dogs shat and fucked. Naked children stared solemnly, watching the dogs, watching Josephine as she ran. She ran in at a doorway, recognising a church. A thick smell of incense grabbed her nostrils. Oversized statues of unrecognisable figures, half saints, half ogres, leered down at her from the walls. They resembled the dolls of the market carvers, grown monstrous to punish her for refusing to buy them.

Turning to flee, her heart stopped when a man appeared, gesturing to her from outside the door. Looking from the gloom of the church into the blazing sunlight she could not see him distinctly; but she could see he was dressed all in black, and wearing a domino mask.

Josephine faltered, then hurried towards him. But he was only a reveller in costume, Zorro the Fox with his hat hanging on his back, a ribboned stick of sugarcane for a sword. He bowed elegantly and tried to grope her as she pushed past him, hurrying back to the safety of her prison.

After that she went out only to the beach, and only after sunset, or in the luminous hour before daybreak, when the only other strollers were lovers or solitaries like herself, poets, beachcombers. She would not swim, but walked along in the shallows, feeling tiny fish nibble at her ankles, letting the warm Caribbean sea sway her into something resembling peace. The black sand stained her legs and clung like mud between her toes. Peacocks shrieked. Days passed. She remained on her balcony, unavailable for lunch, dinner, golf, baccarat or water-skiing.

One day, lying on her balcony with a trashy novel, she looked up and saw somebody watching her.

It was a young woman on one of the balconies opposite. She was slender, with long legs and high, pointed breasts in a maroon and blue bikini. Her face was obscured by a large pair of round sunglasses, her long sandy hair done up in a navy blue bandanna. Her skin was a regulation even Caribbean tan, golden as toffee. She looked about twenty.

She was standing leaning out over the railing of her balcony, her arms stretched out to either side, her weight on her hands. Though her eyes were invisible behind the sunglasses, she was making no attempt to conceal her observation of Josephine. A moment later, she clinched it by lifting her hand and waving.

Josephine, caught unawares, waved back.

Quickly she returned her attention to her book. She had no intention of getting involved in a conversation of shouted inanities across the width of the courtyard.

But the words slipped about on the page, sliding away from her comprehension. She found herself reading the same sentence three times, each time failing to make any sense of it at all. When she did succeed in focusing on them, with a great effort of will, the words seemed more trite and idiotic than ever.

The day was too hot, the book too stupid. She tossed it aside with a sigh. She would go back inside and lie down.

When she raised her head, self-consciously as one will who knows herself under surveillance, she found the girl still leaning on the railing, her hands clasped now under her chin, her face still indubitably turned directly towards her.

Josephine looked away hurriedly. There was something about that golden, luminous figure that intrigued her so powerfully she couldn't even look. She was thinking about her, even while she busied herself gathering up her towel and her sun oil and the wretched book. She carried her frank and curious gaze with her into the shadows of the room. There was no escape there. She decided to go downstairs for a drink.

She sat in her wrap in the terrace bar watching the swimmers, drinking golden rum with fruit in it. In an hour or so, after another drink or two, she could go back to her room and sleep for a while. Maybe tonight there would be an old movie on cable, something chivalrous and predictable in black and white.

'Hello,' said a warm voice at her side.

She looked up.

It was the girl in the blue bandanna. She had pushed her sunglasses up on top of her head. Her eyes were a light, bewitching green. Her nose was short and quite pointed. Even through her tan, the dusting of freckles across it was perfectly clear. Her mouth was small, her lips slightly parted in a quizzical smile. Josephine could see her teeth were white and perfect.

'Hi,' said Josephine, coldly.

'I saw you just now, up there? I gave you a wave?' She was American. Her voice was deeper than you would have expected, making her sound older and wiser than she looked. But it turned up at the ends of her sentences rather in the way her lips turned up at the corners, deferentially, taking nothing for granted. Young Americans, Josephine had always found, especially rich young Americans, had this ability to turn the last five minutes into ancient history, as if they expected everything to be forgotten the instant it had happened.

She nodded. She would give this beautiful golden virgin no more than that, no more than she gave the trim silver-haired market analysts in the hotel casino.

'My name's Cadence,' said the young woman.

'Hi,' said Josephine again, in exactly the same tone as before. She sat there at the edge of the floor, neither guarded nor open, non-committally.

'I'm sorry,' Cadence said. But she did not move away.

'For waving?' Josephine asked.

'For Cadence,' said Cadence; and now Josephine could detect the tiny wince as she said it, as small, sinuous motion of the sleek shoulders, a momentary wrinkling of the nose. 'It was my Mom's idea, I guess.'

Josephine turned her head a fraction to regard her squarely.

'You could change it,' she said.

'I don't know,' said Cadence frankly, as if they had known each other for years, as if they had discussed this very point before and failed to resolve it. 'They say once you get given a name, that's it, that's your name. You can change it, but you can't get rid of it.'

She was leaning on the back of the empty chair next to Josephine's in the same perched, languid posture she had been in when Josephine saw her on the balcony. She had thrown a loose pink sun-top on over her bikini. It was unbuttoned. Josephine could smell the fragrance of her skin, bergamot and warm youth.

'What's that you're drinking?' Cadence asked her.

'Rum,' said Josephine.

'Is that fruit in it? That looks good. I think I'll have one of those.'

She smiled gratefully, as if Josephine had been very generous, helping her make a difficult decision that had been troubling her; and ignoring the waitress beginning to move in their direction, she went over to see the bar.

Amused out of her withdrawal, Josephine turned to watch her go. She walked with a lazy, innocent grace that touched a nerve somewhere in Josephine's abdomen. She took a large swallow of rum, the fruit bobbing moistly at her lip.

Cadence returned, drink in hand. She held it up awkwardly, as though it was a trophy someone had just presented to her unexpectedly. 'Is it okay if I join you?' she asked Josephine, doubtfully. Her hopelessness was as total, as palpable as her delight had been. She expected to be told to go away. After her frank and nonchalant intrusion, suddenly she was shy and unseasoned as a convent girl.

Chagrined by this deference to her chilly disdain, Josephine raised her eyebrows and gave the slightest perceptible nod to the empty chair. Cadence pulled it out and sat down gently. The chairs were tall, high stools with low backs of bent bamboo. Josephine found herself watching the girl's supple flanks, her bottom and thighs, bared by the high-cut bikini pants, as they flattened against the seat of the chair.

To cover her indiscretion, she picked up her glass again and sipped, snagging a titbit of melon with her teeth and chewing it contemplatively while Cadence settled and sampled her drink.

'Oh, it's good!' Cadence exclaimed. Her face lit up with pleasure for a second, then sank again into blankness. She wrinkled her nose again, as if perplexed, and, in an odd but graceful gesture, propped her elbows on the table and rubbed the inside of each wrist with the fingers of the other hand, as if massaging some invisible perfume into them.

Josephine sipped her rum.

'Are you hungry?' Cadence asked her. 'I am. I didn't have breakfast. I guess I should eat something if I'm going to drink,' she said, with a frown and a little laugh, chastening herself.

There was a bowl of macadamia nuts on the table, and one of olives. Josephine pushed both towards her. Cadence smiled radiantly again, as if Josephine had accomplished another great act of generosity, had been and picked the nuts and harvested the olives herself, and brought them to her. She ate a nut. Then, looking into her glass as if seeing it for the first time, gave a little embarrassed gasp and made a face of dismay at her own foolishness. 'Fruit, right?' she muttered. She tried to pick out a slippery piece of guava with her fingers.

Josephine hid a smile. She said nothing. This girlish pantomine of nervousness was strangely endearing.

Cadence lost interest in the drink and the food. She hunched her shoulders and thrust her palms together between her thighs, shifting around to face Josephine at an angle. 'I haven't been here long,' she said. 'I guess I don't know too many people.'

The nakedness of her appeal was heartbreaking. Josephine tried to unbend a little. It was extraordinarily difficult. In her own way, she realised, she was as awkward at this as Cadence was proving to be. 'Are you here on your own?' she asked; understanding instantly she heard herself say the words that she wanted Cadence to say yes.

Cadence lifted her chin and sat up a little straighter. 'My father's supposed to join me, but he never does. Probably he's too busy,' she said, pronouncing it *prolly*.

Josephine nodded, feeling a small curl of pleasure, masking it as sympathy. She surveyed the crowd of happy swimmers below. 'Maybe you'll meet someone nice,' she said, and almost bit her tongue.

Cadence said, 'Oh *God*,' in a tone of mingled distress and panic and longing and rejection, as if she wished all the happy tourists on Dominica would go surfing away together on an apocalyptic tidal wave and never be seen again. She sucked hard on her drink.

'I come here every year,' she said, despairingly, as if the island was a recurring trap she always tried to avoid and always inevitably fell into. 'Really I want to go to Europe,' she said, pronouncing it *Yurp*, 'but he won't let me go on my own. Have you been to Europe?'

'I'm English,' Josephine said.

Cadence lit up again. 'You know, I *thought* so! I *thought* you were. When I saw you, I thought you were from England, I don't know why, I just knew you were English, isn't that amazing?' Her smile invited Josephine to marvel at this miracle of intuition. 'You know, you don't really have any accent, hardly,' she said, complimenting her.

She was from California, though she'd been born in New Jersey. They'd left when she was a baby, she didn't remember it at all. Her parents were divorced, she was living with her father in Laguna Beach, though he was hardly ever there. He was in Washington all the time, working for 'the administration'. Cadence was at college in Davis. She wanted to travel, she wanted to be an airline pilot, she wanted to work with refugees, she didn't know what she wanted to do. Every summer her father booked them both a vacation at the Concord Reef, and every year something came up that meant he couldn't fly down with her. Every year he said he'd join her later, but he never did. Cadence forgave him. Josephine wanted to reach out and hold her, to draw her into her arms and absorb her utterly, totally. She realised she was looking at Cadence and thinking of Jackie, that slender body, that long, spun golden hair. She realised she had passed some crucial threshold suddenly, stepped out of her desolation as completely and irreversibly as she had stepped out of the château and found herself on the beach. She realised she was drunk.

Cadence was saying, apologetically, 'I was watching you up there, on your balcony. It looks so comfortable, kind of peaceful. It's silly, isn't it, they're all the same, probably.'

'I get the sun later,' Josephine said.

Cadence was thrilled by this thought. 'That's right!' she said. 'You do! I don't get any sun at all in the afternoon, hardly. If you go out on the deck –' she gestured clumsily, dismissively, to the far side of the pool, ' – the men won't leave you alone. And as for the guys on the beach!' Her voice brimmed with disgust.

Filled now with joy, with rum, with her unexpected sympathy for this gorgeous child, Josephine understood how bored she truly was, how unhappy. She reached out her hand and rested it lightly on Cadence's where it lay on the table. It felt like a small, naked animal crouching there, under her hand.

'Let's go out in the sun,' she suggested.

Cadence looked into her eyes, uncertain, eager, timid. 'On the balcony?' she said.

'Yes.'

Josephine picked up her key, the remains of her drink. Cadence was already getting down from the chair, scraping it noisily across the parquet, ready to flee the bar at top speed. Watching Josephine, she said, 'Oh. Oh,' and darted her hand back nervously to her glass, picking it up, drinking hurriedly from it, as if she was supposed to finish it before leaving the table.

'Bring it with you,' Josephine said.

'It's finished, nearly,' said Cadence, taking a huge gulp.

'There's more,' Josephine said, smiling. 'In my room.'

They went upstairs. Cadence talked all the way. Her brother was in Hawaii, he was a TV presenter, though he was also 'into exports in a big way'. She hadn't seen him for years, though actually she had been to visit him once. He had a really neat place, one day she was going to go and live there. He wasn't really her brother, he was a kind of a half-brother. Their Mom was in Chicago, living with a black guy who was just some kind of hamburger chef or something, though really she lived in Kentucky. Had Josephine ever been to Kentucky? It was really neat, a really neat kind of place, she was going to live there one day, she knew she was, it was just, like, something she had to do, though she never wanted to see her Mom again ever, her Mom had tried to kill them, her and her brother both, when they were kids.

'Oh, wow, this is so neat!' She strode lithely across the room, fumbled the blind up over her head and went straight out onto the balcony, leaving the slats to clatter wonkily back into place behind her. Josephine straightened the blind, raised it and locked it off, and went outside too. Her guest was leaning on the railing in exactly the posture in which she'd leant on her own. 'That's my room, there,' she said needlessly, pointing across the courtyard.

She sat on the lounger, testing it. 'Can I really sit here?' she asked, doubtful again.

'Sure,' said Josephine, expansively, amused at her, amused at herself.

She went and got the peacock chair, dragged it outside and positioned it facing the sun. Cadence had already taken off her suntop and was lying face down in her bikini, completely relaxed. Josephine slipped off her wrap and hung it over the back of the chair. 'Shall I get you a drink?' she asked her visitor. 'More rum?'

Cadence's low voice was muffled by her arms. 'Sure.'

Josephine went back inside. She poured generous shots of overproof over ice, added pineapple juice. She put the glasses on a tray, put the suntan oil on it too, and carried it outside. She would offer to oil Cadence. Her breathing quickened. She felt pressure in her temples as she thought of stroking that perfect flesh, running her hands down that flat stomach, spreading oil down her thighs, over her bottom.

To her surprise, Cadence was sitting up again, perched on the edge of the lounger. She looked so ill at ease suddenly that Josephine asked, 'What's wrong?'

Cadence glanced at her sideways, guiltily, snatched her eyes away at once. 'I guess,' she said, slowly, her voice light and high with false casualness, 'probably you could sunbathe naked up here, if you wanted, no one could see you, probably. I mean if you wanted.'

'Do you want to?' asked Josephine, neutrally.

Cadence writhed her shoulders in anguish. 'Oh God, I didn't mean. I guess. I mean.'

She looked helplessly up at Josephine, imploring her for rescue.

'Go ahead,' said Josephine, keeping her voice calm. She was better than Cadence at pretending.

Cadence's hands went behind her to the buckle of her maroon and blue bikini top. She hesitated. 'You really don't mind?' she asked, in a small, childish voice.

Josephine smiled. 'Here,' she said, squatting down beside her and reaching to help her.

Cadence dropped her hands into her lap and froze. Her back to Josephine, she sat as still as if she thought someone was going to hurt her.

Josephine unbuckled the bikini top. Putting her hands under Cadence's arms, she slipped the cups from her high young breasts. She did not touch them. She let go with one hand and drew the bikini top back under Cadence's arm, and softly laid it aside.

Cadence's shoulders trembled once. Still with her back to Josephine, she lifted her arms and crossed them across her breasts, covering them. Then she turned awkwardly where she sat, and faced Josephine. Her face was a picture of apprehension. She laughed nervously. She dropped her arms.

Her breasts were conical, her nipples small, and round and brown as berries. The evenness of her tan, continuous over her breasts, showed this was how she habitually met the sun, and welcomed it.

She touched her head, combing stray hairs back under her bandanna. Her left hand, returning to her lap, hovered over her breast as if she wanted to touch herself but couldn't find a reason to.

Josephine nodded.

'Stand up,' she said softly.

Cadence exhaled shakily, gave a sniff of resolution. She got to her feet, looking down at Josephine crouching before her, combing ineffectually again at her hair with her fingers.

Josephine took hold of Cadence's maroon and blue bikini pants and drew them down her thighs, over her knees, down her long slim legs to the tiled floor. She took Cadence's hand to support her as she stepped out of them. Her head was at the level of Cadence's crotch. The hair there was flossy and soft, squashed into a flat mat by the elastic fabric of the pants. Jackie's hair, she thought, was just the same. She wondered fleetingly if she would ever undress Jackie again, if she would ever see Jackie again, and she felt a pang of loss and desire.

Cadence's hands were now hovering, belatedly, in front of her crotch. She kept lifting them and combing her hair. She gave Josephine a grimace of helplessness. She looked extremely uncomfortable. She spread her arms, raising her face to the sun, summoning it to pour down over her. 'This is great,' she said miserably.

Josephine put the bikini pants with the top and eased herself up until she stood upright directly in front of Cadence. She caught the scent of her loins, salty and fresh. She was only an inch or so taller than the nude young woman, though there were so many years between them. She smiled into her eyes.

She unhooked her own bikini top, slipped the straps slowly from her shoulders, peeled off the cups.

She saw Cadence's eyes linger on her tattoo, then rove longingly over the expanse of her breasts. Smiling steadily at her, she slipped her thumbs in the waistband of her skirt and leaning forward a degree, tilting her pelvis, she pulled the skirt down to the floor and stepped out of it.

Cadence had backed off a pace. Her hand was at her hair again.

Josephine kicked off her sandals. Naked, she reached a hand towards Cadence, as if to take her by the arm, but she didn't touch her. She gestured at the lounger.

'Lie down,' she said. 'I'll get you some oil.'

Relieved by instruction, Cadence returned to the lounger. She lay face down, in the same position as before. Josephine sat on the edge of the lounger, her legs angled away. Her bare bottom rested lightly against Cadence's thigh. She poured oil on Cadence's shoulders, and in the hollow of her back. With both hands, she began softly and delicately, then more firmly, slowly, lingeringly, to massage it in.

The scent of jasmine and bergamot rose between them.

Josephine shifted along the lounger, moving down the length of Cadence's body, their flesh no longer touching except where her hands moved down now to Cadence's bottom. It was firm and high, like her breasts. For long minutes Josephine stroked and kneaded her cheeks, then swept her hands down the curve of her thighs, oiling her legs right down to her heels. Cadence lay perfectly passive, not even speaking. Unable to resist, Josephine drew her hand back up the inside of Cadence's left leg, up the inside of her thigh, slipped her fingers into the cleft of her bottom, letting them trail lightly up between her buttocks to the small of her back. She heard Cadence catch her breath.

'Turn over,' she said.

Cadence turned over. Her face was alight now with barely suppressed excitement. She opened her legs.

Josephine set her left hand lightly on the soft swell of her pubic mound. She lifted it and caressed her right breast, her palm barely grazing the nipple.

Cadence reached up to her, but let her hand fall back to her side. Her lips parted in a silent appeal.

Josephine took back her hand. She poured oil into her palm. She rubbed it on Cadence's stomach, on her clean, small feet, rubbing each one carefully between her hands, wiping oil up Cadence's shins, around her knees, up her thighs to their fragrant junction. She teased the matted hair with her fingertips.

Cadence chuckled, tensely. She took hold of Josephine's hand by the wrist, looping her fingers lightly around it as if to acknowledge some real but tentative bond, then dropped her hand again, wanting to be claimed, not to claim.

She rolled her head back, letting Josephine stroke oil up her stomach between her breasts, and up the hollow of her throat. Josephine lay on top of her. Her breasts ached and tingled from the shock of contact after long abstinence. With reverent fingers she oiled the beautiful face, the brow and cheeks and moist, eager lips. She pressed her hand into Cadence's crotch and Cadence shivered. A tiny moan escaped her.

Josephine lowered her head and kissed her slowly, questingly, on the mouth. She tasted of sweet rum and minty chewing gum. Cadence's tongue moved like the brilliant fish in the hotel aquarium, darting in and out with ceaseless, tiny vigour. She began to soften and grow wet beneath Josephine's patient, persistent hand. She gasped again, breaking the kiss. Her eyes were open, electric green as the Caribbean sky before thunder, searching Josephine's face. Her hands crept shyly up onto Josephine's bottom. Then she murmured urgently in her ear. 'What's your *name?*'

Josephine laughed. The floodgates of her senses opened at last. She woke up. She was herself again, making love in the sun to the most beautiful virgin on Dominica.

'I'm Josephine,' she said.

|10|

Cadence was going off on a skin-diving trip with a young gang of Japanese. Last night she had lost to them at table tennis and beaten them hollow at pool. 'Come on, Josephine, you can come,' she pleaded. But Josephine felt detached, aloof from their eager politeness, their freshly ironed J.G. Hook shirts, their passionate knowledge of American pop music.

'I'll see you later,' she said, and kissed Cadence goodbye, kissed her on the lips, there on the terrace at breakfast. Her eyes shining, Cadence took this risqué tribute and ran, the laces of her sneakers flapping.

At a loss, Josephine dared the poolside sundeck, but the ceaseless noise and bustle in and out of the water irritated her. Her room was quiet. She wound up in the bar, drunk by eleven, eating pretzels for want of anything better to do with her hands.

The barman arrived at her elbow with another daiquiri on a tray. 'I didn't order that,' she said.

'No, Miss Morrow,' he said. 'The lady over there.' He nodded in the direction of a deeply-tanned woman in her late forties, drinking alone in the corner. Her greying hair was pink-rinsed, her fat arms laden with golden bracelets and bangles and rings, her ears with huge mineral pendants, her bosom with necklaces and chains. She raised her own glass to Josephine in salute. Emotionlessly, Josephine returned her nod and accepted the drink.

She came over.

'Two women drinking alone at this hour of the morning is disgraceful,' she rumbled by way of a greeting. 'Two women drinking together is just neighbourly.' And she laughed warmly, splashing some of her drink onto the table as she clumsily pulled out a chair and sat down across from Josephine, uninvited. 'Caroline Morgenstern,' she said, holding out her large jewelled hand. 'My friends call me Carrie.'

Josephine recognised her as one of the locals, American retirees and wives of diplomats, who came to play the casino, loaf around the pool and spend their husbands' money at the bar. She shook her hand perfunctorily, wondering how tiresome this was going to be, how soon she would be able to extricate herself without offending the woman completely. 'I'm Josephine,' she said.

'Oh, I know who *you* are,' said Caroline Morgenstern, slightly arch. 'You're the mysterious Englishwoman. Very reserved.' She raised her eyebrows with a mocking grin, daring Josephine to take offence. 'Excuse me,' she said, waving at the air between them as if to waft away the insult, 'don't take any notice of me, I'm just juiced, I say what I think.'

Josephine didn't reply. She drained her glass, set it down squarely on its little quilted paper coaster, then picked up the drink Mrs Morgenstern had bought her. 'Cheers,' she said.

'Cheers,' said Mrs Morgenstern, imitating her accent. 'So you here on vacation, excuse me, *holiday*?'

'Resting,' said Josephine. If she was to be the mysterious Englishwoman, she might as well play it to the hilt. She had no wish for the bored American's company, but there might be some amusement in toying with her curiosity for a while.

Caroline Morgenstern nodded, acquiring a second chin in the motion. Seen close up, her skin was clearly well into the parched, wrinkled old age that comes from too many years spent prostrate in tropical sunshine. 'How do you like our island?' she asked.

Josephine looked around. A gaggle of children were jumping up and down at the poolside, leaping in the water and splashing about. 'There are more restful places,' she said.

'Well, go to 'em,' said Mrs Morgenstern shortly, and Josephine realised she was being ruder than she meant to be. If she already had a reputation at the Concord Reef, particularly now Mrs Morgenstern and her cronies had seen her with Cadence, there was no advantage in courting hostility.

'This is where the credit is,' she said.

Mrs Morgenstern appreciated that. She laughed again, a worldly, nicotine and whisky laugh. 'Got you tied down, has he?' she asked.

Josephine felt her heart stop for an instant. She looked at the woman carefully through her alcoholic haze.

'Who?' she asked.

'Your husband.'

Outwardly Josephine relaxed. Inside, she remembered a cold cell, a pleasant-faced woman, English, saying, 'Who was it? Your husband? Your lover?' She remembered her heavy, bare breasts, her plum-coloured nipples, her bluish tattoo. Who was Mrs Morgenstern?

'I'm not married.'

The brown face opposite her softened, evincing genuine regret. 'Oh my dear, I'm sorry.'

Josephine looked her in the eye. 'I left him,' she said.

This did not produce the cheerful, sympathetic response she expected. Mrs Morgenstern shook her pink-rinsed locks. 'I feel sorry for you young women today with no husbands, truly I do,' she said, in a tone of some severity. 'Women without men, it's not right.' She tapped the tabletop with her finger, then started moving her finger around, drawing in the spilt whisky.

With a chilly start, Josephine felt as if she were floating in the air several feet above her body, looking down on the table.

The shape Mrs Morgenstern was tracing was a figure of eight, elongated, sideways on. It might have been the symbol for infinity. Or the outline of a domino mask.

She saw Josephine looking, and caught her eye. She nodded at her, indicating something.

'That's a very unusual tattoo,' she said.

Looking down at herself, Josephine realised the frill on the bodice of her sundress had slipped down. She was not wearing a bra. From across the table, the little blue-black sigil would be clearly visible.

She made a move to cover it up.

'I suppose that was his idea too,' said Mrs Morgenstern.

Josephine said nothing.

Mrs Morgenstern smiled disapprovingly. 'You young women today,' she said.

Summoning her dissipated energies, Josephine decided it was high time to turn this around. 'You're not so old, Caroline,' she said.

'Carrie, please, my dear,' purred Mrs Morgenstern. 'My bones are old,' she said; and before Josephine could reply, went on: 'Have you seen the island? Not the city, the island. Come on, drink up, we'll go for a drive. Would you like that?'

And Josephine suddenly realised she was sick of the hotel, sick of moping in the bar. If Cadence could go out, so could she.

Carrie drove an old convertible with a pint of Johnnie Walker in a pocket beside her seat. She insisted on swigging from this as they set off, belting up the road onto the ridge above the city, and insisted on Josephine swigging from it too. Josephine told herself there would be no other traffic on this switchback, and that her driver must know the crumbly, unsigned roads blindfold to have lived long enough to drive them with such speed and disregard.

Carrie put her hand on Josephine's leg. 'How do you like it?' she shouted.

Josephine pretended she meant the scenery. 'It's beautiful!' she shouted back. It was. This was the Dominica she had always dreamed of visiting. Lush greenery spilled down the mountainside beneath them, tumultuous with wild flowers. Splashes of bright colour were birds in plumage of a thousand rainbows, flashing up into the trees in alarm as the car thundered round another bend.

Carrie shouted something and pointed down to the left. Craning round, Josephine could see the hotel, already far below them. The sea was every shade of turquoise, sewn with filigree of sunlight, and the beach was shiny black as sharkskin between the palm trees. As it passed from view, Josephine felt exhilarated. Meeting Cadence had relieved her from her gloom, but kept her at the Concord Reef. Knocking back another belt of Carrie's whisky, she realised she had been punishing herself for the failure of her life by refusing to walk out, up into the hills.

The breeze threshed her hair about. Then, jolting and jarring, the car tipped its nose down an incline and went booming out of the trees across a narrow wooden bridge. Only the most notional bamboo parapet kept them from rolling off into white water, a wild river plunging hectically down a steep gorge that opened like a greedy throat below their wheels. Hanging on to the strap handle, Josephine glimpsed giddy depths, vicious rocks, before Carrie brought them banging and lurching onto firm ground the other side.

They emerged from what seemed to be complete jungle onto another thinly-metalled roadway. Houses began to appear among the trees, up the mountainside to their left. Below on the right, Josephine glimpsed rooftops, suntraps, satellite dishes. These were big houses.

'Do you live up here?' she shouted in Carrie's ear.

'You want to see?' Carrie bellowed back.

'Okay.'

Mrs Morgenstern drove for some minutes, then turned off the road onto a rutted track. She hit the horn, twice, and a small brown animal went belting across the road into the undergrowth. Overhead trees hung heavy with fruit. The casual profusion of flowers was almost too rich to believe.

The track ended in a clearing where someone, obviously many years ago, had built an approximation of a grand Spanish villa. Now vines clustered up the white slab walls, and young trees crowded the entrance to the inner courtyard. Carrie parked the car next to an antiquated cart, pulled on the handbrake and opened the door.

'Welcome to Sam's Hideaway,' she said . 'Sam's not here right now, but I'll be happy to show you round.'

Sam was Mr Morgenstern. His absence, like Cadence's father's absence, was apparently chronic. Caroline Morgenstern's remarks about women alone began to make a little more sense.

Inside the house it was cool. The décor was a violent mixture of 'period' funiture, all reproduction, examples of every European age and style jammed together in neglected luxury.

A maid, a local girl, big-eyed and shy, no more than fifteen, came to greet her mistress and know her pleasure. Carrie sent her for whisky and glasses.

She sat in a fifties-style conversation pit overstuffed with cushions, and stuck her blue-jeaned legs straight out in front of her. Before she had started to grow fat, Josephine could now see, she had been what another generation would have called 'a fine figure of a woman'. Josephine sat opposite her and they talked their way through most of the bottle. She kept the conversation to Britain, where her hostess had never been. Carrie had a hundred questions about the Royal Family, with whom she assumed Josephine must be on intimate terms; about Scotland; about Benny Hill and *Upstairs, Downstairs*, on both of which she heaped the most lavish praise.

Then she wanted to know about British boarding schools. Was it girls only, or did they have boys there too? Was it true that they were very strict? Was it true they used to cane girls? Was it true senior girls were allowed to cane juniors? She had heard of something called a tawse, did Josephine know what that was? Had she had any experience of it?

While Josephine was framing a guarded, drunken answer, Mrs

Morgenstern got to her feet and went to the door.

'Isabel!' she bellowed into the passageway; then she turned back into the room and said, in a soft and solemn voice: 'I have a confession to make, Josephine.'

Josephine caught her breath.

Carrie, coming close, stood over her, rock steady despite all she had drunk. She looked down at Josephine, and nodded again at her chest.

'Your tattoo,' she said. 'I've seen it before.'

Josephine's heartbeat quickened.

'My husband Sam has the same tattoo,' said Caroline Morgenstern.

Josephine looked at her in energetic surmise. Her suspicions in the hotel bar rose up again before her. She started to speak, but Carrie waved her brusquely to silence.

There was a patter of slippers in the hall, and the young maid appeared. She curtseyed to her mistress.

'Isabel,' said Mrs Morgenstern with the ponderous gravity of the highly inebriated, 'I want you to go and open Mr Morgenstern's drawer.'

The look on the girl's face was pure dismay. 'Don't worry,' said Mrs Morgenstern, 'it's not for you.'

At that Isabel turned her head and goggled at Josephine; and Mrs Morgenstern shouted, 'Do it, you lazy slut, before I change my mind about that.'

Isabel vanished. Josephine heard her feet scurrying upstairs as quick as she could go.

Carrie bent down and took hold of the frill of Josephine's sundress, and pulled it down over her bosom. Josephine sat passively, letting her examine the tattoo. If the bodice had been any looser, she would have been examining Josephine's nipples too.

Carrie nodded, satisfied. 'My husband wears that identical same tattoo,' she said. 'Him and his friends.' Without apology or further comment she let go of Josephine's dress. 'Come on up,' she said.

They went upstairs.

In the book-lined study the air seemed hotter, closer. A crowded bureau in the corner furthest from the window supported a large oil-lamp, an antique globe and a bust of Beethoven. Isabel the maid had unlocked a drawer in the bureau and disappeared again.

'Sam brought it back from one of his so-called "conferences", ' Carrie said as she made her way to the bureau. 'He won't let me use

it on the servants. Says it's too good for 'em. So he keeps it locked up.'
She smiled broadly, mirthlessly, at Josephine. 'But he don't know that
I know that Isabel knows where he keeps the key.'

Out of the drawer she took an antique instrument case of black
leather, about two feet long. She snapped the brass catches and
opened the lid.

The inside was lined with crimson cushioning. In it nestled a whip.

It was a martinet, four-tailed, its leather thongs black with age. It
had been put away carefully, lovingly, the tails wound precisely around
the handle, which was wooden, shaped to the hand, and inlaid with
chased silver and mother of pearl.

Josephine looked at her hostess. Mrs Morgenstern nodded. 'Go on,'
she said. 'Take it out.'

Gently, Josephine took the whip from its case. The thongs swung
free, and the stock lay comfortably, inspiringly, in her hand. Flipping
the thongs lightly through the air, she felt the superb heft and balance
of the implement. She ran the thongs through her fingers. They were
almost black with age, or with some treatment, starching or pickling,
which had been used to stiffen them; and they had been tipped with
tags like abbreviated shoelace ends, made of silver.

Josephine recalled 'her' martinet, the one she had had to keep
beneath her pillow at the château, a limp, sorry example of the type,
though perfectly functional, she remembered. She had read of the
preparation of a splendid device like this one in the library at Estwych,
but never seen anything half so fine, even there.

'A most particular whip,' she heard herself say.

Caroline Morgenstern nodded approvingly. 'Sam showed me when
he brought it home,' she said huskily. 'I begged him not to use it on
me. He promised he wouldn't,' she said, and looked Josephine in the
eye with a slow, sensuous smile. 'Not unless I beg him to. I have to beg
him three times first,' she said.

Josephine felt the thongs again. 'You never would,' she said.

Carrie stroked her arm, fondling her bangles thoughtfully. 'I guess
not,' she said. 'Unless he was thinking of doing something else.
Something worse.'

They sat and drank, facing each other across the table, the whip in
its open case between them. 'We all go to hell here,' Carrie ruminated.
'America is going to hell. Europe. There's no discipline.' She drank,
refilled her glass. 'You need a man,' she said, as if it were a principle

of the universe, one no wisdom could ever deny. 'Don't care what you say. You have to have a man's hand.' She slapped the table, beating time to her words.

Josephine felt subdued, suddenly, unaccountably sad. She felt as if her identity was unravelling again, peeling apart on the tropical wind. She felt she could get up and open a door in this grandiose colonial folly, and find herself walking out onto the gallery at Estwych, or into the cold chambers of a château, high in the seclusion of the Alps.

'Did your husband have one of them tattoos?' Carrie asked.

Josephine shook her head. 'No.'

'Did he never put you on a spanking régime?' she persisted.

Josephine looked into her drink. She took a deep breath. 'Not Larry, no,' she said. She wondered how much she should or should not tell this woman married to a tattooed man, a woman without a tattoo of her own. 'A régime?' she echoed, musing. 'Others, perhaps . . . women and men . . .'

Carrie was shaking her head. 'If you don't know what I mean, no one ever did,' she said. 'Sometimes Sam puts me on what he calls a spanking régime,' she said grimly. 'Every morning for a week, ten days, as soon as he wakes, he has me across his knee. One day the paddle, next day the slipper maybe, next day the hairbrush — every day something different.'

Josephine felt something move under the table. Caroline Morgenstern, she realised, had slipped off her shoe and was stroking her on the leg with her bare foot.

'Always been that way,' she was saying. 'He says I need it. I guess I do. I guess we all do. Isabel gets hers. She works much smarter after we have her over a stool in the kitchen, taking her skirts up for a licking. Sam uses his belt, mostly. If she gives him trouble, he has me hold her down.'

She took another drink.

'I got something else to confess,' she said. 'I was looking at your butt on the deck the other day, Josephine, you were wearing your little bikini. My God, lady, you have the most beautiful butt I've ever seen. You have a *beautiful* butt. Us, we're just lard, all of us flabby cows that live around here, come dragging our flabby asses down the Concord, hot, starved, mooing at each other over cocktails . . .'

She seemed to have gone off rambling on a private, bitter monologue of her own; but she fell silent, looking at Josephine across the table with open longing on her face. Her voice, when she spoke again, was dry, deliberate, hypnotic. 'Oblige me forever and show me again now.'

Josephine was not under her command. She owed her no obedience, a woman who had been disciplined but never trained, a woman who understood so little it amounted to nothing at all, a woman without even a tattoo. But she could hear the loneliness and frustration in Caroline Morgenstern's voice, as clear as the wrinkles, kisses of a cruel sun, on her face and neck; and she felt sorry for her. She let the melancholy courage of the drink suffuse her, opening her pores to the electricity of the ugly old house.

She pushed back her chair and got to her feet.

Outside in the clearing, a harsh bird was calling. She thought of home, of the pigeons on the penthouse roof. It had been a long time since she had heard them, a lifetime since she had been whipped by a chauffeur and spanked across the knee of another man's slave.

She cast a last look at the whip in its case. Then she turned from the table, turned her back on Caroline Morgenstern, and lifted the skirt of her sundress. She lifted it to her waist.

'My Christ you're so beautiful,' croaked her hostess, drunkenly. 'Josephine . . . Josephine . . . Take your panties down. Oh, please do that for me.'

Josephine obeyed.

Her panties were skimpy bikini bottoms, thin white cotton. She pulled then down below the cheeks of her bottom until they nestled in the crease around the tops of her thighs.

'Oh my God . . .' groaned Carrie.

Josephine heard her shift in her seat, pushing her chair back from the table. She wondered, woozily, if she was playing with herself.

What came next was in a completely different tone, a tone of quiet authority and confidence.

'Bend over and put your hands on your knees,' said Mrs Morgenstern.

So now it was coming. From the hands of a total stranger, an addled, aging lush who liked to help when her husband strapped the maid. Josephine could only hope she knew how to use that villainous little implement. She wondered how fiercely she would use it, how much of it she would be able to take. And she wondered what Cadence would say tonight, when she saw the weals. For Cadence knew nothing, not a thing.

151

Breathing deeply, trying to stop her stomach swirling while her head kept pace in the opposite direction, Josephine Morrow bent forwards, tucking the skirt of her sundress up in its waistband at the back. She put her hands on her knees.

She heard Caroline Morgenstern get heavily to her feet and walk towards her.

She thought it would be pain next, but it was a gentle, trembling touch. Carrie put her hand on Josephine's bent back, and gingerly stroked the swell of her bare bottom, Josephine heard the bracelets jingle.

'Wonderful, Josie, wonderful,' breathed Carrie in her ear. 'Oh Christ, it's a terrible shame for a woman like you not to have a *man* behind her . . .'

She fondled Josephine's buttocks. Her touch was far from unpleasant. She was getting up courage, Josephine thought, courage to pick up the forbidden whip.

'Maybe when Sam shows up,' she was saying, 'you can come visit. Spend some time here. Sam will help you, I know he will. He'll put you on a régime if I ask him. He'll put us both on, you and me together, how about that?' She seemed to think Josephine was her daughter, or a child like Isabel, timid and innocent, needing to be coaxed to the whip. Yet somehow, through her befuddled ignorance, she had discovered the principle of the discipline, the long, hard lesson of total obedience to chastisement. Josephine wondered why Sam Morgenstern had never taken his wife into training.

Carrie's hand was on her arm now. She supposed the whip was in the other hand, poised unsteadily over her bare bottom cheeks.

But Carrie was pulling her upright, urging her to stand up, shepherding her to walk to the door and out of the room, with her knickers around her thighs, her skirt tucked up at the back.

She cast a bewildered glance at the table. The most particular whip was still there, in its case, untouched.

'Bring it,' said Mrs Morgenstern hoarsely.

Josephine went and shut the lid, closed the catches, and took the case by its handle. It was very light; too light for the weight and power it contained.

Wondering what she was in for now, she followed Mrs Morgenstern across the landing and into the bedroom.

There was a double bed, unmade, with a mosquito net poised over

152

it on a pulley. Regency-style wallpaper was peeling in the tropical humidity. There was a grimy goatskin rug on the floor, a scatter of discarded clothes and newspapers. Josephine saw at least one abandoned empty glass. The window was open onto the trees, and the room smelt headily of sweet jacaranda.

Caroline Morgenstern turned to Josephine and took her in her arms. She buried her face in her hair, wiping her nose and mouth through it as if to inhale some precious odour. Then she pressed her mouth to Josephine's, one hand behind Josephine's back, the other groping for her breasts.

Her lips were warm and firm. Josephine closed her eyes and let herself be ravished with a long, omnivorous kiss. She could pretend, for Carrie's sake, to be her daughter, or Isabel, or a slave, collared and passive, ready for whatever pleasure or pain the mistress saw fit to impose on her body. No one would see; no one would know that she had violated the exclusive token of the domino tattoo. She had been rejected, cast out of the castle. She was free.

Caroline Morgenstern let go of her. Her face was drunken, tremulous, her eyes wandering over Josephine's face, up and down her body. She lurched past her and started to rummage amid the litter of cosmetics and coffee cups on the bedside table.

Josephine set the instrument case down beside the bed.

Mrs Morgenstern came up with a framed photograph, which she wiped deliberately on the palm of her hand, then on the sleeve of her blouse. She held it at arms' length, her head on one side, an expression of sodden devotion in her eyes. Then she brought it to her mouth and kissed the glass; which necessitated her wiping it again.

She showed it to Josephine. 'That's my Sam,' she said huskily.

Sam was a mild-looking grey-haired man standing under a palm tree with his arms folded. He wore a tattered straw hat and a dark grey-sleeved shirt. His neck was long, his jaw protruding. He looked like an amiable old turtle.

Carrie would not let go of the photo while Josephine looked at it. She took it back quickly and stood it at the front of the table, pushing the debris back to make room for it. There was the clatter of a teaspoon and a bottle of dried-up nail polish tumbling down behind the table.

'There,' said Carrie with satisfaction. 'Sam can watch us. Here we are, Sam!' She chuckled and gave a little wave. Her mood seemed to have lightened, she was growing playful now. She turned to Josephine and gestured peremptorily. 'Hey, hey, turn around,' she said, nodding. 'Show Sam that beautiful butt of yours.'

Josephine swivelled and bend forward, thrusting her bottom towards the picture. Carrie began fondling her again. 'Oh, Sam would love you, you little honey,' she breathed, wheezily. 'Sam would love to get his hands on you,' she murmured, squeezing Josephine's buttocks lustily. She started to pull Josephine's panties the rest of the way down.

Josephine took over. Bending down, she stepped out of her sandals and pants. Then she hoisted up her sundress, baring her belly, her breasts, pulling it over her head. She stood naked before her hostess.

Imitating her, Carrie pulled at the buttons on her blouse, tugged it open, sweeping it back behind her like a stripper, shoving her bosom up at Josephine. Her breasts hung like coconuts, pendulous and heavy, in a ridiculously lacy black brassière. Her belt was broad brown leather, creased and cracked, with a huge pewter buckle enamelled with the Confederate flag. She opened it with a flick of her thumb, then opened her tight blue jeans. Grunting with effort, she forced them down over her hips and buttocks, her black lace panties sliding down with them. Her pubic hair was dark brown, speckled with grey. It grew straggling up her belly and down her thighs, as though it had been regularly shaved some time in the past and allowed to grow back.

Josephine wondered if she stripped off when they spanked the maid. She wondered where Isabel was now, whether she was hiding in a nearby room, waiting to hear the terrible sound of the little whip. Her eyes flickered from Carrie's large brown body to the case standing beside the bed.

Carrie climbed on the bed. 'Come up here,' she said. 'Come on.'

Josephine joined her on the bed. She knelt there on her haunches, facing her, naked.

'Kiss me first,' Carrie ordered.

Josephine leaned forward, kissed her crimson lipsticked mouth.

'Mm! Mm!' said Carrie, protesting, and pulled away. 'Not there, sugar.' She spread her great thighs and pointed. '*Here. . .*'

Her head swimming, Josephine conceived mischief. She picked up her whisky glass and took a mouthful, most of what was left. Then dipping her back with sinuous grace, she pressed her lips against Carrie's crotch, dribbling liquid gold, burning, stinging, down between her moist and spreading labia.

154

'*Oh! Oh!* Oh my *Go-o-od* . . .' Mrs Morgenstern threw back her head and collapsed back against her bamboo headboard. The bed shook. Laughing, choking on the spirit, Josephine pursued her, burying her face between her fat thighs and nuzzling forcefully at her crotch. Let the woman have something to punish her *for*, she thought lasciviously. Let her burn before she makes *me* burn.

'Oh! Oh!' cried Mrs Morgenstern, clutching Josephine's head twining her fingers in her hair. 'Oh! Oh! Oh! Do it now!'

Do it now? Do what now, Josephine wondered, drunkenly. And she pressed her assault on Carrie's clitoris home even more vigorously.

But that was not it. With a mountainous heave, Carrie pulled away from here. 'Please, Josie, please!'

She was lumbering sideways, one knee up, struggling against the wallowing of the mattress. The wooden frame creaked in protest. She was turning the great larded mounds of her buttocks towards Josephine.

She crouched on the bed, her bottom in the air, and looked back at Josephine. She still had all her jewellery on. With her brown skin and her golden bracelets, she looked like the favourite wife of an Indian rajah, begging her lord and master to mount her from behind.

But that was not what she was begging for.

'Please, Josie!' she cried again, hoarsely. 'Let me have it! I *beg* you!'

Three times, thought Josephine. She was stunned.

'You want *me* to whip *you*?' she whispered, in dismay. Her mouth and nose were full of the mingled taste of whisky and Caroline Morgenstern's cunt. She had abased herself for this woman, stripped for her, let her order her around. And now she wanted *her* to take command?

In a frenzy she dived for the case, wrenched it open, pulled out the little blackened martinet.

But it could not be done.

For a horrified, frozen moment she knelt there on the bed in the hot room, overpowered by the smell of jungle flowers, the reek of Caroline Morgenstern's hungry flesh. She looked at the little toy in her hand.

It could not be done.

Once it could have been done. Once she could have whipped her speechless, corrugated her vast buttocks with the crimson rake of passion. Once. Before.

They had taken that away from her, at the Château des Aiguilles.

Josephine's sight went dark around the edges, the scene on the bed dwindling to a tableau at the end of a tunnel, remote, dim. Then everything was dark. Blood pounded in her ears. She saw a black shape, a solid black rectangle, standing upright on a featureless surface. It was a domino. A double blank.

She heard herself cry out. She could feel a tightness round her throat, like the tug of an invisible collar.

Then she found herself on the stairs, clutching her dress, running for her life.

There was a figure on the landing: Isabel the maid, cowering in the shadow, stumbling to her feet at the naked apparition hurtling down the stairs towards her. She tried to flee.

Leaping down the rest of the flight, Josephine flung out an arm and grabbed her. She pulled the girl viciously towards her.

Her face was full of terror. Her big brown eyes showed white all around the iris.

Josephine shook her. With the hand that held the dress she pointed back up the stairs to the door of the bedroom where Mrs Morgenstern was lying, crying out querulously, calling Josephine's name.

'Get up there, Isabel!' she ordered. 'Go and give her what she needs!'

The maid trembled in Josephine's grip.

'Get up there now,' said Josephine, 'or regret it forever.'

Then she flung the girl aside and bounded down the rest of the stairs and out of the first door she saw, never once looking back.

She ran across the courtyard, past the cart, past the old convertible, startling the yellow birds perching on the folded hood and the upholstery. The packed dirt was hard beneath her naked feet. She ran back down the track, over sharp stones, twigs, mud, heedless. The hot aroma of the forest was all around her. Her lungs felt as if she was running through hot, thick water. She could hear a car engine on the road behind her.

She wheeled around and stood in the way, feet astride. Was it coming this way?

It was. A drab blue Landrover bounced and jolted round the bend into view.

Josephine waved her dress over her head like a flag of distress.

There was a man driving, a native. His eyes were staring, starting from his head. He braked. The car jerked to a stop, still some way off.

Josephine ran to it. She seized the sill of the open window, glaring in across the empty passenger seat.

'Please,' she said, 'you've got to help me.' Even as she spoke, she recognized the man. He worked at the Concord Reef. He was one of the hotel lifeguards.

'Are you going to the hotel?' she asked, urgently.

His eyes looked towards her, ran uneasily over her face and shoulders. He was dressed in a singlet and shorts, a sheen of sweat outlining his muscular frame.

'*Are* you?'

'Yes, ma'am. Yes, ma'am. I'm going to work.'

Josephine grabbed the door handle, hauled the door open.

'You've got to take me,' she said, and climbed in.

The engine was still running, chugging loudly to itself. The man stared at the naked woman climbing into the seat beside him.

'You can do whatever you like to me,' Josephine promised. 'Please, please, just drive!'

The man suddenly flung his hand up over his face, his fingers spread.

'Madam, please would you put your dress on,' he said, his voice intent and low with shock. 'I'm engaged to be married.'

And starting the car, he stared straight ahead through the insect-spattered windscreen while Josephine struggled back into her sundress.

|11|

Cadence had come back from skin-diving and gone out again. She had slipped a message under Josephine's door.

'*Hi! Come to a party — Papillote. Jax says take Traf. Falls Rd., look for the balloons. See you there! All my love, C.*' There were crooked kisses, and little circles for the dots over the *i*'s. Josephine wondered who Jax was.

She didn't want to go to a party. But she didn't want to hang around Concord Reef on her own. She didn't want to be there if Caroline Morgenstern came looking for her. She threw her sweaty, muddy sundress into the laundry, twisted the cap from a bottle of rum and took it with her into the bathroom, where she showered and washed her hair. Her movements were quick, vigorous with renewed drunkenness and determination.

Papillote. Traf. Falls. She had only a vague idea where these places were. She had no money. Taking another pull on the rum, she reached for her shorts, then decided to dazzle. She pulled on black stockings and suspender belt, clean knickers, then a lurid pink halter top and long, loose-weaved skirt of silver and black with little metallic threads in it. She put on her fancy sandals, brushed her hair, made up her lashes and lips. Then she went down to reception to hire a car.

The young white man on the desk picked up the phone. 'I'll need to see your permit, ma'am,' he said. 'Also your passport and US driver's licence.'

'No,' said Josephine.

He lifted his head, with a curious, let's-share-the-joke smile. 'Excuse me?'

'Haven't got any of them,' said Josephine.

His hand paused on the phone. 'International driver's licence?'

'No.'

158

Resignedly he put the phone back down. 'Ma'am, I'm sorry, I can't let you hire a car without your local permit, passport and driver's licence. I'm sorry, that's the regulations.'

Josephine smiled. 'Fuck the regulations,' she said sweetly and distinctly. 'Tell the manager.'

The boy's nostrils took on a pinched, white appearance. With an effort, he returned her smile. 'I'm afraid that won't make any difference, madam, you see —'

Josephine flipped her hand at him. 'Tell him,' she said, and wandered away across the lobby.

Tilting his head sideways with a grimace of swallowed protest, he left the desk, knocked on the office door, and went in.

Josephine looked out of the great plate glass window. The sun was declining from its mid-afternoon pinnacle. It shimmered on the sea, baked the road and the passers-by, glowed through the canvas awnings like red and white fire.

The boy returned to the desk. He picked up the phone, waited, then spoke to someone in a hushed voice. He listened. 'That's right,' he said. 'That's right. Right. Yes, that's right. Thank you.'

He put the phone down as gently as if it was made of china.

'Your car will be outside in five minutes, Ms Morrow,' he said, his eyes downcast.

'Thank you so much, Jeffrey,' said Josephine, reading his name badge. 'And I'll need a crate of overproof.'

His head jerked up, and he shot her a glance of fear and hatred. The very principles of law and order were being violated here by this fancy Englishwoman, and he had to help her. He picked up the phone.

The hire car was a bile green Impala convertible, automatic, four-wheel drive, reclining seats, air-conditioning, stereo. Josephine drove north-east, negotiating trucks and donkeys, looking for signs. Trafalgar Falls was apparently a famous beauty spot, Papillote a hotel of some kind, or a hiking lodge. The bottles jingled continuously in their crate on the back seat as the road climbed into the foothills.

Josephine saw stands of mahogany, tulip trees, grapefruit. Parrots flew back and forth across the road, calling sharply to one another. The road snaked sharply left and right again. She spotted a clump of balloons hanging from a palm tree. At first she mistook them for exotic fruit, calabashes swollen as bladders and pink and blue and green. Someone must have climbed up and tied them in place.

Behind the trees the green-black cone of Morne Macaque appeared and disappeared, geometric as a native painting. Sweat trickled down between Josephine's breasts, cooling as it reached her stomach. The engine of the car whined complainingly as the wheels spun in mud, then gripped again, slewing left and lurching forward. Lianas festooned the trees, swaying above the car like cobwebs at a ghost train.

Two more clusters of balloons, yellow and pink, decorated the corners of a large cardboard sign. 'YOU ARE HERE,' it said. Cars and pick-up trucks were parked both sides of the track, making further progress impossible.

Josephine stopped the car and got out, looking around, shading her eyes against the sun. She heard birdcalls, hundreds of birds, it sounded like; a babble of lazy voices; and somewhere the sound of rushing water. This seemed to be the edge of cultivation, the beginning of the forest.

Slamming the door of the Impala, Josephine walked up through the trees and into the open.

She emerged in front of a sheer cliff of red and black rock covered by a profusion of the flora that she had seen that afternoon from Caroline Morgenstern's car. Up among the rocks was perched a collection of log buildings that looked straight out of a Hollywood fantasy jungle. Above them could be glimpsed a flashing silver column of water that simply had to be 'Traf. Falls', or one of them. And above that were the slopes of the extinct volcano. The light was green and golden as a painting by Gauguin, green as desire, golden as rum.

Across the compound, people were sitting and standing around a barbecue pit outside a picturesque pavilion. Smiling faces, white and brown and tanned, greeted Josephine as she wandered by, looking for Cadence. The trees smelled of ginger and resin, the air of savoury smoke, chillies, sweet lemongrass. Young people sat on the rocks with cans of beer, bottles of wine and plates of lobster creole. Elderly people sat in camp chairs, children ran around naked, swiping at each other's rosy flesh and pulling each other's hair, squealing and laughing. Birds flew overhead continually, alarmed by this sudden intrusion into their corner of paradise. Near at hand, a peacock shrieked.

In one corner, two pools lay cupped in rings of black stone, flows of clear, crystal water bubbling into them through the mouths of symbolic-looking serpents carved out of the rocks. A group of half a dozen youngsters was gathered here, floating and bobbing in the ceaselessly roiling waters. They seemed intent, gathered closely together, with their backs to her. Josephine decided not to approach them, not to interrupt their intimacy. But as she turned back towards the terrace, where people sat at wooden tables, eating and drinking with a will, she heard her name called.

'Josephine!'

She turned her head, looking back at the group in the pool, and saw a blonde head raised, a bare arm waving at her.

'Over here!'

She went, conscious of her footsteps tapping across the stone-paved ground. All the swimmers turned their heads to watch her approach.

'Hey, Josephine.'

It was Cadence, naked, floating upright in one corner of the black pool as if it was her private jacuzzi. The group surrounding her was mixed, two couples, male and female, and a single man. Until Josephine had arrived, coming up behind them, all the men had their eyes firmly fixed on Cadence. Josephine saw now they were some of the Japanese crew Cadence had gone off with that morning.

The young women with them were other guests at the Concord Reef, she thought, one white, one Mexican. Both, she noticed, were still dressed in one-piece swimming costumes. As far as she could see, the young men were all in their bathing trunks. They clutched cups and cans, holding them clear of the water. It was heated, Josephine felt as she walked around the edge to where Cadence was floating. There was a slight haze over it, and warmth rose from it in a moist caress against her skin. It smelled faintly of sulphur.

Squinting against the brightness of the open sky, Cadence looked up at her with a huge smile. Music was playing somewhere, electric rock and roll from a tape recorder, incongruous in this wilderness. The old volcano stood loftily overhead, disregarding everything happening at its foot.

Josephine smiled firmly down at her new friend, ignoring the rest of the company. 'Hello, Cadence.'

'Hi.'

Cadence's voice was slurred by drink, her tone determined, emboldened by the audience of admirers that encircled her in the pool. 'Man, you're all dressed up like a movie star or something!' she

161

exulted. 'Isn't this great?' she said, bobbing up out of the waters, carelessly displaying her breasts and belly to the world at large. She floated onto her back, kicking water clumsily at the nearest of the Japanese boys. He laughed, a high-pitched giggle that made his friends all join in in chorus, deriding him and calling out good-natured insults Josephine could not interpret. They flashed their teeth at Josephine, hoping she was a good sport like her friend.

The two girls assumed expressions of nonchalance, hanging back, holding on to their positions at the edge of the pool. It was obvious that their companions had been prevailing upon them to strip off their costumes and go naked like Cadence, and that they had been holding out on them.

Josephine felt a sudden flash of anger. Cadence, who had let herself be undressed so timidly and passively on Josephine's balcony that first afternoon, was now flirting with everyone and flashing herself at all and sundry. A spasm of jealousy twisted in Josephine's heart, and the sunlight seemed to dim as she squatted down neatly at the poolside, tucking her long skirt decorously between her thighs.

'C'mon in,' Cadence urged her. 'It's warm. Feel.' And she lifted her hand out of the water and grasped Josephine's hand.

Her grasp was slippery and wet, and warm. Josephine squeezed her hand, then let go. She dabbled her own hand in the water, holding it in the stream spewing from the mouth of one of the snakes. It was hot, invitingly and comfortably so, and had the silky feel of a dissolved wealth of minerals.

'I didn't bring a costume,' Josephine said, smiling at the other white girl, who smiled back, uncertainly, and tipped a cup to her lips.

'You don't need a "costume"!' said Cadence rudely, giggling and mocking her. '*They* don't mind.'

'I'm sure they don't,' said Josephine levelly, looking round the faces smiling eagerly at her out of the water.

'I don't mean *them*,' said Cadence, splashing water sloppily and dismissively in the direction of the rest of the group. 'I mean the guys that own this place. Can you imagine *living* here? Isn't this a fabulous place? I want to live here, I mean forever.' She swam a stroke to hang in the water below Josephine, leaning with folded arms on the rocks and lifting her face to her appealingly. 'Come on in, Josephine, you'll love it,' she pleaded.

Josephine's heart softened at the sight of her fresh and freckled face.

In the pure green eyes was a tiny consciousness of disgrace, held in the middle of a complete and oceanic innocence, like a puppy that knows its mistress is cross but has no notion why; that begs only to be forgiven and loved again.

'Hey, have a drink,' said Cadence, and turning, she held out her arm to one of the boys, bringing her breast above the surface of the water again. 'Here, Toto, pass Josephine that bottle. I call him Toto,' she said, and laughed, unconscious of any offence she might have given. 'We had such a great day,' she said wistfully. 'I wish you'd've come, Josephine.'

But Josephine, remembering what her day had been, said only: 'That's nice,' and nothing more.

The bottle proved to be empty. It had spilled in the water, said another of the young men excitedly; No, countered the one Cadence had called Toto, defending his honour: Consuela had drunk it all. A jerky, repressed fight followed, as Consuela attempted to duck Toto in the water for slandering her, the other boys cheering her on and laughing ashamedly, while Toto tried to make the most of her assault by groping and fumbling at her body under cover of the water, pawing at her breasts and buttocks, then snatching his hands away.

'Come on, Josephine,' Cadence pleaded, making big eyes at her. 'Come on in.'

Josephine gave her a mock frown. 'I'm all dressed up,' she said merrily. 'I'm not getting undressed again.'

'Aaahh . . .' sighed the boys, disappointed, minute by minute growing bolder with this beautiful stranger.

'I'll just sit and put my feet in,' she told Cadence, who looked delighted.

Josephine slipped off her sandals and stood in her stockinged feet on the warm wet stone. She hitched up her skirt, to unfasten her suspenders; but she paused. She looked around the little group in the pool. All eyes were turned keenly, unblinkingly, on her.

She smiled gracefully, holding her skirt where it was, not drawing it an inch higher.

'Why don't you boys go and fetch the rum from my car?' she asked sweetly, in the mild but steely tones of a scoutmistress. 'The green Impala. On the back seat.' She gestured towards the far side of the compound.

Chattering, laughing shamefacedly, admitting defeat, Toto and one of his compatriots climbed lithely from the water. As Josephine had suspected, they were both modestly clad in swimming shorts, brightly coloured with bold designs. They glanced at her, at the third young man, who was hanging back.

Josephine caught his eye. 'There's a crate,' she told him. 'Plenty for everyone.'

Bobbing his head in deference, looking away, he waded in an ungainly fashion through the water away from the white girl whose hand he had taken. Pressing with his muscular arms on the rocks, he pushed himself straight up out of the pool. The waters slopped and lapped at the rocks. The three boys jogged off towards the car. The afternoon sun beat down. Josephine calmly hiked up her skirt and unfastened her suspenders.

While she carefully rolled down her stockings and peeled them off, Consuela and the other girl drew nervously closer together in the pool, murmuring. Sensing something, some awesome secret, between the drunken, loud-mouth Californian and her mysterious English friend, they sought refuge in each other, pretending to be preoccupied with looking for something amongst the various belongings discarded around the pool — Cadence's clothes, empty cans, cameras and bunches of car keys. The white girl came up with a pair of sunglasses. Were they Consuela's? No? Then they must be hers. And so on.

Josephine gathered her flashy skirt at her thighs and sat delicately on a rock near where Cadence had been floating, one high enough to still be dry after the horseplay. She sank her battered feet gratefully in the hot water, and sighed.

Cadence smiled uncertainly.

'Feels good, doesn't it?'

'It does,' Josephine said warmly. 'Mm. It truly does.'

She shut her eyes and leaned back on her hands, turning her face up to the blazing sky.

She felt Cadence's touch, tentative and shy, on her foot. She wiggled her toes, then, opening her eyes, slid her foot through the water to touch Cadence grazingly under her left breast.

Consuela and her friend were climbing from the water, talking to each other in tones of anxious casualness, reclaiming their clothes. 'We're going to get something to eat,' said the white girl loudly, in a North European accent, German or Dutch. 'See you later, Cadence, okay?'

'Okay,' called Cadence cheerfully, dismissing them as easily as she had taken up with them. 'See you later!'

The girl looked nervously at Josephine, shading her eyes. 'Nice meeting you!' she said.

'Bye!' called Consuela, already scampering off towards the terrace.

'See ya, Connie,' shouted Cadence. 'Bye, Jax!'

Josephine smiled and waved.

Alone with Cadence, she reached down into the water and cupped her breast in her hand, and bent her head down to kiss her on the lips.

'You're not mad at me, are you?' asked Cadence, after the kiss.

'No, my love,' Josephine said, relaxing back in the sun and closing her eyes again. 'I've just had a wild and crazy day, that's all.'

She felt Cadence relax beside her. 'Come on in, Josephine. They've gone now, you can do it,' her deep, husky voice urged her. 'It's really relaxing, Josephine.'

'Leave me alone!' laughed Josephine. 'Just tell me when they get back with that booze.'

'You're smashed, aren't you?' Cadence said, pestering her. 'Did you drive here drunk? Oh boy, you could have got in real trouble. You could have got yourself killed!'

She prattled on, and Josephine tuned out, listening to nothing but the happy, sensuous, adoring tone of her voice. They were together again, and nobody knew where they were, not even Caroline Morgenstern.

The water bubbled and lapped reassuringly at her tired feet. Caroline Morgenstern and the Concord Reef Hotel seemed a million miles away. She lay and listened to the ceaseless squalling and cheeping of the birds in the forest. She wondered if there were any big wild animals in there. Idly she imagined the dead volcano suddenly rumbling into life again, the ancient caldera boiling up the subterranean fires that had heated the water in the pools. She could almost feel the heat of the flaming lava as it rushed down the jungle slopes of Morne Macaque to sweep away Papillote, to cauterise the green earth and burn it clean of all human corruptions and complexities.

She heard children's voices, shrill cries of pleasure and splashings in the other pool; then adult voices too, in indolent, fragmentary conversation. She opened her eyes and looked to see if it was the boys, returning with the crate of drink.

She saw a group of people, white but tanned, moving towards them from the flower garden. Like Cadence's friends and most of the other people at this party, many of them were wearing only jeans, or bathing trunks and suits. Josephine felt slightly self-conscious, overdressed in her make-up and party clothes. She watched them go by. Behind them she glimpsed a short blond bare-chested figure, a man, walking away among the flowers. For a moment she saw his torso plainly. He was wearing a tattoo. It was too small to see clearly at that distance, with people walking in between. But Josephine didn't need to see it clearly. She knew what it was.

The sign of the domino mask.

Sam Morgenstern, she thought at once. But she had seen a picture of Sam, he was a middle-aged man, grey-haired. Raising her body upright, and craning her neck, she saw this man again just before he moved away out of sight. He was young, she was sure of it; no older than Cadence's chums. His hair was blond and curly.

Her heart began to hammer. Caroline Morgenstern had spoken of 'Sam's friends', who shared his tattoo. Was this one of them? Was he looking for her? Had he come to give her what Carrie herself had not given her? She wondered how it would be. Would he come and drag her away from Cadence, back to the house in the forest? Was her Caribbean idyll over now, so soon, and would she never be free again?

For the second time that afternoon she felt as if she was fainting. She gripped the rock with one hand, Cadence's shoulder with the other. The heat of the day seemed to vanish, erased by the wipe of a cloth, and in its place was winter, an eternal winter. Josephine Morrow was not lounging by a pool but squatting over a drain; the buildings that loomed around her were stout and built of stone; and the mountain that divided the sky was not a volcano, not of any age. They were not flakes of barbecue ash that whirled and drifted by on the breeze, but snow.

She was looking across a cold quadrangle at a group of half-naked people passing, totally unconcerned with her existence or presence. And one of them was a young man, a boy – no older than twenty, nor any taller than five foot six. He was white, with fine blonde hair that grew in curls.

He was not wearing a peaked cap then; nor a chauffeur's uniform, crimson jacket with mandarin collar, black frogging and polished brass buttons. Nor was he now.

'Josephine! *Josephine!*'

Someone close by was calling her name in tones of annoyance.

'Josephine, you're hurting my *arm!*'

She came to, and found she was gripping Cadence tight enough to bruise her.

'Cadence, I — I'm sorry, I've just seen someone — someone I think I know. I must, I've got to catch him.' She was babbling, pulling one of her stockings back on and fastening it up. Stupid, stupid, she thought with another part of her distracted mind, you don't need stockings here, and she almost ran off as she was, but another part, equally loud, said, how absurd to run around anywhere in only one stocking. So she pulled the other one on too, and shoved her feet into her sandals.

Cadence's voice was anxious. She didn't want her companion to go and leave her alone in the pool. 'Josephine, where are you going? Who is it, Josephine? I don't see anyone.'

Suddenly Josephine was filled with concern for her young lover. 'Stay here, Cadence,' she said. 'Don't follow me.'

And with that she ran off through the compound into the garden, pushing past oncoming people. 'Excuse me — excuse me, please —'

Orchids surrounded her, mocking her with their flesh, their nauseating scent. She saw a bare back through a stand of bamboo, then lost it again. The paths confused her. She stood surrounded by blazing canna blossoms, looking frantically to left and right.

There was no sign of him with the diners, nor among the people around the barbecue pit. She wondered if he was staying here at Papillote, if one of the rooms in the wooden house was his, and if so, how she would find out which before someone who belonged here stopped her and asked her what she was doing.

'Hi!' said an embarrassed voice right beside her, and another, in the same tone, 'Hi . . .'

It was Jax and Consuela, each with a can of beer and an expression of hurriedly assumed pleasure.

'Jax! Have you, either of you, have you seen a boy, a young man I should say, around here? Blond hair, curly, not too tall — wearing shorts? Kind of snub nose . . . deep-set eyes . . .'

Her voice tailed off. Both girls were looking at her vacantly. They looked at each other, as if to say, What is she *on?*

'No . . .' said the one called Jax, uncertainly. 'I don't think so. . .'

Before she could turn away Josephine reached out and grabbed hold of her wrist. 'This boy, he has an unusual kind of tattoo on his chest,' she said. 'Like this.' And with her other hand she dragged down her halter top into the space between her breasts, and showed them her domino tattoo.

They both recoiled, from the strangeness and suddenness of the action rather than from the sign itself. Jax jerked her hand back quickly and clutched it to her bosom with the other hand, as though she was afraid Cadence's crazy friend might try to snatch her hand right off her wrist. 'No!' she said sharply. 'We haven't seen anybody! Come on, Consuela —'

But her friend was still looking at Josephine with a small frown, trying to remember somethng. She shook her head at the tattoo, but she said, 'Very smart guy? Jacket, looks like silk or something? And crocodile shoes?'

Josephine shrugged. Could he have got dressed while she was struggling with her stockings and running around the garden like a headless chicken? It was possible. 'Maybe . . .' she said.

'I saw *him*,' said Consuela, taking a swig from her can and wiping her mouth on the back of one slim, nut-brown wrist. 'Down there.' She gestured with her can, back towards the track where the cars were parked.

'There,' she said.

Josephine whirled and searched the scene.

There was the boy, or someone who looked very much like him from the back. It was true, he was no longer dressed like a messenger, or a slave, or a sunbather. He wore light-coloured slacks and a tan jacket, unbuttoned, that flowed lightly from his shoulders as he walked.

Not even stopping to thank the Mexican girl, Josephine ran back across the compound. She passed the Japanese, still toiling up from her car with the crate, their progress not helped by the fact that they had already opened one of the bottles and were passing it around between them, with much shoving and boisterousness. They shouted out merrily as they saw Josephine, saluting her with the open bottle and joking in Japanese.

Ignoring them, she ran by.

It was him, she was sure of it. She had seen him from the back, never in tropical sunlight, and never dressed like that, but leaving the office in grey, chilly London, and in the bleak cloisters at the Château des

168

Aiguilles. She called after him. He did not turn around, nor slow his pace. In fact, if anything, he walked a little faster down the slope.

She caught up with him and laid a hand on his shoulder. It was a silk jacket, Italian silk. Not what a slave might be expected to wear. But neither were her clothes, her Fortuny skirt, her Lapotaire lingerie.

He turned his head. He was wearing sunglasses: circular black lenses in black wire rims, polished steel hinges, nose and earpieces. It was him. It was.

'I've got to speak to you,' she said.

He took off his glasses. His eyes were as blue as television, as grey as northern seas.

It was him.

There was no recognition in his blue grey eyes.

'You know what happened,' she said. 'You know why. Please, you've got to tell me!'

'I don't know what you're talking about.' It was his voice, though she'd only ever heard a few words. It was!

'Who was it?' she demanded. '*What did I do wrong*?'

'I don't know,' he said quietly, and prised her importunate fingers free from his jacket. He rubbed the fabric where she had gripped it, as though to smooth wrinkles from it. 'I'm afraid you've mistaken me for someone else.'

He had a slight accent, she thought, continental European, Swiss or Austrian.

'You remember me,' she told him. 'You do! In London. My flat. And at the château. I called out to you. Your keeper was angry.'

He shook his head. 'I've never seen you before in my life,' he said.

But his face was bland, expressionless. He showed none of the puzzlement, amusement or annoyance a total stranger would have felt at being accosted, here in broad daylight, by a madwoman from the other side of the ocean.

For the second time in five minutes she tugged down the front of her halter top to show her tattoo. His eyes narrowed as she bared the upper slopes of her breasts, but the sigil itself still produced no visible reaction.

'Open your shirt,' she told him. 'Just do that for me. If you're not who I know you are, you'll have no tattoo. Just show me. Show me you haven't got a tattoo like mine and I'll apologise, I'll go away, I'll never speak to you again, I promise.'

He made no move.

'If you don't show me, then I know I'm right,' she said, her voice low and tight.

Behind her the birds squawked, music played, the waterfalls boomed. Josephine was deaf to them all. People had begun to dance, a haphazard conga to and fro among the flowers. She was oblivious. There was a cone of total darkness, impervious and absolute, around her and the boy where they stood, separating them from the sky, the earth, the world of barbecues and driving permits and nature reserves.

She was sure he was the messenger, the boy who had searched her flat, the chauffeur, the slave she had shouted to across the freezing quad. She had taken him for a servant when he whipped her, but he had turned out to be a slave too. And he too had failed their masters, like her, and been abandoned here, like her. What did he think he had left to hide from her?

Perhaps to speak to her would be to acknowledge his failure, his exile. Perhaps he genuinely did not recognise her, and was unsure why she was demanding to see his tattoo.

No, he was stalling. He was lying. She knew it.

She reached for his open-necked shirt.

He seized her hands as they closed on his shirtfront, his reflex as swift as his grip was strong.

He held her no less imprisoned than when he had put her in handcuffs.

'Leave me alone,' he told her. 'Go away. I don't know you. How many more times? I don't know who you are. Go away now.'

Perhaps they had been intended to meet, Josephine thought as she hung helpless in his grasp, unable either to obey him or to continue in her intention, unable to move at all. If not, why bring them both here, why here, with all the islands in the Caribbean presumably, quite probably all the islands in the world, to choose from?

Perhaps – it occurred to her in a sudden, crashing realisation, like the crashing of the waterfalls – perhaps Dominica was not their prison at all, but their final test.

He gave her a sudden push, and let go. She stumbled backwards, trying to to keep her footing in the soft ground. He turned and walked quickly to his car, a white Mazda. She saw him get in and turn the key.

She ran along the line to her own car. When the Mazda swept past her, she pulled out after it.

The Mazda was heading back the way she had come, bumping down the road between the overhanging trees. A party of strollers got between them. Josephine sounded her horn, but here no one was in a hurry. They waved and laughed, and one of them, a young black man, grabbed hold of the side of the car and jogged along with her, trying to entice her into conversation as she nosed the Impala ahead. She put her foot down and he lost his grip, whirling and almost tumbling headlong in the road; he laughed and kicked up his feet and gave her a wolf-whistle as she drove away.

The falling sun flared on the windscreen. She hunted for sunglasses. Now she was coming up on a woman on a donkey, leading a string of goats. Where were all these people coming from? The Mazda was a white shape ahead, slipping between green branches.

She followed it onto a road she wouldn't have thought was even a track, let alone a road. Greenery enfolded her, long leaves slapping and trailing over the windscreen, into the car. She ducked and cursed, wishing she'd put the roof up. Branches heavy with huge blossoms went down under the bonnet, were crushed into the mud. The track zigzagged around the trees. Had he drawn her into the jungle to strand her there and be rid of her?

She came out onto a ridge, the forest a still and sweaty mass of green behind and below her. A real metalled road snaked away down to the sea. The Mazda was there below, putting distance between them, zipping up along the coast. Josephine took the right-hand corner in a swerve that threatened to fishtail the car as the muddy wheels slid onto the tarmac. Little white sails dotted the blue sea, far out. The low sun shone orange and vermilion on a fringe of distant cloud.

The coast road was firm and clear, no goats, no donkeys. She passed a cluster of white houses where ragged children perched on the wall, waving to her as she went by. She felt uncomfortable, tight, enclosed like a snail in its shell. The Dominican day was growing calmer, settling towards evening, and the island called her to relax, to shuck off her clothes and lie back in the hot springs, to wander through the trees, picking fruit and watching the brilliant-coloured birds that flashed into the air, to laugh and laze with the people over a lobster dinner, a jigger of rum, maybe a marijuana spliff. She was not Caroline Morgenstern, punishing herself for the failure to uncoil. Her senses were open, she knew the gates of her own desire.

171

But the boy in the white car held the key.

A truck passed her on the right, laden with white and red chickens in rickety cages. The aged driver grinned and made eyes at her. She was coming into a fishing village, old stone walls, a church with flags, plaster peeling from soft brick, a cobbled street, a fat woman with a baby on her shoulder.

She almost drove straight past the Mazda.

It was parked just beyond the village, at an angle to the road, in the shadow of a tumbledown shed where ancient nets hung on rusty frames, waiting for the mending they would never receive. With a squeal of brakes she pulled off the road, leapt from the car and ran back.

The Mazda was empty, but for a pile of clothes on the back seat. Josephine tried the door. It was open. She turned over the clothes, automatically noticing the labels. Tan Giorgio Armani silk jacket, linen Sarrgiorgio slacks the colour of wheatstraw. White cotton ankle socks sat limply, one in each of a pair of Polo crocodile mocassins. Why had he undressed? Had he gone swimming?

Quickly she ran back across the road and scanned the beach. A long line of black cloud was advancing from the north, like a curtain being drawn across the sea. There were no blond young men.

The shed held the hull of an old boat, tins of paint, tarred ropes, scattered fishing floats of perished cork. Nothing else. There were empty bins that released a powerful reek of ancient fish.

Beyond the Mazda a trail went up into the hills.

Josephine took it.

It led her up between glistening black rocks to the bank of a little stream, where it ended. She stood alone among flowering bushes, looking once again into the green maze she had just escaped. A bird called, a five-note tune that rose at the end as if beckoning her.

She looked at her fancy sandals, her stockings, her party skirt.

She splashed down into the stream, forded it, and at once found herself on the faintest of tracks leading up into the jungle.

She followed it.

|12|

She was sure he had come this way. There were footprints in the muddy ground. He had paced surefootedly ahead where she now slithered helplessly, grabbing at roots and branches, her fancy sandals sliding out from under her feet. Her stockings were laddered within fifty yards, her skirt snagged on twigs and low branches. Flies plagued her. She continued, determined to pursue him, to track down the truth he held and know it for her own. Perhaps it had been worked out beforehand, by the supreme masters. Perhaps they knew she would come to this. Or perhaps the game was already over, the opportunities of her body discarded, her potential examined and discounted. Either way, she would know. She would.

The forest baffled her with forty thousand shades of green. Was she still on the trail? What seemed near might be far, what seemed firm evade her grasp and leave her slipping feebly down the bank. The shadows of the sinking sun made a maze of their own, paths of golden light woven between hedges of dark, drawing her in and closing behind her. When she turned, she saw only the shaggy forest canopy, no sky, no sea. A toothed breeze sliced through the foliage, warning her of heavy weather. Her cheery pink halter top seemed meagre protection against exposure in a raw tropical evening. The sweat of exertion cooled and dried even as it ran down her back.

Aromatic trees scented her passage. A hundred phantom scents, frangipani, marigold, frankincense, lime, came lilting by as she heaved and stumbled her way up into the forest. Salmon-pink bromeliads brushed her cheeks and shoulders. Strange syrupy saps hung congealed on the rough grainy bark of the trees like wax on church candles. Birds hooted and flapped their invisible passage through the gigantic leaves overhead.

Suddenly the sun was gone. The swift tropical night had begun, or the clouds had closed about the sky. The breeze stiffened. Her lungs laboured from the climb. The orchids seemed to redouble their attack on her senses. She thought she heard monkeys shrieking. The ground fell away to her right and she realised she was high up, on a sheer face far above a lush valley now thick with shadow. Doves mourned, flying insects thronged, a stone slid under her foot and her sandal skidded, wrenching her ankle. She cried out, in frustration as much as pain.

A hummingbird came to investigate her, buzzing fearlessly in front of her face, close enough for her to see the pulsing of its purple throat. She wanted to speak to it. It was the reigning elemental of the forest, supervising everything that went on in its domain, each ingestion, each devouring. It was the imperious queen of bromeliads, the spirit of hibiscus. Before she could address it, it whirred away, its verdict unknown.

The sky went black.

Josephine tore a sandal strap clambering over an exposed tree root. The ruined shoe flapped beneath the sole of her foot like a useless appendage. After a few more paces she let it slide away and went on barefoot, digging her toes in the soft, granular soil. Soon she lost the second sandal, by choice as much as chance.

Was she still following the mysterious blond boy? She had no way of knowing. Perhaps she was penetrating the region of the hummingbird, the territory of some hideous *vodoun* deity, all teeth and ears, who eviscerated unwary little girls.

It started to rain.

The first drops fell large and cold on her neck, her cheeks and shoulders. They merely spurred her to greater efforts. She forced herself along a precarious ledge at breakneck speed, as if she knew there was some destination to which she was inevitably headed. The hummingbird would not permit her to get lost. She was the sacrifice. She too wore a prominent stigma on her breast. The devoted were saved.

She wished she had kept back a bottle of rum.

The soles of her feet were out of her tattered stockings. She would have stopped to peel the remnants of the wretched things from her legs if she hadn't been in a hurry.

She had not sighted the boy since leaving the road.

The rain thickened. Josephine's hair grew damp, then wet; it clung coldly to her skull, dripped down her neck. Her halter was no protection. Rain sluiced her face, beading in her eyelashes; it coursed down the sides of her nose, across her cheeks, ruining her party make-up. She wished it could wash away every trace of her dull, indulgent life since arriving here in Dominica. She felt like a more than usually animate slug, pulling herself along the forest trail in search of a predator.

The rain was heavy now. The drops lashed her back, her muddy legs, her cowering head. She looked up reluctantly and squinted against the storm, water pelting pitilessly on her face. Was there no shelter?

Nothing was guaranteed. No one in the world, she remembered suddenly, knew where she was. Unknown dangers might surround her on all sides. A mountain lion could emerge, prowling out of the undergrowth, summoned by the hummingbird, and tear out her throat with its teeth. A mudslide could swallow her and leave her bones for the sun to bleach. Possibly no other human had ever set foot where she now hobbled.

No other but one.

Her calves ached. Had he any idea what he was doing to her? Had he any idea she was still there, on his tail? The rain pierced through and through the forest canopy, fogging visibility, pelting her, drowning her senses, stupefying her altogether. Nothing could be worth this.

Without this, there was nothing. There could be nothing. Only the withered life of Caroline Morgenstern, living on gossip and cocktails at the Concord Reef, wondering when *he* was coming home. Looking for substitutes for Sam. In this weather, Carrie and Isabel would unite, pressing their faces to the window with their arms around each other's shoulders, anxious to know: were they safe? was the hurricane returning?

From here the sea looked like zinc between the trees. The rain zipped spinning down from the clouds, each fat drop seeming targeted. Her clothes were soaked through. Lightning snapped in the purple distance, and thunder opened its throat. The trees conspired against her. She shouted through the storm.

'*Damn you!*'

There was something, she saw, among the trees ahead. Dashing water from her eyes she hurried forward, tripping, stumbling with fatigue. It was a building, a thatched hut; not large, and not new. Its walls leaned at odd, unplanned angles. Their logs had married the

175

forest, giving footholds to leaf and vine. Thick veils of moss, translucent in the stormlight, hung dripping from the eaves.

With a will she dashed for the verandah, dragged herself up the steps and pushed open the door.

It was hot and dark inside, and smelt of decay, green mould, damp. Square outlines of dim green light showed where shutters had been raised over unglazed windows. She heard the rain battering on the roof and, inside, the skittering of tiny creatures disturbed by her arrival.

The lightning flickered and flared again, and she saw him.

She saw him all at once, completely, before the darkness swamped them again. He was sitting in a tall-backed planter's chair, his hands resting on the arms, his feet flat on the floor. He wore skin-tight trousers of black leather and high-topped boots streaked with black jungle mud. A canna petal clung plastered to one, like a coloured kiss. Around his waist he wore a broad black leather belt with a steel buckle that looked like a spring trap. Above the waist he was naked but for a black collar with blunted steel spikes and a domino mask over his eyes. His skin was shining wet, his hair darkened by the rain.

In the black darkness after the lightning, a luminous green afterimage of his domino tattoo hung in space before her like a signature of infinity.

'I didn't tell you to come in,' he said.

'I'm here,' she said flatly. She shivered a little, despite the closeness and heat of the dead air. She sniffed, blinked water from her eyes, shook a shower of raindrops from her hair.

'Why are you following me?' he asked her. His voice seemed older in the darkness, patient, the voice of an examiner or judge.

'You know,' she said. 'You know why. You know who I am.'

'Not even you know that, I imagine.'

The lightning came and went again as he spoke. This time she saw nothing but his lips, the lips of a boy, and his tongue between them moist and cherry pink.

Something was building in her, some tension, something like fury, like loathing. It was pent in her body like power. She realised she was waiting for the thunder. It crumbled and broke above them, indescribable and huge. Her ears rang with it.

'Will you answer my questions?' she asked him.

'You don't need questions,' he said.

His slow voice seemed to prowl round the room, sniffing her like a black panther, invisible in the dark. One wrong move and its patience would evaporate. One falter and it would spring at her head.

'If you answer them, I won't have them any more,' she said.

There was a brief pause. When he spoke again he sounded amused, as if she had bought a few more seconds of his tolerance because she had amused him. 'Do you bargain with me?'

'I have nothing to offer you,' she said. She said it carefully, like a woman stepping across a treacherous floor in a dark room, not knowing where it might give way beneath her. She heard this tentative quality in her voice, and knew as she spoke that she was hoping what she said was not true.

'That's true,' said the boy.

He spoke calmly, with the merest hint of annoyance, as if warning her it was not amusing to be told obvious things.

Her knees were trembling. Her anger turned in on herself like a knife, becoming misery. She felt it in her stomach, driving deep into her womb. She would ask him anyway, whether he would answer or not.

'Why have I been rejected?'

'Who –'

The lightning slashed through the room again. The boy had not moved in the interim. Josephine sensed furniture in the green dazzle, a low bed of rope on a primitive frame of wood and lashings, some kind of upright frame like a loom. She saw a collection of unidentifiable equipment, metal, shiny leather.

He was still speaking.

'– told you you were rejected?'

The thunder crashed.

Dizzy, she seized on the first thing she thought of, absurd, trivial. 'They took my passport away.'

'You don't need a passport,' he said. He emphasised the pronoun, slightly.

'I've got no money. I'm here illegally.' She hated herself for the banality of her concern. 'In exile!' she said savagely. She wiped her wet face on her wet arm.

'The world is exile,' he said, once more sounding older than his years.

The lightning flashed, and there was silence until the thunder rumbled, suddenly far away. The rain came down unceasingly. She

177

could almost see now. Either her eyes had become accustomed to the dark or there was a strange glimmer in the hut, as if some fungus there were phosphorescing, giving back the radiance of the lightning charge.

'You have all you need,' he said, as if it were his final word.

She thought of the manager of the Concord Reef, smiling, bowing. She thought of her dalliance with Cadence, scratching the itch that would not let her sleep. She thought of Carrie Morgenstern and her uncomprehending despair. Was that to be Josephine's fate, to wither here in the sun, waiting, hoping that perhaps one day *he*, the supreme master, would arrive, or send for her?

'Your clothes are ruined,' the boy said lightly, in a parody of polite sympathy, the concerned host.

She was in a mood for metaphor. 'I am ruined,' she said, not sounding absurd, even to her own ears.

'Take them off,' he told her.

She lifted her head. Rain dripped from her hair. 'My clothes?' she asked.

'Everything.'

The glow in the hut was growing stronger, all around. It appeared to be seeping from the floor, up the walls, as though trays of quicklime had been ignited under the floor, their baleful, unreal light leaking through the joints and cracks. She saw a lizard poised on the wall by the bed like a jewelled brooch.

Everything. The past, the future, truth, identity, hope, despair.

Josephine pulled the sodden fabric of her halter from her shoulders. The fastening parted in her hands. Her breasts lolled free. She dropped the wet thing on the glowing floor.

She unhooked the waistband of her skirt. The burr of the opening zip was inaudible beneath the roaring whisper of the rain. The skirt fell about her feet, its silver threads glinting, weak as expiring fireflies.

Her breathing was deep with that unnamed passion still welling in her. Her breasts rose and fell. Methodically she unclipped her suspenders, stripped away the rags of her black stockings, unhooked her suspender belt and threw it after them.

She peeled down her panties, as wet as the rest of her clothes.

It was light enough in the hut to see his eyes now. They looked at her body unblinking, as unconcerned as when he had dressed as a chauffeur and intruded into her life. She locked her gaze with his.

178

Their wills met, mated, merged.

He had only to lift a fingertip from the arm of his chair and she came to him, leaving the rags of her past behind her on the floor.

She stood at his knee.

He lifted his whole hand now, extending his index finger, rested it lightly, demonstratively, on the sign tattooed between her breasts, the sign they shared.

'This is all you need,' he said simply. 'Your passport. Your money. Your law. Your residence. Your name.'

He dropped his hand, seeming to sit back, relaxing, though his body never moved.

'The rest you will find on the chair over there,' he said.

She had not noticed the small wooden chair. It was as if it had not existed until the moment when he named it. It was very like some chairs she had had once, in her kitchen, when she had lived in a flat high up above a great and ancient city.

There were some small things lying on the seat of the chair.

It was a wrench to move away from him, to step across the shining, crooked floor, even though he had directed her to.

She picked up what was on the chair.

A black leather collar, fastened by a silver buckle, and furnished with a silver ring at the front, in the centre.

And a black velvet domino mask.

She stood facing him, her hands at her side, one of these things in each hand.

'Put them on,' he said.

She buckled the collar around her neck, slipped the elastic of the mask behind her head and adjusted it.

Through the eyeholes of the mask the room looked no different, though now it was lighter she could see what the rest of the furnishings and equipment actually were.

She faced the boy on his throne.

Her voice caught in her throat. Yet she had to speak.

'Will you answer one more question?' she asked.

He considered. 'You will pay dearly for the answer,' he said. It was a warning, an announcement, a promise.

'Who sent me the domino?' she asked. 'The double blank?'

'I did,' said the beautiful boy.

After that he got up from his chair and fastened her to the upright

179

frame that stood behind him, with a clear space all around it. He fitted cuffs of soft black leather around her wrists and drew the chains of the cuffs up through stout eyebolts at the upper corners of the frame, stretching her arms up over her head until she stood on tiptoe, then locking the chains in place. About her head he fastened a snug bridle of strong, fine leather and steel, with straps that rose diagonally in front, taut across both cheeks and over her ears, joining at a point at the back of her head. The bit of the bridle went between her teeth, gagging her and pressing her tongue to the floor of her mouth with hardened leather reinforced with slender, rounded ribs of steel. The straps of the bit he drew tight around her jaw and locked them to the fastening of the upper straps.

Then she felt him tug her head gently backwards by a chain that he clipped to the bridle. It was warm, but still she shivered as he ran it down between her buttocks. Then came a violent pain of heat and immolation. He was forcing something into her anus. It felt huge and smooth and metallic. She wanted to cry out, but the bit silenced her. She felt as if she was about to evacuate convulsively, yet she knew this was an illusion. She remembered the device from the rose-scented room at the Château des Aiguilles. It was a silver egg, and when it was finally, firmly settled in place, as it was now, its upper end pressed the root of the clitoris through the wall of the vagina.

She felt the boy's hand coax her legs apart. The egg shifted in her and she shuddered with the shock, feeling again that any instant now she would lose control of her bowels.

The chain from her bridle was fixed to a strap that he now pulled tight between her legs and forward through her crotch. The strap was fastened to the base of the egg. It was heavy. She felt warm metal press against the mouth of her vagina. Another spasm. Pain and more pain. A silver ball was pressed up inside her. She felt she would be split.

Gently, insistently, he pushed the ball up and in. It felt enormous, there was no room for it. Her eyes filled suddenly with sharp tears of pain. But now he was pressing the ball up from below, pushing it further in. He was pressing the first ball up with the second. Didn't he know she would burst?

The second ball pushed the first up and up until it nestled perfectly under the tilted egg. Her entire belly seemed to swell and throb, contracting in on itself, and with each contraction, pummelling and shocking itself to another contraction. Her mouth filled with saliva, unable to escape. It trickled down her throat.

He pulled the leather harness up in front. A two-pronged silver nub slipped easily between the swelling lips of her vulva and forked neatly around her clitoris. She arched her back, feeling the lightning of the jungle storm now blaze through her spine. She was to be spared nothing. Not now, not any more.

The straps of the harness fitted around her hips, fastening in front, beneath her navel. She felt how the design of the array violated her totally, yet left her buttocks bare. Hanging from her wrists with her head pulled backwards to the full extent of her neck, she had only her legs still free. She felt them kicking beneath her, distant from her, detached from her paralysed and useless will. There was a smell in the room, strange herbs burning. Unaccountable shadows slithered on the phosphorescent wall before her eyes. Demons had come to watch.

His hands took hold of her left ankle. He must be stooping, kneeling. He should not kneel to her. Yet his will was all. He provided no servant, no maid to attend to her binding. It was his will to lay his own hands on her, to set his seal on her openings and dispose her limbs correctly himself.

His hands closed a thick, soft leather fetter around her ankle. Every touch transmitted itself to her groin, her rectum, and thence to her abdomen, to her straining shoulders. She rode high on a wave of suffering, of fear and exultation. He fastened a chain to her anklet. While he carried her leg across to the corner of the frame, the muscles of her thigh moved the muscles of her hip, and the balls rolled inexorably within her vagina. Her eyes were starting from her head with the wild churning in her solar plexus. The room seemed to be full of fragrant, bitter smoke. Her right leg was flexing like a live thing. She wept for the smoke, for the pain, for the disobedience of her own body. Her quim oozed helplessly, her waters spilling out around the edges of the punishment harness.

He fastened her right leg to the frame.

She tasted metal. There was a crackling roar in her ears which was perhaps the rain, the fire, the protest of her own blood. There was no further distinction between inside and outside, between herself and the forest, between the forest and the world. The roof of the hut had vanished, rendered unnecessary by these new laws of space. Strapped tight to the confines of its own flesh, her nervous system filled the black tropical sky with the slow wheel of the stars. When the supreme master reached to touch her flesh, electricity arced and cracked across the gap. On the smouldering ground of her hip his handprint burned white-hot.

He kissed her shoulder. His lips dripped venom. She burned with shame, with horror, with desire. The smoke in the room was the steam of their own wet bodies, released by this inhuman heat. The smell of bitter herbs was the scent of unknown hormones, the coded signals of the new creatures they had become, king and queen serpents of the jungle. The volcano was reawakening. The lips of its crater smoked and smiled.

The master did not speak. His breath hissed in her ear. The hiss was the roar of the sea, far below, the rain falling on the empty sea, into the fiery pit of the volcano. It was the language of the circling stars.

He thrashed her then. He laid a long, slender wooden switch across her naked bottom, measuring his stroke, saluting her, preparing her. Then he thrashed her, and for a while, forgetting, she became herself again, spread and penetrated and chained to a creaking wooden frame in a derelict hut on a mountainside. Her flesh insisted it was flesh, not fire, not space, not the raw virgin landscape of a new creation. The slopes of her bottom were not wooded scarps but dressed only in their own vulnerable skin. Her flanks were not the flanks of the mountain, they were hers, Josephine Morrow's, their abused nerves shrieking with pain she could not express. With each jolt of the switch, cruel devices of leather and silver ground inside her, battering the membranes of her womb. Then she lost this old, irrelevant illusion, and passed again into the wild dark of myth. The switch fell across her thighs, and the nutmeg groves burst into flame. Small creatures ran about in frenzy. The switch fell again, and fields of sugarcane flared like exploding torches.

He exchanged the switch for a whip, and the lash licked across her back, lightly as a caress, then powerfully, slamming her forward to the furthest extent of her bonds. The tip of the lash swept round and caught her right breast, stinging like a hornet. He lashed her from the other side, expertly, symmetrically. The lash danced upon her skin. She flew up out of her prison and circled high above the dark forest on a plane of mirror. In the mirror she saw the face of the supreme master, which was the true face of the universe. It was her own face.

Fainting, she fell into his arms. The illusion was gone. They were two again, separate, unknown to each other, supreme master, supreme slave. He was unlocking her, taking her down. Leather bonds split and shrivelled in his fingers like sloughed snakeskin. Chains slipped away at his touch, melting, made of mercury. Too slight to carry her bodily, he supported her, eased her over to the low bed. The punishment harness kneaded ceaselessly at her loins, but when he placed his hand between her whipped thighs she arched like a tightened bow.

She lay beneath him, her hands locked together above her head. He bowed his head over her, and his soft young mouth fastened gently on her left breast. Another jolt of lightning blasted through her body. She moaned in her throat, into her gag. His hand was on her right breast, caressing, squeezing, while he sucked at her nipple, grazing it again and again between his teeth, then breathing on it, cool and warm, teasing it with his cherry-pink tongue.

She was thumped back into her body as if she had been away. Tears sprang from her eyes, sweat from every pore of her body. She wanted nothing. She had given him everything, her will, her past, her future, her name, everything. His beautiful lips traced the outline of her domino tattoo.

He unfastened the buckle that was like a trap, and put aside his belt. He unlaced the front of his leather trews. His penis sprang out, erect and imperious, its tip cherry-pink like his tongue, and glistening as it peeked from the crinkled foreskin.

He came to the head of the bed and unfastened her bridle. The wet gag slipped dribbling from her mouth like a spent phallus from a cunt. She could feel the taut lines of the straps on her face, itching and burning like the marks of the whip on her back.

He got up on the bed on his knees, planting one either side of her head. She lay in a fervid aura of leather, sweat, the odour of his arousal. His penis dipped towards her face.

'Caress me with your lips and tongue,' he said.

He tasted of snake, dark meat, thick juices. She nuzzled the slick underside of the shaft, straining her neck and shoulders upwards to reach the rim of the glans, nestling the tip of her tongue into the groove. At her touch the prick kicked powerfully, twice, arcing away from her. She swept her tongue back down the shaft and rubbed her lips lightly around his balls.

His fingers were unfastening her harness. The silver spheres responded, sliding and tugging inside her. Crying out in ecstasy and complaint, she lost hold of his penis. The leather of his thighs engulfed her face.

They rolled over, he on his back on the cot, she crouching over him on all fours. She dipped her head and arched her back to graze on his prick, batting it lightly from side to side with her tongue. Working with his hands up above his face, he unfastened the last catch of the harness and smoothly, ruthlessly, dragged the dripping balls from her vagina. She felt them go, a rude shock of delight in her aching flesh. He grabbed her bottom, making her shriek as his fingers clasped her whipped flesh, and pulled her hips down on his face, clamping his lips on her swollen quim.

Together they sucked and slavered, drank and fed. Still deep in her rectum, the silver egg circled and bobbed with every move they made.

Then he smacked her hard and pushed her off him, rising up on one elbow at her side, climbing off the bed.

'On your knees,' he said.

She crouched down, cuffed hands stuck out in front of her, head turned sideways on the cot, sore bottom high in the air.

In one swift, agonising motion, he pulled the egg from her anus like a stopper from a wineskin.

In torment she begged him grant her five minutes to run outside, into the bushes, and relieve herself in the way all the inflamed nerves of her belly were demanding; but he struck her again with the switch, making her cry out, and before she knew, another firm invasion of her rear was taking place.

'Oh! Oh! *Aah!*'

He drove himself into her anus, impaling her on the prow of his desire, using her as he would any serving-boy. His hips pounded against her fiery bottom, the dangling laces of his leather trousers flapping and slapping lightly between her thighs. His hands ran urgently up her sides and seized her breasts where they lay beneath her, squeezed against the ropes of the bed. She could not breathe for sensation. His thumbs mashed her quivering nipples cruelly, making her croak helplessly, deep in her throat, bucking her hips and forcing him deeper in. There was a centre in her still, the heart of the volcano, that he had not plumbed.

He drew slowly and steadily out of her anus in a series of heart-stopping shocks. He took up his switch and began to beat her again.

By the sixth searing stroke, she couldn't stand it any more. She heaved herself off the bed, arms still pinioned in front of her, and fled from the hut into the rain. Naked, in the nearest bush, she squatted and emptied herself in a single scalding rush. She wept and panted.

He strode out after her, stepping slowly from the verandah in his high boots, stalking through the undergrowth to where she crouched. The two masked creatures glared defiantly into each other's eyes. Then, with his switch, the boy drove the woman from her mess, away from the hut and further into the wet and clinging greenery. The rain pelted down on them as though it was the will of heaven that it should rain and never stop; the dancing switch rained blows on Josephine's thighs and back and bottom and breasts, whichever way she turned and floundered. He drove her back against a tree, where, with a thud, she landed, sprawling, her legs spread wide. Bounced back against the trunk by the impact, she saw a flutter of black rags swirling in the branches overhead; a swarm of bats, driven from their perches by this violent and unprecedented interruption.

The master dropped to his knees. His erection had subsided in his pursuit of her. Josephine sat up against the tree, reaching forward with her cuffed hands. She cradled his cock, stroked and cosseted and slapped and pinched it back to hard and blushing life. Then she lay back again and pulled it down and put it inside her.

He hugged her tight, his moist mouth caressing her cheek, her neck, the side of her face. His hands seemed to search out the pattern of the whipmarks, pressing and squeezing each one until it grew red-hot. She was rigid, threshing in the wet leaves. The smell of their congress was inextricable from the reek of the wet jungle. Rain pelted them, mud was in their hair and fingers, oozing up into the crack of her bottom. He slid his penis out, all but the last half-inch, and poised, delicately. Then he laughed and plunged back into her again.

They rolled over in the mud, her cuffed hands imprisoned awkwardly between their bodies, crushed between her breasts, his arms around her and her legs high up his back, thighs sliding under his armpits. She heard him bang his head, but he did not react. She swivelled her pelvis, dragging again and again and again at his cock, willing him to spend himself before she found her own climax. He was her obedient master, and she was his imperious slave.

Somehow they were upright, standing under a smooth-barked tree. Her back was to the trunk, her legs braced, her hands unlocked. She held his bottom in her hands, clutching him to her, squeezing him into her cunt. His voice sobbed and swore into the jungle night, crying lustily and desperately like an animal neglected at the naming of beasts. The bats zipped and fretted in the air above, their squeals so shrill she could hardly make them out above their own screams and moans. The rain hissed down over and around them like cold water on hot metal. The metal was their blood, the lava of the volcano, the semen of the beautiful boy which gushed suddenly, pumping into her vagina and flowing down over her fingers, clutched beneath his balls.

He dropped out of her and stood huddled up to her, his arms about her, his cheek on her shoulder, human, young.

She caressed his blond curls, flattened and darkened by the rain. After a moment she supported him as he had supported her from the whipping frame, leading back through the undergrowth to the hut.

Back in the open the rain washed all mud and seed and foulness from them in seconds. Trapped between earth and sky, Josephine planned her own release.

She took him to the cot and laid him down. She went and kicked the door shut, then returned to the inert boy. Kneeling at his feet like a slave, she stripped off his filthy boots and his leather trousers, dumping them on the floor, then lay down with him, cuddling him, feeling his hairless chest rise and fall beneath her arm. Their masks were gone in their tumble in the bushes. All that remained were their collars, hers featureless and slender, the collar of possession; and his broad and spiked, the collar of assumption. She traced his tattoo with her finger, then pressed her tattoo to his, rubbing her breasts in circles over his chest.

Then, for the first time, they kissed.

She put her mouth to his, feeling his lips part sluggishly under hers, and fastening her lips to his. Her tongue quested gently between his lips, brushing the tips of his teeth and diving beyond, sliding over his tongue.

At the same time she reached down with one hand and lightly slipped it into his groin, circling his penis and scrotum with finger and thumb.

His tongue, not stunned but resting, rose to hers.

And his penis began to swell again as she coaxed it with her fingertip, stroking it up the underside again and again, returning each time to the base.

With that kiss she woke her prince, and took back the power she

186

had given him.

She felt it flow into her like honey, like snake venom. It was not hot but tingling, the essence of every stripe and cut he had given her.

She took it back and sucked it in, letting it well up through her spine.

She was a giant, kneeling up now and straddling his body.

He looked up at her, smiling, taken aback. 'It's yours!' he said, breathlessly.

Her own smile was cool, powered by pity and a distant, discriminating love. 'I know,' she replied, chiding him.

She drew his knees up to his chest, exposing his bottom. Then she found the switch and beat him until he begged her to stop. Then she turned him over and beat him on the back, and on the soles of his feet, and then on the bottom again. Then she positioned him on his back, and squatted down on him, caressing his hip with the inside of her thigh and slipping herself down over his penis.

She kissed away his tears and rode him until the rain was done and the night well worn, the peach-pink tropical moon sinking low behind the trees.

And her orgasm, when it came, was not a volcano; not a whirlpool; not the forked lightning that splits the mountain peak. It was not the end of the world at all.

It was quiet, and silvery, like mercury all along her nerves, and she curled back her lips and threw back her shaggy head and keened with delight, feeling herself somersault through space and drop down like a descending goddess, breaking through every glassy plane, all the way from heaven down to earth, where she landed lightly, on her feet, ready to begin again.

Everything, all over again.

Afterwards, she asked him: 'Was I a long time at the château?'

He shrugged. His flesh was warm beneath her where he cradled her in his arms, her head on his shoulder. He said, 'Everyone there takes all the time they need.'

The hut was lit by a single black candle, set on a spike beside the bed.

'Why here?' she said. 'Why Dominica?'

'Dominica . . .' he said. 'Domino . . .' He caressed her flank. 'No special reason.'

She shifted her chin to look up at his face. From this angle he looked terribly young. She found herself wondering how often he needed to shave. She wondered what his name was.

'But did you know this was my dream island?'

His grasp tightened around her back. He looked down his cheeks at her. 'We know everything about you, Josephine Morrow,' he said in his wise, magisterial voice.

She hid a smile against his chest, turned it into a kiss. The arrogance of men.

But she couldn't stop asking questions. 'What would have happened if I'd whipped Caroline Morgenstern?'

'Who can say?'

'But she was one of yours? Of ours? Part of the test, I mean?'

'Oh yes.'

She was not at all convinced he wasn't lying.

She stretched her legs, beginning to feel hungry. A faint light was growing in the hut, the purely natural light that ushers in the dawn.

'And what about Cadence?'

'Your young American friend?'

'Mmm . . .'

'She has possibilities.'

'I'm glad you think so.' She reached up up to his mouth and they kissed, silently, for a long time.

Later, pointing across the steadily lightening room, he said, 'You forgot something.'

Josephine turned her head, her hair swaying out behind her, feeling the ache of the whipping as the muscles stretched across her bare back. The boy bowed his head and kissed the tracks of his cruelty. She looked where he pointed. On the chair, where the mask and the collar had been, something glittered.

She got up and went over to look at it.

It was a tiara of black diamonds.

She picked it up.

The supreme master stretched out his hand. 'Bring it to me,' he said.

Josephine smiled.

'No,' she said.

And bowing her head very slightly forward, she put it on.

THE END